the
lonely
crowd

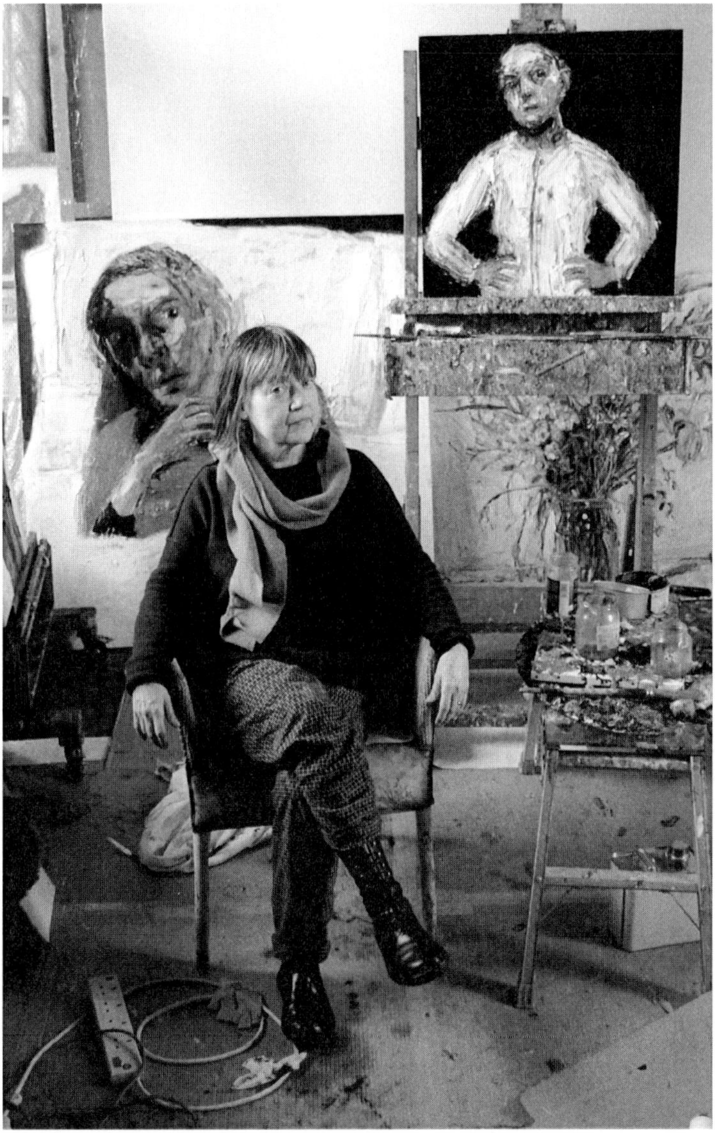

the lonely crowd

publishers of fiction, poetry & photography

Editing & Design John Lavin
Advisory Editor Michou Burckett St. Laurent
Contributing Editor Dan Coxon
Frontispiece: 'Shani Rhys James' Jo Mazelis
Front Cover Photo: 'Richard Cowell' Jo Mazelis
Back Cover Photo: from 'Mametz Wood' Rob Hudson
Cover Design John Lavin

Published by The Lonely Press, 2018
Printed in Wales by Gwasg Gomer
Copyright The Lonely Crowd & its contributors, 2018
ISBN 978-0-9932368-9-1
*The Lonely Crowd is an entirely self-funded enterprise.
Please consider supporting us by subscribing to the magazine here*
www.thelonelycrowd.org/subscribe

Please direct all enquiries to
johnlavin@thelonelycrowd.org
Visit our website for exclusive online content
www.thelonelycrowd.org

Contents

An Interview with Robert Minhinnick John Lavin - **9**
Two Poems Robert Minhinnick - **18**
Barafundle Anna-Marie Young - **23**
Four Poems Martina Evans - **26**
A Gift for Abidah Courttia Newland - **35**
Five Poems Matt Rader - **63**
Eclipse Stevie Davies - **73**
Three Poems John Freeman - **82**
Actors David Hayden - **88**
Three Poems Bethany W. Pope - **97**
Lovebirds Armel Dagorn - **103**
Two Poems Rhea Seren Philips - **109**
Waddington James Clarke - **111**
Three Poems Louise Warren - **120**
*Into the Woods: An Interview with
Rob Hudson* Jo Mazelis - **123**
Thenar Space Gareth E. Rees - **146**
Four Poems Sarah Doyle - **164**
Edward Elgar Rehearses the Powick Asylum Staff Band
Nigel Jarrett - **170**

Two Poems Michael Ray - **177**
The Good Poltergeist Ronan Flaherty - **180**
Two Poems Natalie Ann Holborow - **196**
The Driver Tanya Farrelly - **200**
Two Poems Kate North - **210**
Mummy Derwen Morfayel - **214**
Three Poems Susanna Galbraith - **224**
Sound of the Riverbed Dan Coxon - **228**
Two Poems and a Photograph Jo Mazelis - **234**
Detroit Anne Hayden - **239**
Celebrating the Past John Freeman - **248**
*Forty Years of Editing:
Some Do's, Some Don'ts: 1978—2018*
Gerald Dawe - **256**

About the Authors - **273**

issue nine

An Interview with Robert Minhinnick
John Lavin

Robert Minhinnick (b. 1952) has been called 'the leading Welsh poet of his generation' by The Sunday Times. He has twice won the Wales Book of the Year for his collections of essays, Watching the Fire Eater *and* To Babel and Back. *He edited the magazine,* Poetry Wales *from 1997 until 2008 and founded both Friends of the Earth Cymru and Sustainable Wales. He has won the Forward Prize for Best Single Poem twice, for 'Twenty Five Laments for Iraq' and 'The Fox in the National Museum of Wales'.*

While Minhinnick's latest collection Diary of the Last Man *(shortlisted for the T. S. Eliot prize) is rooted in the dunescapes of the author's hometown of Porthcawl, it is also a work that is intrinsically internationalist in outlook. The long title poem is a wry, standing-ovation-worthy requiem for humanity, predominantly set on the Welsh coast but it could be argued that Minhinnick reserves his most powerful poetry for when he casts his eyes abroad.*

The searing 'Amiriya Suite' revisits 'a bunker in Baghdad destroyed by the USAAF on February 13, 1991', in which 'over 400 civilians were killed'. The reader is introduced to a female survivor that acts as a tour guide to the 'charnel corridors': 'one body with four hundred souls.' The collection draws to a close with 'Aversions', a series of translations / interpretations of Welsh, Arabic and Turkish poems, all of which conjoin with the rivers of desolation that sit at the heart of Minhinnick's poetic vision.

*

John Lavin: Could you tell us something about your early life and your beginnings as a writer? Was there a moment when you knew that writing was what you wanted to do? Or was it something that you came to more gradually, over time?

Robert Minhinnick: My parents both wrote, also my twin sister. My father wrote short stories and some were published in journals such as *Herald of Wales*. I wrote three novels, if I remember, around 1970. Really young! Then a 'verse drama', 'The Night Before Winter', 1972, recently rediscovered. Writing was… natural.

JL: And to follow on from that, can you remember a first significant breakthrough? A piece of work that made you think that writing was something that you could make your career?

RM: About 1976 I was approached by Cary Archard to submit a manuscript of poems for the 'Triskel' series he was editing, on evidence of poems I was publishing around that time. I recall walking through Bridgend in the snow, having come from Penyfai. Then Cary invited me to attend a 'poetry reading' in, I think, what was Barry College of Education. The manuscript should have contained a suite of poems, 'Scrap Iron Sculpture', based on my experience of working for Bird Brothers, in Cardiff. That scrapyard and its people were a formative experience. I'm still using it as a source for writing.

JL: Do you have many memories of your first collection, *A Thread in the Maze*, and its reception? Do you see similarities between the writer you were then and the writer you have become?

RM: The collection appeared six months before I was married in late 1977, and I was already being introduced as 'a poet', publishing in magazines. But I've only ever thought of myself as a 'writer'. The book contained poems about the scrapyard and the world around Penyfai. Evocations of what was a rural world and a 'manorial'-type estate, Cwrt Colman, and the people who worked there. I still write in similar ways, homing in on tiny particularities, but the focus can also be broader, created by travel and politics.

JL: 'Amirya Suite' in your new collection *Diary of the Last Man* sees you return to the subject of Iraq, a country that you have said 'changed your life' when you first visited it. Amirya was an air-raid shelter that the Americans destroyed during the first Gulf War, killing over four hundred innocent civilians. You introduce us to Umm Ghada, 'who goads God with her grief and the ghosts she carries', by living on the site and acting as a guide to visitors. It's an extremely moving poem, dealing with subject matter too painful to contemplate. It's also rare for British writers to write about events in the Middle East like this. Could you perhaps tell us something of how and why you came to write the poem, and perhaps also a little about your relationship with Iraq?

RM: Since 1980 I've been a part of the environmental movement. I became aware of the issue of pollution caused by 'depleted uranium' around 1995, via the HTV programme *Grassroots* for which Margaret Minhinnick was presenter and researcher. Margaret and I worked on scripts from Saskatoon library, where I was a writer-in-residence. Eventually 'depleted uranium' used in armaments meant Margaret, myself and our daughter, Lucy, interviewing UK soldiers in Barry and Birmingham, then travelling around the USA, making a film.

We consulted government officials, pressure groups, and native people from the Navajo, Hopi and other indigenous nations.

The next stage of the film was myself entering Iraq with Beatrice Boctor, a funder of the project. We smuggled a Sony digital camera and lots of medicines into Iraq on a bus across the Badiet Esh Sham desert. Terrifying place. One of the places we visited was Amiriya and the poem relates what had happened there. There's also a film excerpt called 'Black Hands' linked to remixed classical Iraqi music. It's part of my essay collection, *To Babel and Back* (Seren). Probably I'll never go back…

JL: When I interviewed you for Wales Arts Review's *A Fiction Map of Wales* series in 2014, I remember you saying that 'you were obsessed with what sand conceals and reveals', something that is born out both by *Diary of the Last Man* and by your poem 'Old Boots' in this issue of The Lonely Crowd, in which the protagonist 'watches a pyramid / of sand build suddenly'. Could you tell us about this preoccupation and why it has become such a significant subject in your work?

RM: I've lived in Porthcawl since 1977. The town lies between two of the biggest dune systems in Wales, and I often climb the highest dune in Wales, Cog y Brain. If anyone explores the area they find sand unavoidable. I love sand because of the history it conceals and then, overnight, can reveal. Climate change is helping here, as the dunes are disturbed. 'In the dune nothing stays a secret long' is a line I constantly reuse. As to the boots, they showed all the evidence of my explorations of the area. They told an actual story. The boots were a document. Sand is both sullen and mercurial and I like its instability…

JL: Revisiting our interview from 2014 made me think of your contribution to *Fiction Map*, 'Long Haul Road', which you revealed was part of a series of apocalyptic prose writings entitled 'Mouth to Mouth', set by the rivers of Ogmore and Cynffig in South Wales. Did the work for those prose pieces feed into or inspire the poem, 'Mouth to Mouth: A Recitation Between Two Rivers', in *Diary of the Last Man*; and indeed the title poem itself, which feels as though it is set in a similar scenario to 'Long Haul Road'?

RM: Every piece of writing feeds into something else. The two poems here were written on the same day, which is most unusual for me. But nothing comes from nowhere. All writers are walking around with a headful of tunes. Sometimes you find the energy to write them down. I've been thinking about my 'boots' and that overgrown back lane for years. I owned a pair of Dakota boots in Saskatchewan and have written about those.

Because I think it an extraordinary place, the three miles between the mouths of the Cynffig and Ogwr are often where I locate my writing. And when you've been to Saddam Hussein's Babylon or the old totalitarian squares of Tirana, you don't need to invent new worlds because it's already impossible to do those factual places justice…

I think it's almost inevitable for me, as I've been part of the environmental movement for years, to be fascinated by 'apocalypse'. Not the world 'ending' but significant change. In a way apocalypse is natural. In a way apocalypse is good. After all, we continue to live with nuclear energy and weapons… And there's cultural apocalypse. A gradual atomization. I like John Barnie's recent lines 'some say they loved each other / but they loved the Earth too late', which is a sweet epitaph. But I wouldn't have written it. Too pessimistic for me.

JL: It seems to me that a lot of your work is interconnected – certainly the poems in *Diary of the Last Man* – and I wondered if you could tell us a bit about your working methods? Do you write every day? Do your different projects come out of writing which is ongoing, or do they begin more from moments of individual inspiration and a conscious desire to take a new direction? Going back again to our previous interview, you spoke about editing a long poem that you were working on and said that 'It's like putting a film or a novel together. The editing is everything.' It reminds me of William Trevor's approach to short story writing, which he likened to sculpture. Trevor would often take away much more than half of the work that he had originally drafted when completing a story – and yet he felt that the original, dramatically longer draft was essential to the truth of the finished, shortened version. Is this something you find yourself? And when you edit work, do you find that superfluous material finds a new purpose elsewhere in other works?

RM: Yes, I edit and rewrite but rarely throw anything away, believing it can become something else. Words should be recycled. Sculpture? For me it's music, a headful of tunes, as I've said. But maybe I don't have enough notes. Or film perhaps? Writing for me is fluid and organic. I write in my head every day but I'm sure all writers do the same. I'm also fascinated by digital editing and the possibilities it creates. And the remix possibilities of music are endless.

JL: Speaking of film, Eamon Bourke has made an arresting piece to accompany *Diary of the Last Man*, showing you wandering those 'three miles between the mouths of the Cynffig and Ogwr' that we have become accustomed to visualising through your poetry. Indeed, watching it made me feel that, in a sense, you are the 'Last Man' of the poem's title. Whether this is the case or not, the film undoubtedly adds another layer to our understanding of these poems, while also being an intriguing, standalone work in its own right. How did you come to collaborate with Bourke? And how did the collaboration work? Do you see yourself making more films like this in the future?

RM: In Iraq I was responsible for charging the camera, a vital job. I wasn't thinking enough about what the film should look like. We filmed for many hours but it was generally too dull. Also, there were tough restrictions, so filming in Iraq was dangerous. Eamon Bourke [for more information see www.park6films.com] has worked for the charity, 'Sustainable Wales' and other green organisations. Eamon wishes to make other films about writers and I will suggest names. He had complete control over *Diary of the Last Man* and I was happy to go along with his ideas and editing. The film follows a walk between the two river mouths and, yes, stands alone. I'd be happy to be involved in other park6 films but not on screen. Anyway, all writing to me is autobiographical, even criticism and biography. I am the last man and of course I'm not.

JL: There are some very beautiful translations of poems by Fatima Naoot, Karen Owen & Nese Yasin towards the end of *Diary of the Last Man*. Could you tell us a little about these writers and what drew you to translating them?

RM: I try to be honest to the writer's original intentions, but my versions of Fatima and Nese were written in translation hothouses on the isle of Jura and in Israel, courtesy of Literature Across Frontiers. I was signed up to translate even though I didn't know Arabic or Turkish. Karen is different as I have some, but not enough, Welsh. My versions of her work are part of a contract signed years ago, though some of it has not yet appeared. I particularly like Nese Yasin's poems as she clearly described them and I worked from her verbal descriptions. No text. No crib. *Diary of the Last Man* is a mosaic of little songs. And of course poetry can be used in stories. I like disguising poems.

JL: When approaching a project like this, do you set out to simply translate the poems as accurately as possible, or do you seek to imbue them with a sense of your own poetic vision and aesthetic?

RM: Making a good poem in English is always my intention. However, my translation is not slavishly rendering into another language, it's trying to make a valid piece of art. Too much translation is bureaucratic copying. I treat the poems like mirrors. Smash the originals and try to put them back together. Of course I can't. A broken mirror reflects light differently. That's why I find translation exciting.

JL: Carrying on from this, are there any contemporary writers that have particularly inspired your own work, or that you greatly admire?

RM: Of course, lots. I allow myself to be influenced. Influence is healthy and necessary. I came down on the train from Glasgow recently, reading two novels. One, *Apple Tree Yard* by Louise Doughty, was a BBC TV series. The other was *Suttree* by Cormac McCarthy. If I was a filmmaker, I'd choose *Suttree* for its teeming life in distinctive places. *Apple Tree Yard* possesses drama but lacks poetry. It becomes tedious. *Suttree*, for all its faults, explodes, and remains thrilling.

JL: Finally, are you working on new material at the moment? You're also an established novelist these days. Is there a successor to *Limestone Man* on the horizon?

RM: I'm now thinking about my own experiences of different places. Thus Saskatchewan is a possible subject for prose, as is the Middle East. I love islands such as Malta and Sicily. Maybe linking them with home is a possibility.

Two Poems
Robert Minhinnick

Old Boots

He pulls the right one
off, its lace made in some
Vietnamese sweatshop,

fourteen eyelets though he uses only
six, and 200 joule impact
for the steel toecaps,

which must be good he thought
when he saw them years ago
in the Army & Navy, guessing

what it meant, but you don't find those shops
so often now,
and yes they're cracked but not

split and the tongue is
seawater bleached,
all those places he walks,

the margins, over limestone
razors, through
pools red with corallina,

difficult because a continent
is drowned here
and a continent begins,

and he has the polish,
a rind left in the tin
of Carr & Day & Martin,

he should take
greater care, and he pulls
the left one off,

always difficult the left,
yes, in greater need,
the left, a mosaic of scars, but the sole

on both sufficient when he
considers the punishment
of the journeys he makes,

the difficult vocabulary
that rock always uses
and him a learner,

always a learner practising
sandstone's syllables, its quartzite
verbs, and he tips the right

and watches a pyramid
of sand build suddenly
and from the left the same,

perfect he thinks, in their way,
and now he smacks
the heels upon the floor,

and then both soles, and there's more
than he ever thought,
those grains collected

on his expeditions
up to the edge, but next
he sweeps them all away,

dark as violets, white as brass
and wonders as he knows he must
how much might fill an hourglass?

Ragwort

First time in six
months I unbolt the gate
but find the lane

locked by brambles
yards across, an
apology of roses.

Smokers' Lane, the kids
call it, where the world
is supposed to happen.

And who are these?
Lovers, I suppose, as if on cue,
he ahead, the horny

tyke, NY ballcap
perched impossibly,
she behind, eyes

to her samsung,
belly pinned by
an iron butterfly,

grass to their waists,
and bored already
or afraid maybe

but resolutely mute
the three of us
as I pick the thorns

out of my jeans –
thorns the size of fingernails –
and they vanish, this pair

through ragwort's
dishclout perfumery,
into their future.

Barafundle
Anna-Marie Young

That flat summer light. Across the grass she moves towards her friends, and watching, I know what that feels like. The deep sinking tread of moss, the whispering crocosmia, and the part shade from the turning walnut leaves. She sits heavily, glass in hand, dress too wide for the seat, light reflecting off the spray in her hair. Her friends are on ringed sections of pine I cut and left to dry in the late May sun. They are dressed in themed celebration too. Tigers and dogs and elephants and fish.

I sit by the house, my back to the whitewash, and warm my bare feet on the slate. I watch. His arms. The chatter-scream of swifts dipping into the bowl of garden. Next to me, Dad leans against the wall too and takes up my gaze. After a while he says, *I like him,* and the garden and the marquee and the birdsong blurs.

*

That night we decide not to stay. Pack the car in the June twilight with a tent and blankets and drive to the coast. We're running out of time to make it with daylight and so we don't stop, barely talk, load ourselves with bags and hike up the coastal path, over three fields and down a walkway to the beach. Barafundle.

There's music in my head from the dancing and the faint tang of alcohol behind my eyes. In the fading light, sad and melodic. The birds fly low over the headland as we make our way and the sea rushes at the shore, making a show. The dog runs in the dunes smelling rabbits, maybe snakes.

And it's just us and the cool sand and the wind.

It isn't right. It's brittle. Something has happened to us, and so quickly everything is desperate. I don't know what to say because I'm afraid of solidifying it. I look out at the sea and the way the water breaks and then foams up and licks the beach, the way the waves run up the cliffs and leave a darker shadow of damp on the rock. The way to one side a dry stone wall marks the walkway we've come down and, at the other end of the beach, the path leads into woods. The tops of the tree branches shiver in the wind.

And even so, I'm waiting.

He drinks from the bottle, a little frantic, and night falls quickly and softly and brings with it the deep smell of the outside. Fresh and stinging and animal. In the dark of the tent we lie next to each other not touching and he turns his head and begins. And the words blur with the outline of his face and how the sand is lying in ribbons beneath me and how heavy my limbs feel and then, obscenely, how familiar my pillow smells. Like when I was tired as a child.

But however much my sad, shocked body concentrates on the external, I still echo the words. Like syllables to a song I don't know the meaning of. Quiet and strong and painful. As if speaking them aloud casts a spell.

Before I'd met you.

She's keeping it.

And I curl myself around the curve of his spine and hold his shaking body and tell him it will be alright. And later, when he is quiet, I let go. Separate myself from the scent of his body, from that warmth I know, and slowly face away. Listening to the sea hushing the sand in repeat.

Hours later, when the light comes up, that noise is still there: constant and familiar and life-giving. Reminding my heart to open and close and rush blood around my body. Reminding my diaphragm to pull air into my lungs.

We pack in silence and at once I want to get away and also never leave, because this was the last place we were whole. But the gulls are cawing, and the sun is painfully bright and the broken shells cut the soles of my feet as we walk.

And briefly I hate it all.

Four Poems
Martina Evans

Nighttown

Up all night in the Mater pushing
an X-ray machine through the fluorescent light –

I'd waited eight hours for the last coronary bypass
and when it came back, I'd given up

and gone to bed so I had to come down
again in the old cage lift from the Doctor's Res

to the heart arrested in ITU, the body bucking,
the surgeon from Dubai shoving past me as I angled

the X-ray tube and my cross of light on the sunken
sternum, his neat brown fingers cutting into

my picture, chopping the stitches with the side
of his hand, he took out the heart and massaged

it in front of me while I heaved in my forbidden
open-toe sandals. I'd stopped wearing shoes

after my first 24 hours on call in Cork Regional.
They rang from Casualty, *RTA* –

get up out of that quick! the porter who knew
the whole of the Yangtze River menu by heart

shouted there was two stretchers coming up
from a road traffic accident. I sat at the side

of the narrow bed, felt for my shoes only
my feet were tender watermelons that refused

to go in. Forcing them, I couldn't manage one
step – like an ugly sister or a step-mother

dancing in hot iron shoes. I hoped bare feet
wouldn't be noticed in an emergency.

And is it a gypsy you are now so? the A&E
Sister snapped out of her blue lead apron, as I padded

around the immobilised blood & alcohol
smelling bodies with my sandbags and cassettes,

marking right and left with my metal marker,
concentrating on not mixing them up like I had

before. That bossy Sister noticed everything I did.
Next day I woke at half four, in the stuffy

on call room, my day off already disappeared
into November darkness as I hurried

to the shoe shop in Wilton Shopping Centre.
The assistant told me that feet never stopped

growing, *Half a size for every year,
I'm telling you, girl* – sleepy and bewildered

I bought a big size seven. It was only when
I revived over beans & toast at eight o clock

that it hit me – by that reasoning I'd be size
eleven at the age of thirty, with many yards

to go ahead of me. *The coffin that would hold me
hasn't been made yet!* I shouted in the empty

beige kitchen. Back in the shop next day
for an exchange – no sign of the first assistant.

The bee-hived older woman said she'd never
heard of her.

You Can't Go Out Like That

It took Liadain a long time to forgive
me for saying her yellow-tongued pumps were
like something that a prostitute would wear.
Later, I bought MBTs for plantar
fasciitus, convinced by the testimonials
for foot-cures powerful as the touch
of a saint's bone – and just as good looking.
Liane said they were supposed to *give you
a tight butt* but I wanted comfort. Wrapped
in fake fur, ear muffs, blue cross and chain,
I rocked by the hall door on my giant
trainers and Liadain said, *Mum, you can't
go out like that, you look like a rapper!*

The Ambulance Driver Said She Didn't Like My Crocs

And I was at her mercy not wanting
to say that I'd been proud

to get my tea-towelled bloody foot
into any kind of receptacle.

They both moaned from the bottom,
Why is it always three flights!

*Overwork? That's what happened to the
last one. He worked himself to death.*

*Literally. He was a cold – purple literally
– cab driver, just sixty. Dead in his cab.*

She'd be annoyed, she said
if it was neat and tidy when

I unwrapped my fifty-six-year-old foot
implying that there might be a case

for me being a malingerer,
just angling to be carried out

for my Big Night on the Homerton.
A feather-quick exam of my foot,

(later revealed to be full of glass)
and they had me on my feet.

Stumbling, following them down
my own stairs as if they'd been called out

because I'd lost my sense of direction.
This was what walking on knives might be like.

And my foot didn't care for it, burst
its red geyser at the bottom before

I was helped over the bright syrup
clotting on the front steps

and into the van where my blood pressure
was taken and me and my glass

bound tightly together for the take-off
through the streets of Hackney.

In Casualty a zombie-like fleet worked
on computers without lifting their heads

as the two of them wheeled me here
and there, looking for takers.

Politics, politics, she was smiling
with the proof of what they were up

against. It was past midnight when they
found a nurse station open for business.

Those horrible Crocs, she laughed again.
She'd had enough. She was taking a sick day

tomorrow which was today *literally*.
Good Idea, I called after her from

my wheel chair, finally delivered.

the madwife brings a flower in her bag

after Pier Paulo Pasolini's Love Letters

i forgot
from the belly
the madwife brings a flower in her bag
no the midwife comes and in her bag
she brings a flower
your uncle brought you?
the stork brought me
i was born under the blankets
i was the eachtar, the runt
there was a want in me
nobody told me
sent from god
collected at the hospital
sent down by an angel
in a yellow buttoned cardigan
a small nun all in grey
with a pale pink baby sock hanging
off her four knitting needles
i didn't ask for it
never be ashamed
go for help
you can go away quietly
and they will arrange
for it to be adopted
jesus gives it to the stork
i know
i won't say

found crying
in a confession box
a shoe box
blue
thrown in a well
she was nursing in england
and the letter was found
said it was fully-formed
when they took it out
the stork put it in the basket
the madwife comes
and in her bag
she carries a flower

A Gift for Abidah
Courttia Newland

Night softens their clothes, gentle against bare skin, quiet compared with the clamour of the airport. The hum of unseen insects, a hesitant croak, reminds him of tender breathing. Their driver's a thin man, grey hair and grizzled cheeks. He wears an open blue shirt over a white vest and doesn't have a sign. He simply waves with a limp hand, taking the bags from their grasp saying, Please. Please.

Adam's silent for the drive. One arm loose around her shoulders, watching unfamiliar streets through the open window. A rippling blast of warm air. A run of worn and broken shops, the occasional bright moment, fanned with people standing or sitting on bruised kerbs. The sudden blare of music, receding. Faye sleeps against his shoulder, oblivious. She snores and wakes, lifting her head, lowers. He's used to this and doesn't mind. It's the same every journey. With time, he's grown to enjoy the feeling.

He's unaware how long it takes before they turn off the main road, along a bumpy track that makes the car rock, their driver grunt and Faye wake a final time, rising to shift over to the window. Coconut trees arc above. Mute lights, a figure standing by an open door. Sathya. Her pale blue sari's not as pretty as the pictures. She doesn't smile, or wave. They look elsewhere, hands on thighs. When their driver shuts off the engine they get out, waiting for him to pop the trunk and release their bags.

Her greeting's warmer than her body language. She bows, palms pressed flat, and they attempt a hurried imitation, failing. Four young men appear, thin in T-shirts and shorts, wrestling a herd of bags from the boot. Their driver grins, occasionally helping the boys with a particularly heavy item, mostly waiting until Adam remembers. He digs into his pockets, producing oily notes. He hands the driver the amount that Sathya tells him until the man smiles, bows, says Yogi. It takes until the next morning for Adam's quiet epiphany. It's the driver's name, not his occupation.

Their room's not what they expect, yet they've travelled enough for surprise to be a familiar, first night feeling. A low double bed, a sofa in one corner, a single in the other, an easy chair and coffee table, a seventies-style TV. The walls are lumpy porridge oats, pocked and creamy. Jet lag settles into a fog. They wander in small circles, nodding, saying Not bad, not bad, until Sathya waves from the porch, and their young porters shut the door, retreating to whatever rooms they keep. Laughter occurs, shrill as night birds. After some time there's nothing left but the busy silence of a tropical clime.

They undress, brush teeth. Climb into the thin skin of bed sheets, bodies sticky with heat, pressed tight. Adam's head swims. He remembers the air hostess explaining a game she'd played as a child, catching frogs and blowing them up with straws until they exploded. Faye stopped listening, going back to her film, barely disguising her distaste. Adam hadn't laughed even when the hostess did. He wonders if she'd thought him strange, and falls asleep to Faye's baritone snores, a tickle of hair against his cheek.

They wake in a few hours to perform the whole thing in reverse; dress, brush teeth, leave the room. At the door, loud music shocks them to a halt. Echoing drums, the screech of an electric guitar, brittle organ keys. They peer over a crumbling wall and can't see a thing, so they carefully make their way past the pool to the dining room.

You're late, a slim waiter says, wiping tables, but take a seat. We'll get you something. That's very kind they tell him, and hover at the nearest table, lowering into their seats as if hung over. The loud music is closer. There's a man on a crackling microphone singing in Malayalam, seemingly out of tune, only it's difficult for Adam to tell. Sometimes the voice is on their shoulders, then it trails on the wind. Faye winces, gritting her teeth.

God.

A bit much yeah, he says, grinning.

So what d'you fancy doing? After?

Her shoulders are rounded to ward off another verbal assault, dark eyes lit hazel by a metal wall lamp. Strands of brown hair hang in smoky wisps around her face. She looks beautiful. Adam follows her gaze. The sea is dark contrast to the bright expanse of beach. The sky is velvet black. He's torn between going back to their room to make love and catching the night's festivities.

There's that beach festival? We could get there before midnight.

Sounds good.

She's nodding, face blank. He's not sure if she's disappointed or jet lagged. The waiter, another young boy, perhaps one of the quartet who carried their bags, returns with two empty cups and a sweating bottle.

Rod said it gets quite rowdy. Not the usual Hindu affair.

He waits, in anticipation of their order. There's a shallow nick above his eyebrow camouflaged by scar tissue. His hair's cut short and square, jet-black. His clothing, on inspection, hangs from him.

Faye giggles, blushes. Adam grins wider.

Sorry. Didn't see you there.
No trouble friend. No trouble. Would you like drink?
Yes please. Kingfisher?
Very good. Madam?
I'm fine with water thanks.
Very good.

He turns on his heel, leaving the bottle and cups. Another blast of music. Adam leans over, one hand cupped around his mouth.

Hold up mate, can I ask something?
Yes sir?
Poised two bare tables from them, waiting.
What's that racket next door?
I beg your pardon?
The music? Next door. What's going on?
Ah. The church. They're Christians. They celebrate New Year.
Oh.

Adam gives Faye a look. She raises her eyebrows.
What do you know, she says.
Thanks mate, he tells him, and their waiter disappears. Fast talk can be heard from the kitchen. Metal clatters. They splutter laughter, trying not to be noticed again until the food arrives.

He booked a moped with their room, a Yamaha. They collect the keys and helmets from the reception. Sathya's gone, but the nightwatchman doesn't mind being woken. It's waiting in the small car park alongside a team of six others, all forlorn and a bit overused. His bike is cornflake yellow. Its thin sides are dented, rust flakes at the wheels. Adam feels sorry for it. It reminds him of their waiter, and then he feels guilty. Beyond the wall church drums are pounding fists.

There's something intensely satisfying about riding into the night, Adam always feels. It goes undiscovered until the streets flash past on either side, though he never fails to recognise the triggers. Their billowing clothes, the engine roar. The thick smell of burning fumes. Faye's arms around his waist, her body hot and yielding against his. The traffic at this hour is light, yet constant. He uses his iPhone to get there, oblivious of the cost. Adam's too preoccupied to see the few sights offered by the city, yet Faye points them out, ignoring being ignored until she gives up, and keeps them for her own memories.

His phone tells them they've arrived at their destination some four hundred yards before they do. Brine stings their nostrils, ahead there are lights. He follows the broad road until it curves left and they can see the bright expanse of sandy beach, the crash of waves against the shore and a dark shroud of people. Hundreds of Indian families as far as they can see, to infinity. Floodlights blaze white from the opposite side of the road. There's a makeshift funfair, just a merry-go-round, a bouncy castle and trampoline. The tinkle and coloured light of children's toys, a sweet smell of frying. He rides mindful of huge cars and toddlers trailing their parents as they weave through gaps in traffic. Faye clutches tighter, laughs with glee.

He parks and they walk hand in hand, taking their sandals off when they get to the beach. There's a crowd lined before the sea, facing the horizon, and they wonder what they're doing, worrying the subject until they sneak their way through people sideways on, apologising, feeling more British than ever. On the other side, they stand as the Indians do.

Oh.

Wow.

The sea is foaming, venomous. It rushes to the shore, a bully slapping and pummelling the ankles and thighs of the bravest beachgoers, most screaming and running, clothing sodden. Kids have the most fun, jumping the tide knees high. Adam and Faye exchange rueful smiles. She rests against his shoulder.

After you.

Yeah right.

It's wonderful. Good choice.

She kisses his neck, squeezes his waist. A dishevelled man stumbles, finding it difficult to gain a footing on the crumbling sand. He wears a creased shirt and blazer, no shoes. He stands before them, staring. They are the only non-Indians on the beach.

Wife? he says.

Yes, Adam nods. They'd learnt the right answer on previous trips when it became difficult to book rooms with a double bed, if at all. Now they even have rings, Faye's slight and deep yellow, Adam's a silver Native Indian engraving he'd bought in Vancouver.

Good, good. The man grins. Faye looks out to sea. Happy New Year!

He's gone. When they dare to turn, he's stumbling towards the main road, almost falling.

Christ. Well done.

I suppose we will attract the odd nutter. I always thought they didn't drink.

Oh well. At least he was harmless, she says, relaxing against him again. She sighs deeply. I love you Baker.

I love you Mitchell, he says, kissing her head, inhaling coconut shampoo.

There's a roar from the crowd. The kids wave toys, coloured lights smearing the night. The adults shout in unison.

Is that the countdown? I think it's the countdown! She's bouncing with excitement.

I think you're right, he says, and then they can't hear each other, so he roars something wordless as fireworks scream and explode, and they kiss in total oblivion until they remember where they are, but the crowd is too distracted to notice.

Happy New Year! Happy New Year!

It's the most English they've heard since they arrived. The sky is bright and crackling. A young girl smiles at Faye, so she smiles back, waves a little. Her family nod, waggling heads like toy puppies. He takes it as a sign of approval, feeling better.

Look at them.

He follows her finger. A young couple, fully clothed, up to their waists in seawater, rocking with the firm tide, arms wrapped around each other. He wears slacks and a shirt, she wears a sari. The fabric spreads flat, a cotton water lily.

That's so sweet.

That's dedication.

She gives his arm a light slap.

Bet you wouldn't do that for me.

I would.

Is that a promise?

Someone jostles his elbow, filling empty space.

Mister?

The drunk. Faye stiffens, ignores him.

Look mate. Can you bugger off somewhere else?

Happy New Year!

The drunk raises something. A water bottle. The contents are milky. The drunk grins.

Try! Try!

No thanks. Please, just go.

A gift! New Year!

I don't think he's going, Faye says, her voice tugged rope.

Quite.
Gift sir!
Just take it. Maybe he'll leave.
Sir, try!
OK, OK. Namaste. Namaste.

The bottle is warm, a little sticky. There's a blur of smudged prints on the plastic. He tips it to his lips and more comes out than he expects; the liquid is thin, burning at the first swallow, worse at the second. He doesn't know why he takes a second. There's a taste he recognises so he downs more, a third, a fourth, a fifth, then it's like hot chillies. He spits the final mouthful onto the sand involuntarily, coughing. Faye rubs his spine. The taste thickens his tongue. Coconut.

Good! Yes, good!

He shoves the bottle back, annoyed, only the drunk can tell now. His grubby face falls. He stops shouting.

Namaste, Adam says, Happy New Year.

It's too late. The man wanders into the crowd.

Are you OK?

Yeah.

He wipes his stinging lips and sees the family behind her. Each mouth is a thin hyphen of disapproval. The young girl stares at her toy.

They explore a short length of the beach and go to the funfair, but the magic has disappeared much like the drunk. They watch the open-mouthed horses spinning mid-prance, their skin white and glistening, the music a sharp melody in his ears and Faye's hand soft in his, until he realises the swift lights are blurred, his eyes half closed. Shit. He's only tipsy.

Halfway back to the moped a man sells Chai. Adam buys two. They sit on a low wall, pushing their bare feet in cool sand.

Faye talks about that first trip to Thailand, the magic of Had Yao. So amazing, so different. He listens for the most part, because whenever he attempts to speak his tongue feels thick and revealing. His head spins. It was only a few sips. What the hell was in it?

He drinks from the polystyrene cup, saying nothing, warm hands cradling the tea. After a while, Faye realises.

You OK babe?

Yeah. He smiles. Jet lagged.

You look a bit pale.

Her eyes are focused, clinical. He's seen that look in the pharmacy. She feels his forehead.

We should probably go.

Finished?

Yeah.

She takes his cup to throw in the nearest vomiting bin. When Adam stands, he feels himself sway. Don't do this, he whispers. Don't do this. Faye comes back, unaware of young men staring as they pass them.

Let's go, she says.

The moped takes three attempts to start. Faye's patient, thinking it's the bike, but it's not. It's him. He can barely hold the bike's weight. The world is a carousel. There's an ache somewhere between his eyes. Every few moments the lights, Indians and buildings coalesce into a kaleidoscopic blur until he squeezes his eyes shut tight and normality returns. He just has to get them to the hotel. If he rides slow and keeps away from other vehicles, he should be able to do that.

It's a good plan, the best of a bad situation. He rides at twenty most of the way, slower when the streets blur, ignoring beeping taxis, the rush of wind and roar of engines as they overtake. Faye strokes his waist, and she's tense, he can tell, but she doesn't say anything. He's glad to have her. She's a good woman. He should marry her, his parents always say it and he laughs them off, but it's true. Who else does he trust? Nobody, that's who — he's a loved-up Scarface. Adam chuckles, squeezing his right hand just a bit harder so he can get her home.

They almost make it. They're so close. The iPhone tells him that in half a mile they'll reach their destination. When he looks up, dark streets merge with bright lights, just as another bike passes close on the right and he hears voices to the left, a large group it sounds like, but he's already veered that way to avoid the overtaking traffic. His hand twitches in shock. The moped leaps forward. He's trying to control it only he can't see anything but the blur. Faye screams close in his ear, frightening him, and he feels a bump and knows what it means, that he's not on the moped anymore, he's not on anything, just riding empty space.

It's almost peaceful. If anyone had told him that he'd say they were lying. There's nothing to see but tarmac shooting beneath him. He's not breathing.

Then he lands, the air punched from his chest, everything coming back, his vision, the noise, his pain. The bike lies on its side not far from him, wheels turning like the merry-go-round, engine growling anger. Faye sits just beyond it, being pulled to her feet by Indian men. More come his way, fingers wagging and they're shouting. On the pavement, half on and off the kerb lies an old woman, mouth open, her thin and dusty sari draped high about her waist. Beneath her grey head, Adam sees blood.

No, no, no…

And they're on him.

The first kick is to his thigh. Before he can react another connects with his bruised ribs, making him gasp, and he's covering his head, curling on the ground as blows land everywhere. They're shouting so loud he can't hear if Faye's screaming. Please don't let her scream. His teeth strike the road, his mouth fills with blood. He's kicked in the head, repeatedly. A heavy boot slams into his stomach. He can't breathe. He's dizzy, he retches. The blows intensify until he can't tell where he's being hit, everywhere hurts. There's more shouting, the whistle of an object scything air, the thud of something solid hitting flesh, and the kicking stops, leaving him to the throb of his pain.

He's lifted to his feet. He yelps with agony. His feet cry *shush* as he's dragged along the street. There are noises, something he should know but does not, and he feels the cold of metal against the broken skin of his cheek. He calls out, the animal sound of his voice echoing in emptiness and the noise comes back, yet he knows it now; the sliding of a van door, followed by a crunch. There's sobbing somewhere over his head. Faye. He feels her beside him, crying and screaming and he knows it's really bad.

They're separated until morning. Of course he doesn't sleep. He lies on the polished floor of what seems like an interview room, wailing, bleeding onto wood. When the sun appears, Adam tries to lift his head only to find his cheek stuck. He shouts as he pulls away. The combination starts him bleeding again. He sits up, rocking, tears stinging the wounds on his face and lips. No one comes.

What feels like hours later, the door opens. A small, unsmiling man enters. He's balding, although the hair at his temples and the back of his head reaches his shoulders. He's short and muscular, wearing baggy slacks and an oversized shirt, carrying a small leather bag. Adam retreats while the man pays him no attention. He opens the bag and begins to pull out bottles, cotton wool, scissors, gauze. Adam relaxes. The man points to a chair and when he sits, examines him without a word, grunting when he needs him to turn, grunting and gesturing with a hand when he wants him to stand. He's quick and thorough. Although he's strong, he takes care not to hurt him. Adam follows his instructions with caution, every move causing pain. The doctor wraps gauze under his arms and around his left leg, applies stinging ointment to his cheeks and the back of his head. Done, he grunts and stands, returns everything into the bag.

Nothing broken. Rest.

Adam nods. He can't even look at him.

And the old woman?

The doctor stares out of the grated window, places both palms together.

Namaste, Adam says.

His eyes well, overflow. He makes a rough, unbidden sound in his throat he hasn't heard since childhood. The doctor knocks on the door. Someone unseen opens it. He leaves without looking back.

Adam lies on the floor, using every muscle that still works to lower himself, sucking air between his teeth until he finds a position that hurts least. He has no watch. Sometime later, groaning as he feels for his waist, he realises he has no belt. He tries not to think about Faye. Eventually he sleeps until the opening door wakes him.

It's a tall, portly Indian. A full head of hair, greying at the forehead and temples, jowly cheeks. He's squinting. His eyes are dark-rimmed, deep. His stomach flows gently over the belt of his trousers and he's dressed in full police uniform. His shoes glisten in the sunlight.

Adam sits up. The movement makes him sweat.

Good afternoon young man. I trust you feel better?

He's not sure where the question might lead, so he nods once, looks at the floor.
Have you eaten?
No.
That is not on. We will arrange it.
I'm not hungry.
We'll arrange it anyway. He smiles. What a terrible, terrible business.
Adam's shoulders tremble, and he sags. He moans, attempting to stop the sounds with a fist. The man squats beside him. His shoes creak.
Please. Don't be so hard on yourself. We understand it was an accident. A simple accident.
He tries to speak, can't. He waits, the policeman's hand on his shoulder, rubbing like a brother. In time, he controls himself.
It's OK. Ha? You shouldn't worry yourself.
I… I just… It's so…
Do *not* worry yourself. I won't allow it. We'll take care of everything.
Adam looks at his big, jowly face, sniffling. He swallows snot, what tastes like blood.
I am Superintendent Khatri. I've assigned myself to your case. Being that I know the family of the injured party, we thought it best I come in and deal with matters.
Pardon me superintendent, but where's my wife? Has she been charged?
No, no, no. Khatri booms laughter, hands on his thighs. His mirth echoes against the walls. You're wife's fine, she waits outside. She's innocent, we understand.
Adam's hands shake. His chest rises and falls.
Thank God. He breathes, throat rattling. So you know the family?

Many years, yes.

How is she?

He doesn't want to sound like he's pleading and he can hear the intensity in his voice. It's the only thing he wants to know after Faye's condition.

We understand, and are grateful for your concern, but unfortunately the lady was very old. Very old. I'm sorry to tell you she passed away sometime during the night.

What? *What?*

I'm afraid so. I'm very sorry.

Jesus Christ. Jesus Christ.

He thinks he might break down again but strangely enough, although he feels the emotion and even pushes hard to release it, nothing emerges. He's very aware of Kathri beside him, peering close, the strength of his aftershave and the big rough hand on his shoulder, maybe that has something to do with it? His headache intensifies. He blinks rapidly.

What now?

What now? Katri leans back, dark ridged palms open. Now it is over. You're finished. Your lady has taken care of everything. Very kind woman. *Good* woman. She understands.

Excuse me?

You're free to go. We took the necessary tests. You were not over the limit. This was not drink driving. It was a simple accident. It could've happened to me.

He beams wide. His teeth are very white, almost perfect.

But…

Yes?

Adam pauses. He wants to say there were no breathalyser tests done that he's aware of. He can't.

You assigned *yourself*?

Yes?

He opens his mouth, thinks. There's a twitch above the superintendent's eyebrows, a beating involuntary muscle. Something tells Adam to stop. He closes his mouth, gasping with slight pain.

Thanks for your help.

Very good. Please enjoy the rest of your stay. And you mustn't worry. You're a good man. Your wife is a good woman.

He swallows. It hurts as though it's solid. Kathri stands, gestures.

Please.

Adam gets to his feet. It's difficult, but he manages. Kathri doesn't offer a hand, or help. He strides to the door, banging with an open palm. The repeated noise makes Adam wince.

They're escorted back to the hotel in a police car. Adam prefers a taxi but isn't about to argue. Faye sits in the rear with him and at the same time doesn't. She's distant, in complete silence, holding his hand in a loose grip. Her head is turned and she looks out of the window. She's been like this since he came out to see her sitting on a polished bench, red-eyed, attempting not to focus on the whispers of waiting Indians. He tries to communicate by caressing her fingers, gets no response. In the rear view, the eyes of their driver stay his tongue.

Sathya waits on the reception steps when they pull into the car park. It takes them both an age to get out. Faye jumps when something thuds like a fallen body behind her — a coconut, dropped from a nearby tree. When they try to locate it, Adam sees lowered heads, whispers, the whites of janitors' eyes. Younger boys stood on one side, watching. Holidaymakers make obvious attempts to ignore them, chatter ceasing. They walk in silence. He tries to pull Faye to him only she's bamboo stiff. Sathya nods at the dust, escorting them to their room even though they all know it's unnecessary.

They can't walk as fast as she does, so every few metres she stops, waits. The resulting journey takes far too long. The sun is gleeful, merciless. The swimmers at the pool make every effort to look elsewhere. Faye struggles with the room key while Sathya remains wordless, gazing at dark wood. She was pretty once, perhaps recently. Her hair is black and straight, reaching her knees. Her skin is one shade removed from the deep brown of the wooden door. Her lips are full and sculpted, yet sadness rests in her long-lashed eyes, creasing the corners. She moves to help as the door opens and they're inside. She takes one step into darkness, no more.

I am sorry you are injured.

Adam mutters half phrases. After all, they're relatively unhurt and can walk, albeit painfully.

We must all do what we can to make this easier. I will do what I can.

We're really, really sorry, Faye says. She's crying. He wants to go to her only his limbs won't.

It will be all right. You must stay at the hotel for a few days. I will let you know when it's good to leave.

How long will that—? Adam starts.

Sathya's outside, sunlight flooding her until she closes the door. They stand together in darkness. Birds twitter beyond their windows. He opens the curtains and can see.

Babe, please.

He holds her. She shudders into his neck and this is bad too, although better than her distant silence. He rocks her, feeling cold tears against his neck, until she's finished. He leads her to the bed where they sit with their arms around each other. When she relaxes, Adam goes into the bathroom, returning with a handful of tissue. Faye grabs the wad, pawing her face.

Shit.

I know, he says. From the pool there's a huge splash, laughter.

And it's my fault.

What are you talking about?

I told you to drink the bloody thing, she says between dabs.

Yeah, well, I didn't have to. Anyway, didn't that superintendent say it wasn't drink driving?

She's frowning, nose and eyes red, glistening.

How would he know?

Adam shrugs, gasping at the shooting pain.

Maybe they did a blood test?

When? This morning? Did that doctor take any blood?

He sees her expression, shakes his head.

Right. And you never saw a doctor last night either. I kept asking, but one never came.

So… Look, I don't get it. What reason would he have to lie?

He knows why, along with his reason for asking. He wants to hear it. He wants it out in the open, to inhabit the room. He wants it to live. Faye's open-mouthed. She thinks he doesn't get it.

Because he made me give him money, that's why. He got that driver guy to drop me at the ATM so I could get forty thousand rupees. I had to use the joint account and mine.

OK, Adam says. OK.

He sits very still, hands on his knees.

OK?

Yes, OK. Meaning it's a lot of money. Right? Meaning it's over, thank God.

But what about that woman?

Look, I know—

She was bleeding! She hit the floor, and there was this massive crack, and it was awful!

Faye... Faye! He grabs her arms, painful as it is. He can't hold on for long, and when she pulls away he's forced to let go. Listen to me. I understand what you're saying. Of course I do, it's terrible. But what would you rather? Me in jail, right now? For something I didn't do?

What do you mean 'didn't do'?

The way she looks at him. Piercing. She's never had that look before. He wants to take back what he said, say it was stupid, only he's told himself the story since the interview room, and it's gained meaning. Kathri's words have become his own. Now, more than hours ago, he owns them.

It was only a few swallows. I wasn't even drunk.

She sneers, actually sneers, turning to lie on the bed, knees against her breasts, unblinking.

I wasn't. I swear.

Go away Adam. Please. Go.

He sighs. Pulls himself up trying not to groan in case she thinks he's attempting to illicit sympathy. The most he can muster is a series of breathy moans that to his mind at least, sound worse. He rustles around for his book and goes onto the veranda. The heat is a five-pound weight against his chest. He lowers himself carefully into the sun lounger, rests his head. Pool chatter falls into silence. He swears beneath his breath, finds his page. The headache returns.

He reads until the light fades and consults his scuffed watch. He looks around, remembering where he is. The pool is barren, water laps. Hanging bulbs and lampposts glow. He goes back in. She's still there, a bed sheet wrapped around her. Crumpled shorts lay on the sofa. He climbs onto the bed, wincing, getting under the covers. He spoons her, kissing her neck. Her eyes are closed and she's breathing lightly. She's warm against rough denim.

I'm sorry.

You don't have to be.
It's not your fault. It's mine.
It was an accident. That's all.
A soft knock. She eases out of bed, pulls on her shorts and opens the door the tiniest crack, wider.
Aw.
She goes out and comes back holding a tray in both hands. Two metal covered plates, two paper covered glasses.
How sweet.
It's very kind.
I told you she was all right.
Next time I'll trust your female intuition.
You should.
They eat on the sofa with enthusiasm. After all that's happened they've forgotten hunger. Sathya left them twin biryanis, one chicken, one vegetable, and freshly squeezed lemonade. She even remembered their dietary requirements. He reminds himself to check any bad feelings towards her. When they finish he stacks their plates and leaves the tray between the sun loungers, on the wicker coffee table outside.
That night the sea thunders violence. The Christian music begins late, going on until daybreak. The preacher's voice echoes. He lies on his back, eyes open, listening to crows shake trees with their movements. He tries not to wake Faye, knowing she's listening. He sees the steady advance of blood, a dark halo on paving slabs.
They don't want to go for breakfast but in the morning, no tray waits. They walk uncertainly to the dining room to find it full. It's a shock. They very nearly turn back. Other holidaymakers try not to stare even though they don't have to, and the fact no one looks their way except for a coloured couple in the corner makes it worse. The couple glare them all the way to their table. This time their waiter is a young woman, her

expression a blank wall. She takes their order and leaves before they are done. When Faye goes to the kitchen to ask for a mango juice, she tells Adam when she returns, the waiter from their first night stands in a corner arguing with a chef. He won't look at her either.

Sathya enters the dining room. Adam knows it's rare, because the waiting staff halt, mouths open. She comes straight to their table, wishing them good morning. After they thank her for last night's meal, she says that they're very welcome and they must see her after breakfast for a chit-chat, as she calls it.

Before that, they walk the beach. The sand's already hot. They pick their way through broken coconut shells and sun-browned palm leaves, remarking how unlike the cleanly expanse of Bondi Beach it is. They're sweating. Not far from the water's edge fishermen haul their boat onto the gentle rise of higher ground, and as a team, prepare to transfer a full net of shimmering fish onto a tarpaulin sheet they've laid and secured with heavy rocks. Adam and Faye watch. The fishermen fall silent. They stop pulling at the net to stare. The couple look away, growing nervous. A man in a red shirt steps away from the others, coming towards them. He shouts, a finger raised, shaking with pure anger. Faye pulls Adam back, he stumbles on loose sand. The man screams at the sky, fists clenched, an elongated war cry. Tears spread on his red shirt like ink spots. He almost reaches them when his colleagues wrestle him to the floor, and yet he fights to stand. It takes eight men to hold him down. They shout, waving them away. A big man walks up to Adam before they can react and pushes him hard in the chest with his palm. Adam falls on his arse, awakening bruises. Faye weeps. The big man waves him away, going back to his friends as Adam clambers to his feet. They stagger to the hotel where a mangy dog, half brittle fur and half rose pink skin, barks at them in turn, turning circles at their feet.

Sathya listens to their story, producing a box of tissues from a drawer to give Faye. Behind the hotel manager Adam sees a black stone and green tinted statue of Shiva. His golden countenance matches Sathya's. She's infinitely calm, both hands laid flat on her reception desk, possibly to avoid the distraction of her jangling bracelets. Adam's put out by her lack of emotion. He expects some level of outrage, but there's none.

Perhaps you could offer something? They're a poor family. Funeral costs will be difficult, she tells them. A small contribution might ease their loss.

He stiffens, one arm around Faye. Her head is bowed. She touches her eyes with swollen tissue.

You mean pay them off?

Sathya's head rocks, deflecting inference.

If you like.

But how would we do that? We don't know who they are...

They don't live far. The man you saw is Azmat. He's related to the woman, Abidah. She's his great-aunt I believe. If you want, I can speak with him.

I don't know… I wouldn't know how much to give, I really wouldn't. This is all so…

It might help Azmat's hurt.

Seriously?

Her poise remains unchanged.

It's the least you can do.

Adam gets to feet. He takes an inward breath and waits, holding the desk. He doesn't like the way she regards him, with contempt, disinterest. She's stopped trying. If she ever had.

OK Sathya. Thanks.

They go back to their small room, which has shrunk in size. Faye lies on the sofa. Her short legs hang over the edge. Her arm covers her eyes. Adam limps from the single bed to the television several times. She ignores him.

So? What do you think? You haven't said a word.

She removes her arm.

I think we should.

Really?

It's the custom.

Really.

What does *that* mean?

She turns on her side, shading her eyes.

I just… It seems a bit silly, don't you think? You saw how he went for me. You really think money will make things better?

Sathya thinks so.

Oh yeah, that old ice queen would really know something about empathy wouldn't she? What?

The light. It's in my face.

He moves to the sofa, waiting for Faye to curl her legs. Sits in the space she's created.

I've nothing against it in principle. It just seems a bit redundant.

I don't know what your problem is. It's very simple.

I told you what my problem is. Besides…

What?

Oh, nothing.

No, go on. What?

He chews a hangnail on the edge of his little finger, bounces his knee. Her neck's craned forwards, her mouth slightly open.

It's… He sighs. Look, we've paid right? Already?

Faye clasps both legs and brings them to her chin, pressing her forehead into her knees. Adam watches, tugging at the hangnail between his teeth.

*

They laze on the veranda listening to the insects and the Christian band tuning up. Beyond the pool, a clink of plates and metalware, chattering voices, a warm glow from the dining area. They've just finished their own dinners when Kathri appears on the curving white path, head tilted at the night sky, arms behind his back, whistling. He sees them and makes a gentle, unconsidered turn to stand before their veranda steps.

Good evening sir, madam.

The air fills with a rich musk of aftershave.

Evening, Adam says. Faye's greeting is so low even he can't hear it.

Enjoying the night?

Yes, very much. Yourself?

Kathri inhales a deep breath, sighs. His broad shoulders sag.

I'd like to. I'd like to.

Adam's hands shake. He sits up.

What is it?

I was at the house. Terrible thing. She was elderly but still, it's unexpected. The family are in such shock.

He's forgotten to breathe. Faye's stiff beside him.

I'm very sorry.

I know you are. It's not your fault. We understand that. But you see, Sathya mentioned you'd had a conversation, and I began to wonder… Whether you might have… He drums his fingers against his belt, frowns. A response.

The words take time to settle. When he looks at Faye, her eyes are wet and she doesn't turn away. He's never wanted to kiss her so badly.

I have. I think we both agree with Sathya.

Good. Very good. Kathri leans forward, one foot on the top step. Do you have plans? If not, we could leave immediately.

They're upright, trying not to seem nervous. Adam can't help noticing Kathri's polished shoe, a gleaming black beetle.

Really?

If you don't mind.

Sure. You don't mind babe, do you? OK. We'll lock up and be with you.

Please. Take your time.

Adam secures their door. Facing the superintendent, he looks over his shoulder to see if anyone's watching. The windows and paths are empty. The breeze lifts, palms nod.

Excellent, Kathri says, placing a hand on his shoulder.

His eyes are like the dark spots on a coconut, small and flat. Everything tells Adam to say no. Everything. Only his guts feel light, and he might vomit. His mouth tastes sour. He senses Faye's presence. For the first time he knows fear.

Good people, the superintendent says.

Kathri takes the main road, making one stop for the money, one turn off. The houses here are singular, spaced wide apart, most too dark to see into. Families sit cross-legged by open doors. Old ones move nothing but their mouths, chewing with bovine rhythm, otherwise in deep mediation. Young ones perform cartwheels or leap small fires while their parents lean against dark grey walls, penetrating night with their eyes. Light is far behind them, confined to small spaces, fighting for survival. All is dark, and as much as they sink into their seats with entwined fingers, there is also a sense that no one shares their concern. Indians walk the unlit street as though the sun blazes. Windows are solid black squares, the spaces beyond as immune to curiosity as closed blinds.

He pulls up beside a high white wall. Opposite the car, various forms separate and merge with the background of a ground level house. Each form is a shadowed chameleon. Kathri gets out. Adam and Faye follow. He walks towards the small flat-roofed house shouting Malayalam. Azmat emerges from the gloom, wiping his hands on a blue checked tea towel. Faye's breathing fast. He pulls the money from his pocket closed in a fist.

While the Indian men talk, the family, three young girls, an older woman who could be their age, and an old skinny man with an open shirt and hollowed chest, treat them like museum pieces. He tries to track what's being said but can't follow the conversation. Kathri throws an arm back to include him. He steps forward, feeling shadows envelop him as the superintendent pulls him close.

It's difficult to see. Azmat's red shirt is open. He wears a thin glistening chain of gold, the most visible thing beside the whites of his eyes. Adam opens his mouth. Instead of words, a sob. He bites back, stammering. Kathri pats and rubs his shoulder. He's shaking. It's awful. Azmat speaks, the family murmuring a chorus. The old man chatters at no one, nodding towards the broken teeth of floorboards. Adam remembers the unhurried orbit of the merry-go-round, the song of white horses, the drunk stumbling on powdered sand, arms flapping for balance.

I… I don't know how to tell you how sorry I am. There's nothing I can say to get that across. I did a foolish thing, and I… He bites a fist. He refuses to cry before these people, he has no right. I'm so sorry. Truly. Please forgive me.

Adam holds out the money. Azmat looks at Kathri. Soft fingers touch the back of his neck, clasping. Faye. When the superintendent speaks, Azamat faces Adam. Shadows make his features a dark blank. Kathri prises the money from his fingers, passing them to the man.

It's not enough. Nothing is.

Kathri translates for Adam. Awful silence follows. Azmat nods, speaks. Raises the money to eye level, returns inside the forlorn house.

It's done, Kathri whispers.

He returns to his car with an even, unhurried step, leaving all of them silent, insignificant metres apart.

Everything's too loud. A chorus of insects wheeze dyspnoea. Crows jostle tall trees, beating wings against palm leaves. Hours afterwards the church music takes over, the preacher roaring eternal salvation, the bass throbbing at walls and cymbals clashing ocean waves as high tide rocks its patient, vocal time against the shoreline. Adams lies on his back, the stark room visible as daylight, cheeks damp with his tears. He dares not turn to Faye in fear of communicating his dreams.

They wake early and take the first taxi out of the hotel, which happens to be Yogi's. His leather seats are painfully hot so they sit on crisp white towels. She rests against Adam's chest, holding his hands. The palace is an hour's drive. When they arrive tourists are already queuing. They stand in the shade to buy tickets, opting for the tour.

In dark and cool rooms, Faye rubs his back, or pushes an arm around his waist. He kisses her hand and she caresses his chest. Once, when their small group climbs a compact square of staircase, she wrestles his head to meet hers, pulling him down, bruising their lips. Her mouth is open, tongue firm. They pant in each other's faces. Adam sees glimpses of other tourists ease past, heads down, half-smiling. Ah, the English, he imagines they say. A small boy watches, playing with his belly button, clutching an armless Captain America.

For lunch, Yogi takes them to the beach where it all started. When they ask him why, he says his cousin's restaurant is the best. They swap worried looks. Yogi doesn't seem to know. After all, nobody does. When Adam meets his eyes in the rear view he perceives his first clearly identified expression of sympathy. Yogi slows to accommodate the passage of beachgoers. A right-side mirror says, 'Objects in the mirror appear the same as they seem.'

They eat and walk on sand while Yogi rests in the back seat with his bare feet up against the door, his blue shirt over his eyes. The sea is calmer, not enough to swim, although people bath in the shallows. The merry-go-round spins, serenading all. They spread out a small blanket, lying down. It's peaceful. They sleep and when they wake the sun has fallen like a stone. In the taxi, Adam tries not to look at Yogi's cracked and yellow toenails, the hardened white of his heels.

Adam wants to walk the beach at sunset. Faye's less sure, and only agrees when he promises not to stay until dark. They cross the hotel grounds, ignoring everybody, exiting through the back gate and stepping onto cooling sand. They've made it. The sun is an orange ball. Seabirds strut on thin, knock-kneed legs. Dogs lay on their sides, their stomachs expanding and contracting bellows. Fishermen haul two boats up the beach. Ropes are tied around the bow and stern. The men are bare-chested, chanting a communal song, and as they raise their voices to the Alphonso sky they pull, bodies dripping seawater and sweat, muscles stretched.

Faye stops, Adam continues. He kicks sand, heeling the sandals from each foot, jogging down to the men, all too busy with the task of beaching fishing boats to notice. He finds an empty space at the nearest boat, slips in front and grasps rope. It's rough against his fingers, solid. Some wear gloves, most don't. One leads the chant, others answer, and in a rhythm he begins to anticipate they lean back, plant their feet, heave. Listen for the leader, sing skyward, heave. Gulls circle, wings reaching. Adam grits his teeth and leans. He doesn't look at the men. The song doesn't stop or lose a beat. He sings only the words he can manage, first beneath his breath, then loudly as they do. Up and up the beach. His hands sting. His T-shirt is damp. Sand scratches his feet. He pulls until the boat climbs the incline and the song fades into the lonely voice of a single man, the leader. Ropes drop.

 The leader climbs into the boat and throws out tarpaulin. They spread it flat, placing rocks on corners. Adam lets go, massaging cracked skin with a thumb. He helps them lift the nets of busy fish onto slick material and they let him, yet no one acknowledges his presence. He scans faces to see if any are Azmat, ashamed he doesn't know him well enough to say. None are wearing a red shirt. He stands further away, hands on hips, breathing hard.

 When he remembers, Adam turns to see Faye waiting. She claps silently, lifting his sandals high. Sathya watches from the hotel gate. Her arms are folded, and her long hair resists the breeze.

Five Poems
Matt Rader

Yarrow

The delicate open-
Work of yarrow
Knitting

White doilies
Among fescue
And ladybirds.

Would you believe me
If I told you
Achilles staunched

Battle wounds
With a poultice
Of yarrow?

I say the best
Orientation
Is disorientation.

You say nosebleed,
Oldman's pepper,
Woundwort.

Who wants to
Half-see, you complain,
The underlying

Surface of things?
Who wants
To be without

Pain? In the Hebrides
A yarrow leaf held
To the eyes

Gave second sight.
From our bent coign
Of vantage we see

Through the lacy gaps
Of flowerhead
Airglow, earthlight.

Trembling Aspen

What's here is not
Only what interacts
With light,

What I know
Of myself, what I can
Show. The shimmer

Of aspen
in a tipple of wind
That rises now

Like evidence
Of nothing
That can be

Spoken
Then falls back again.
The thimblerig

Of Juncos
In a cup of sun
And shadow. Death is

Part of the body.
You can touch
It and do.

But mine is only one
Of many
That are also mine,

Said the quaking aspen,
Within its quiver
Of selves. Here

I am again
And again
And again. In spring

The 1000-year-old
Aspen grove leafs out
All at once.

Black Cottonwood

How often you talk
To yourself
When you're alone

In your poems
Or walking
Between the shadows

Of two cottonwoods
You've never
Named. What powers

The Sun is a process,
A sequence,
That yields all matter.

What regret taught me
Then desire.
How in bed for hours

We unmake
Ourselves
In the other's image.

Feelings
For people don't change,
You said—

The wind moving
Two shadows
Across the window—

They just become
Something, nameless.
How even now

The cottonwoods loom,
Empty, silver.
Through the embrasure

Of branches
Light falls like arrows
All around you.

Riparian

Black leaves
And mud at the edge
Of a season.

The cedars
Suddenly rung
Suddenly more

Among the empty
Birch and willow,
Emerald

Boughs preened
And gleaming
In the wet,

Like tail feathers
Of something
Enormous,

Mythological,
Something
Forever

Turning away
In the photo.
Only the icy, blue

Spruce now,
The paper sky
The early sun

Is just starting
To burn through.
Can we reconcile finally

What's shored
With what's riven?
Between the wires

Of the fence
The radiant fog
Moves.

Cantor

At the third bridge
We stopped
Midway

Above the creek
While the dark path
Continued on

Without us—
Turned one way
It was onslaught,

Turned the other
Abandonment.
From where we stood

We could see nothing
Coming down
The dirt road

Into the valley.
Only the open land
We recognized

As property,
The austerity
Of birch trees

And willow
Huddled
Along the banks.

When the owl called
I did not
Believe

It was an owl. Only
The cantor of evening
Singing like one.

Eclipse
Stevie Davies

'Hige sceal þe heardra, heorte þe cenre, mod sceall þe mara þe ure mægen lytlað'.

Violets and primroses have powered up between the paving stones of Beth's London garden.

'They appear so fragile, don't they?' she says, at the open window, her face to the light. 'But violets are tough as old boots. They just hang on in there and don't take no for an answer.'

Lee and Beth have been getting memories out and looking at them together. They all lead to or from the eclipse. It's thirty years since they slouched in the back row of that Anglo-Saxon lecture — and the following day Beth warned Lee about the eclipse. That's how Lee remembers her first inkling of what was to come, somehow marked by the weird little drama that concluded the lecture. Byrthnoth the warrior had just taken his death blow. He raised his shield and lo! the men of Maldon fell in gouts of blood by his side; the Vikings were upon them.

They rarely speak directly of the eclipse. They chat their way round the subject, occasionally darting in to dab at it with their fingertips.

Holding out a hand which Lee takes in both of hers, Beth says, 'You know, Lee, I was lying awake last night for ages.'

When Lee sympathises, Beth shakes her head. 'No, it can be lovely if you don't have to get up in the morning, just to lie and meditate and see the people you've loved in your mind's eye. Strange — at that hour, there is a great stillness.'

On the train home to Wales, Lee sees Beth there by the open window, saying that there's a great stillness. She's seen that in her, the stillness. She's unsure whether it comforts her, she thinks it does. The train isn't full: Lee has the luxury of two seats to herself. Sipping coffee, she glimpses her face shadowed in the pane as night consumes fields and hills. Somewhere within the dark reflection of Lee hovers the pale stillness of Beth, remembering.

Next day the email springs out. 'Our friendship — it's so dear, it links the time before the eclipse with the time after. Everything else just separates them. I know you used to grieve that I couldn't love you in the way you wanted — and I couldn't, and I can't — but, Lee, what could I do about that? It was better to stand on my own feet anyway, as things turned out. Lying awake the night before you visited, I remembered looking out of the Georgian window in Carey's flat in Bath, the morning after he finished with me. I was back there seeing what I saw then. But what was it I saw? A fatal fluke of the light, impossible to describe. I'd packed my bag, I was ready to leave for the last time, my heart was convulsing, but I just stood there looking. Quite calm. Carey got up, hoping I'd gone most probably, and asked, all hangdog, was I all right? I just shrugged and picked up my case. When I got back to Bristol I sat down at the piano and didn't play. You came in with a mug of tea; you put your hand on my shoulder. You didn't plague me with questions. You were just there. We've come through a lot, you and I — disappointments, estrangements. We're like family, Lee, we always will be.'

As she reads, Lee sees Beth peering out of Carey's Georgian window (though Lee never visited his posh flat and is not even sure what a Georgian window is like). At nineteen Beth was slender and tall, hair all down her back, eyes lustrously dark, her whole life ahead of her. In imagination Lee stands behind her, a silent eyewitness of this private moment. A pearl of a moment, kept for a lifetime. But what was it she saw?

Lee tries to reply but deletes everything as being fatuous and artificial.

*

Waking before dawn Lee is left with the hem of a dream: Beth in a system of reflections, framing one another to vanishing point. She's looking out of that Georgian window. Wondering whether Carey still owns the flat, Lee hunts down the address and googles his name: yes, there's a Carey Wardman listed in Bath.

On the train, looking out into the misty morning, she wonders whether Carey will even recognise her now. Will he let her in? There's only one way to find out. The sun's burning off the mist and the city is honey-yellow as they draw in to the station.

Until her legs have carried her there, Lee's unaware that Carey's is *the* address in Bath: Royal Crescent, exclusive, opulent. She never liked Carey; Carey never liked her. At least they saw eye-to-eye about that. When he visited Beth, Lee would clear off for the day. Carey wasn't all that bright on the emotional level but he smelt her contempt and was doubly gracious. Beth loved Carey so much, Lee never grasped why. He was an ex-public-schoolboy who still affected his school scarf. And he didn't love her enough: Lee never understood that either. Surely the whole world must adore Beth, she thought — not just her dark, amazing beauty but her incomparable heart. Lee crept away like a wounded dog when Beth told her finally, after the eclipse, that it was never going to happen between them. It's not the way I'm made, she said: I can't help that. But don't go away, I don't want you to go away.

The vista here is breathtaking: the sweeping curve of the famous Palladian façade, ochre in sunlight, facing the green. Some houses in the crescent have been linked to form an opulent hotel with a white-gloved doorman in a top hat. Tourists cruise the pavement, craning up at the many-paned sash windows. Lee pushes open the wrought iron gate. There are three bells, one for each apartment. What's she going to say? Hi, Carey, you won't remember me, why should you, I'm a mad person who just wants to look out of your window, do you mind?

She thumbs Carey's doorbell. A woman's voice: 'Had you booked to view, Madam? I'm about to lock up — but I can allow you a brief glimpse.'

Which is all Lee wants. To see out of Carey's space, along Beth's eyeline. The property has been on the market for some time, the estate agent says.

These windows are treasures in themselves, Lee's informed, for this is original glass, over two centuries old. The Princess of Lamballe and then the Duke of York and Albany looked out of these windows: it gives them a value. Lee treats the estate agent to her basilisk blue stare. Nevertheless, the agent feels Lee may be interested to know that the planet Uranus was discovered from this very back garden or it might have been the next one along. Angling herself beside Lee, she appraises her frayed jeans and her window obsession.

'Of course a view like this is worth, literally, millions,' she says, in case Lee hadn't twigged that the apartment is likely to be way out of her league.

Unqualified light streams through soaring panes into the eggshell blue, high-walled interior. For all her irksome spiel, the agent's face is calmly luminous and the green weave of her suit collar turns emerald, reminding Lee of when her mum's cataracts were removed and she'd study the nap of a cushion as if absorbed in a book; also unfortunately decoding the stains that had lain undetected in the fabric for, presumably, years. But whatever met Beth's eyes eludes Lee.

'Have you seen enough?' the estate agent asks. 'Make a formal appointment to view at leisure, if you're genuinely interested.'

'I've seen plenty.'

One final glance at Carey's expensive view.

The sunlight's suddenly milky; colour wanes. Mist spreads across the vista of lawns and trees, swallowing into its softness and silence people and dogs and taxis and a passing gull; a mist so dense as to dissolve altogether the grid-like bars of the Georgian window, clouding the interior of room and eye alike.

That mist was what Beth saw.

*

Lee had spent half an hour binding up Beth's hair in a complex weave of plaits, tiny side-plaits tributary to the thick braid falling from a knot at her crown. Beth's face without its framing tresses looked bare and tight: well, it was tight because the plaits pulled. Her eyes watered and narrowed and her eyebrows seemed to lift in frozen surprise.

He'd been got rid of apparently. Bloody Carey. So Lee might stand a chance.

Up there in the back row of the auditorium, you were sure of being inconspicuous. Tiers of terminally bored students ranged down to where the dark-gowned professor was repeating what he'd said annually for decades: surely he'd actually been present at the Battle of Maldon, a craven scribe annotating verbs as mail-coated warriors slaughtered each other. The guys along the row from Beth and Lee were licking their thumbs to flick through the sports pages, tempting

Professor Hapgood to eject them. Which he never would, for Happy lived in mortal terror — of students as a Viking mob, and even more of students as individuals.

Nobody really listened. Happy was a musty and muttering old bookworm. He'd not yet said anything that might make a difference to anyone's life.

And then he did. It was electrifying.

'Failure,' he said. 'The poem celebrates failure.'

And he stepped out from his defensive position behind the lectern. Pausing, Happy removed his reading specs and confronted the two hundred and fifty pairs of eyes. The slumped audience sat up and took notice. At which Happy retired to the shelter of the lectern. Coughing, er-hem, he covered his mouth and slicked back his oiled hair, what there was of it. He searched, blinking, for his place.

'Ah yes. Here we are.'

There was something funny about the shape of Professor Hapgood's head. A dint in his forehead. No scar, just a reminder that something had banged rather catastrophically against his learned skull at some earlier date. In the war perhaps, though it was hard to imagine Happy bearing arms.

'To continue. Now, the thanes, you see, the thanes can only stand and die. That's it. They've driven off their horses so there can be no retreat. *Come swiftly to us, warriors of war,* Byrthnoth invites the Norsemen.'

Snaring his lapels with his thumbs, Happy began shambling to and fro behind the lectern, murmuring.

Beth paused in the task of unravelling her painful plaits, half her hair curling snakily, the other half still in chains. 'Has something happened?' she whispered and squinted, craning forward. 'I can't see.'

Three paces west, two paces east. Then the murmur ceased. A standstill. He abandoned the lectern altogether.

Professor Hapgood hadn't an original bone in his body. He'd never trusted himself to venture a view without remarking that Sprott or Quail had opined this or that. Whatever it was that prompted Happy's breakout — and weeks later the stroke that carried him away — it must have been a searing wound that thrilled through every nerve in his body and dwarfed the constellation of fears he'd carried through life. Later it was rumoured that he'd been declared Dead Wood by the Dean: a relic of an anachronistic scholarship.

'My dear young people,' said Happy — and he stood in his nakedness before the phalanx of students. He tilted forward, a short man with a paunch, on tiptoe. He opened his arms; the dusty gown became a pair of black wings. 'Consider Maldon. The heroic moment. Consider what the dying Byrthwold tells the dying troops: *Hige sceal þe heardra, heorte þe cenre, mod sceal þe mara þe ure mægen lytlað.*'

They stared over the throng at a tiny actor on a distant stage. Beth rubbed her eyes. 'I can't *see*,' she said.

It meant, so Happy explained, that our will would be harder — our hearts keener — our minds more determined — as our power lessened.

For lessen it would. It could not be otherwise.

Happy gave a curious little jerk. And another. A pencil rolled off the lectern and the clatter of its fall echoed through the auditorium. Folk were all round him in a moment, sitting him down, offering water, but Happy bounced to his feet, wiping the cold sweat from his forehead. 'Ha ha, not dead yet,' was the last thing we heard the professor say.

'That was amazing,' Lee said.

'I couldn't see properly,' Beth complained.

'No, I couldn't really. We should've been at the front.'

Next day Beth confessed: 'Lee, there's something badly wrong with my eyes.'

'Is it conjunctivitis? Let's have a look. Can't see anything.'

Lee hung around in the corridor of the Eye Hospital while they shone lamps into her friend's dear, beautiful eyes. Her parents came and wept. It turned out she'd been denying the lessening of the light for nearly a year. It had been a gradual thing and the doctors could eke out Beth's power to see for some time yet. She said, I'm glad Carey and I finished, Lee. I'd have leaned on him and he'd have withdrawn. It's better this way.

And Lee agreed, with hectic fervour, for somewhere within the passionate sorrow of Beth's catastrophic loss, she thought it gave her a chance.

*

Beth's not expecting Lee. Even if she's at home, there's likely to be a student with her, deep in study of some complex sonata that may take half the day to explore. If so I'll wait. She's learned patience, waiting for Beth. Hanging around beyond the time when it made sense to wait, for any fool could see that the case was hopeless.

Lee lets herself into the back garden, long and narrow, secured by copper beech hedges that keep a rustling remnant of the old year's leaves while new buds break open. The carpet of violets and primroses, well past its prime, still offers patchy vestiges of colour. The piano sounds from indoors: some modern piece Lee can't pretend to understand.

Wandering to the end of the garden, invisible from the house, she curls up on the bench near the ivied wall where one year Beth showed her the sparrows' nest. Lee gets comfortable, bunching up her cardigan for a pillow. She drowses, then she must have slept. Because when she comes to, the low light is auburn on the wall and her friend is crouched at the border braille-reading the blue and white starry faces of anemones. Lee has no idea what she's come so urgently to tell her.

The student has gone and the music is over and they are entering late middle age and, Lee thinks, here I still am beside her.

Three Poems
John Freeman

At Wentworth Place

The smallness of the space and its proportions,
which feel right, like the golden mean and section,
help make this public room feel intimate.
Lying in bed, before and after seeing
the colour of the arterial blood
he had coughed up and asked Brown for a candle
to be sure of, and told him he could not be
deceived in it, it was his death-warrant,
he saw the door at the bed's foot on the left
and the single large window on the right,
just as he was to when he got to Rome
and spent his last months in a room like this one,
though less well lit, and with a higher ceiling,
and with, instead of trees beyond the window,
the murmur even in 1821
of passers up and down, and people sitting,
perhaps, as they do now on the Spanish Steps,
a sound not unlike that of the fountain
which, when human noise is stilled, still rises
from the Piazza di Spagna, Bernini's
Fontana della Barcaccia, and soothed him,
prompting him to compose his epitaph:
Here lies One whose Name was writ in Water.
Despite those differences between the rooms

I wonder if their similar dimensions
as well as having held, asleep and waking,
the same inhabitant at different stages
of his vibrant life, and final illness,
contribute to my feeling, in both places,
something powerful and unexpected
I have not found the like of anywhere,
even in the most secret country churches,
except in these two rooms with half of Europe
between them, and in my case with decades
between my visits to them, so I am struck,
made momentarily almost breathless
by finding it again, this atmosphere,
arresting, charged, an absence like a presence.

Julia's Cakes

My cakes are never as light as Julia's,
she said so sadly that I had to tell her,
you have other talents, but she answered
so does Julia, she paints, she used to paint,
she used to paint the most marvellous landscapes.
I don't like baking, she more than admitted —
affirmed, a rebellious declaration.
I always feel it's such a waste of my time.
There had been a family get-together,
she said, and I thought she meant in the village,
knowing her son had been about, her daughter
so much in our thoughts I wasn't certain
whether she had been at home as well,
convalescing from her operation.
But she said it was in Kent, she liked Kent,
but didn't know it well. It was in Deal,
on the coast, she said, and I would have asked her
to tell me more about it, the occasion
she travelled all that way for with her cake,
and what it was in Kent she saw and liked,
but conversation faltered and veered off.
She looked cold, I noticed, standing with me
in the car park where to my surprise,
and hers, I'd come face to face with her,
busy at the open boot of the car
in the space next to mine, putting in
the last things or the only things she'd bought.
I'm left with the picture of her sitting
on trains from Wales to London and then out,

and in between getting from Paddington
to St Pancras, surely, on the Circle Line,
carrying as I imagine it, as well
as a bag with a few necessary things,
ceremoniously, a large, round tin,
through the underworld like a talisman,
the focus of an ancient ritual,
filled with all kinds of aching heaviness,
family love, family distances,
the self-reproach of not being able
to bake a cake as light as Julia's,
but also the reluctance overcome,
and flour, and butter, eggs, and jam, and sugar.

Keeping A Welcome

I don't come this way on a road to nowhere
for the fun of hearing the distorted chimes
of the Mr Whippy ice cream van, playing
over and over again the first nine notes
of We'll Keep a Welcome in the Hillsides, but
there it is, butter-coloured, blocking the lane,
and there's a harmless, stooped, grey-haired woman
having a chat while she is buying something,
and here's me thinking, it must brighten her day,
no-one else calls here, perhaps she's lonely.
Though I can't see the driver properly
I get a sense of him, quiet, middle-aged,
struggling to make a living probably,
and years of indignation at this pling-plong
heard in city streets, even more denatured,
louder, played more frequently and longer,
count for nothing, my heart set against it
softens to the consistency of ice cream.
I sidle past the van and walk on down
across the ford, back up the other road,
and hear the tune again, unseen this time,
and a front door opens. Two children run out
down to their gate with their faces lifted,
open-mouthed and pointy-nosed, blinking like moles
sniffing out signals, and I can't help melting
at the sight of them, with their laughing mother
in jeans tumbling out of the house behind them,
especially as their snouts are pointing up
instead of down the street, the wrong direction,

and I call out to tell them where he is,
adding that he's coming this way, which he is,
and in so doing I realise I've changed sides,
and cheered for those to whom the ice cream jingle
is something to be glad of, not resent.
To my old self I plead in mitigation
that the volume is down, the repetitions
few and discreet. I hear the tune once more
near the end of my walk, and am able
to tell from the sound that after doing business
with those children, Mr Whippy wound uphill,
past the church, the pub, then down through the estate
of new houses, and either in to the town
or the other way, out towards Bridgend.

Actors
David Hayden

Hair frothed over a sharp white collar onto his denim jacket, brass buttons shone, cuffs neatly folded back, once. The actor sat. Jeans — winter sky blue, neither too tight nor too loose — ended in clean white plimsolls with flopping tongues and no laces. He lounged back on the orange vinyl sofa waiting to go in for his callback. He looked out through the window, as a nameless white bird flew by, and back at the receptionist. She looked up. They both smiled, weightless smiles. Some distance away his siblings gathered with their stories.

M., on his way home from work, was dragged off his bicycle by two strangers. The men stamped on his face and hands, breaking his nose and several fingers. T.'s boyfriend pushed her hand into a fat fryer. He left her to bring up their son alone. He is happy now with his new family. D. works part-time as a kitchen porter in a near-derelict seaside hotel. He could sleep in any of the abandoned rooms, with their slippy walls and mildewed bedding, but he prefers a crawlspace in the attic where, each night, he can turn and turn in his sleeping bag. D. has not spoken since 1987.

A man pushed through the swing doors and rushed forward.

'I'm *so* sorry. I'm *so* late.'

He was wearing jeans, a denim jacket, and a white T-shirt spotted with tomato sauce.

'Yes, you are. Do you have the updated sides?'

'Ah...'

'The ones I emailed you last night? No? Take a seat.'

He span round, a stricken look turned into a smile. He approached.

'Nick…'

'Will… Here… there's a photocopier in the corner.'

Nick took the sheets and returned a moment later.

'Above and beyond, Will. Thanks.'

'There's a cold-read as well.'

'You'd be mad not to want this part.'

'It's a part.'

'Didn't I see you in…'

'Possibly.'

Nick arched his eyebrows and settled back in the chair, flapped the sheets about for a moment then began to read. Will noticed the concentration, noticed his attempt to conceal the concentration.

M. is fifty-five years old. He has been working in kitchens since he was thirteen. He is a good chef. He was recently declared bankrupt after the garden centre café he owned ran into difficulties. Everybody was paid. M. was thrown out by his wife. There was drinking. M. was thrown out by his wife. M. has had surgery on his ruined feet and can no longer stand for the full duration of a regular shift. T.'s son plays the saxophone. T.'s son is episodically psychotic. He has beaten her up, twice badly, once he tried to throw her from an upstairs window. D. has spoken little since 1987.

The phone rang and the receptionist answered. The actors looked over.

'In you go.'

Nick rose with Will.

'Not you,' she said.

Nick sat down and Will left.

The studio was dark except for a white spot in the corner where the director, her assistant and an older woman, unknown to Will, sat.

'You can begin,' said the assistant.

'The leaf and the shadow fall together and meet at the ground. Winter never arrives or departs entirely. The feeble sun, the clotted cloud, the nameless scree in the gutter, the grey sweep of filth on the windscreen, salt stains on unpolished boots, snow holding, holding on high and never falling. Heavy season. We chew on our breath, our lips crack and warp. Heavy season. Blood moves thickly through our feeling, our thinking parts. You are waiting for the story to begin? Wait on.

'Hands are concealed in the cold. How can we trust gloves? How small are these hands? What might these hidden fingers do? Do again what gives us pain? No need to fear. Time will lend you time and take all eternity to do so. There is a rumble underfoot that might be the subway or distant trouble approaching or children, many children, all the children — digging out of the ground with their fingers, their soft and tiny fingers. Greet them with love so that it exhausts you and fills you with longing for loneliness, and the sun will depart and there will be a long cold moment until permanent darkness. That agitation of your heart is the memory of sunlight and how you failed to, how you could not, embrace it all. Every ray was yours but you did not. You knew this at the time.'

Will took a silent breath.

'Now the story begins.'

There was a hush of carpet as the door opened. Nick walked in and over to the group. He stood opposite Will and turned to face the director who nodded. Nick spoke.

'What was your plan?'

'I tied a shoelace around the mechanism of the ironing board.'

'What happened?'

'My wife was tired. It was the end of the day. The children were asleep. The dinner had been made and cleared away. The dishes washed and dried and stored. The laundry had been washed and dried and folded. Clothes to be ironed had been separated into a pile. She took out the ironing board, pulled the lever and tugged the board up, which jammed about a third of the way. The black plastic cap that covered the lever was missing. I forgot to say that.'

'Had you removed it?'

'No, I had not removed it.'

'Continue.'

'I intend to… My wife leaned over the board and, not seeing the shoelace, pulled harder. She lost her balance somehow and fell over the board. The lever punctured the skin next to her shin and, as she tumbled, the metal ripped up her leg, only just missing a major blood vessel. "It was as if my leg had been unzipped," she said later. To the children.'

'Where were you at this time?'

'I was upstairs painting the bathroom.'

'What colour?'

'Primrose yellow.'

'Matt or gloss.'

'Matt.'

'Go on.'

'My wife lay on the floor. Blood poured out, yellow fat, the bone, visible in her ruined leg. She pulled herself across the floor to the kitchen, leaving a wide crimson streak on the carpet…'

'Does she have a name?'

'Yes… She pulled a tea towel from the oven handle, folded it around her leg and pressed as hard as she could until the bleeding slowed. I came down the stairs and into the living room. She cried out. I walked over to the sink with my jam jar filled with brushes. She caught at my trouser cuff as I passed and she pleaded. I pulled away and washed out my brushes. I returned to the bathroom where I continued to paint, finishing the section above the picture rail. An hour, two hours later, our daughter came down the stairs and found her mother mostly unconscious on the kitchen floor. An ambulance was called. An ambulance arrived. My wife recovered. My wife contracted bacterial arthritis. But that was later.'

'Had you intended to hurt her?'

'No. The shoelace was only meant to annoy, to confuse. To throw her off balance, in the other sense. The accident was just lucky. But they all — my wife, my children — thought it was planned. Deliberate.'

'Why would they think that?'

'Because I once said: "I would kill you if I could avoid prison for doing so". Because of everything else.'

'So, after she came out of hospital, your wife left you, right? Were the police involved?'

'No one talked to the police... My wife did not leave me then. My eldest daughter and my son, my youngest, bought a house together a year later. Their plan was to convince their mother to leave me. She told them that she was scared that I would kill her. Eventually. That I would kill her, eventually. They sent her money, which she hid in her left shoe underneath the insole. She left me without... notice. I let her stay away for two weeks and then I visited. I stood on the doorstep and looked up at my son. "Has it come to this?" I said, knowing it was a hackneyed phrase, and I bit my bottom lip for good measure. My daughter, I learned later, stood hiding a few feet away, teeth chattering, body shaking. My son said that this was what his mother wanted. The next day she returned to me carrying the small suitcase with which she had departed. She did not leave them a note. I was concealing myself behind the living room door when she answered my son's telephone call.

There was a long silence. "I... I love him," she said, and hung up the receiver.'

'Tell me about love.'

'I could dance. I could play the piano. I could sing. I looked good in a suit, in swimmers, without them. But that was later. In the dormitory... Where was it? Out west. I could make the others cleave to me. Everything was grey — the barely-suspended sky — or green — the distanceless fields — or brown — the itchy uniforms. There was no glamour until I arrived. I brought the colour, the blood, the necessity. And what was that which came to me as my due, if it wasn't love? A tender age to learn about possession, it was — for all of us.

'There was a drainage channel at the northern limit of the grounds. The boy was found floating there, a pathetic figure in his cap and shorts, his woollen socks still pulled up to his knees. He was alive, just, you know. But they agreed that I should leave. I left for love. That's what I know about love.'

'Tell me about death.'

'My mother died. My father died. He died in my armchair. A half a mogadon was left untaken, a cup of tea untouched. He proposed marriage to my daughter. She brought him tea and a half a mogadon on a saucer. He proposed. She left the room. His heart failed. She returned to find him dead.'

'Tell me about death.'

'I had an aneurysm. I left hospital two weeks later against the advice of doctors, without their knowledge, in fact. I was in the kitchen when my brain, when it finally broke and my head filled with blood. I collapsed onto the cold yellow lino and died there. I was discovered days later. It was a cold September.'

'Tell me more.'

'I can't. I've run out of lines.'

'Thank you,' said the assistant. 'You can wait in reception.'

Nick pointed to himself and looked at Will, who had pointed to himself and was looking at Nick.

'Both of you,' said the assistant.

*

Nick and Will sat on the sofa.

'Went rather well, I thought,' said Nick.

'You were good,' said Will.

'Well, don't sound so surprised.'

'I'm not surprised and you know it. You're a terrible actor when you're not acting.'

'You say the sweetest things,' said Nick.

Will looked out the window. Nick bit off a hangnail and looked at Will.

'Are there two parts, do you think? Because…'

'You've not read the play.'

'No.'

'There's one role. In two parts.'

'Oh.'

Blue flowers were arranged in a too-large vase that rested on a stand opposite Will. He tried to remember the flower's name and nothing else. His family returned.

M. spoke.

'I threw the garden fork clear across the yard and it landed in D's pump, the left one. The tines went clear through the canvas and pinned his foot to the mud. I didn't mean anything by it.'

T. spoke.

'I sat in the car. I was already late for my exam. The sea rose and fell a short distance away. He wanted to know. He wouldn't let me go. He never let me go.'

D. spoke.

'It was safe in the coal shed. Everyone would pretend that I wasn't hiding in there.'

*

A buzzing noise came from the desk. The receptionist looked down and squinted to read, looked up and called over.

'You're wanted.'

Will and Nick looked at each other.

'Both of you.'

The men stood up and walked back to the door of the studio.

'Are we going to be alright?' said Nick.

'I think so,' said Will.

The older woman handed a ragged yellow sheet of paper to the director who handed it to the assistant who pushed it towards the actors.

'Read, please,' said the assistant.

Will held the sheet and Nick stood close by him. 'Left,' he said. 'Right,' said Nick.

'Involuntary against the dark.'

'The depths charged.'

'The mass, each a petal…'

'Falling, floating, shivering.'

'What agitates the sea.'

'What moves the eye.'

'I have never scintillated.'

'Never come to the boil.'

'The cold deep, the held, withheld.'

'The sun, unrisen.'

'And night waits, waits.'

'And again, waits.'

'The movement against fear.'

'The telephone used to ring.'
'Language and its shadow.'
'Time and its shadow.'
The actors paused and spoke their line.
'We came together.'
The director clapped, the older woman and the assistant joined her.
Will looked at Nick.
'It's all ours, Nick.'

Three Poems
Bethany W. Pope

Black Wings; Sharp Teeth: A Modicum of Love

My first Autumn in the orphanage, I
worked lifting bales of hay onto the bed
of a large truck. The bales were square, and bound
with rough twine. They weighed seventy pounds.
I weighed ten pounds more at that time (I was
twelve) and it didn't take long for the nerves
in my palms to deaden completely. My
skin split open, red and lush, right across
my love lines. One day, I snuck off early,
skulked the five miles back to the cottage.
I hadn't heard from my family in weeks.
My father had stopped writing. I felt numb.
The sky was that odd blue I later saw
in Giotto's frescoes: cobalt, with gold
beaten down in sheets underneath it.
I stood on the back porch in a daze,
gaping up through the naked bones of an oak,
before knowledge and fear drove me back
into the house. Walking to the door, I
saw something small, something furry and dark,
clinging to the riverstone wall. A bat;
insectivorous and trembling. I scooped
it up and it lay across the bloody
river that my fingers branched from, swinging
it's sharp-toothed head like a bauble on a spring.

It was definitely rabid. I didn't care.
I brought it indoors with me, hid it in the box
containing my letters. It was something to love.
It lay in the bottom, blind and shivering,
smelling strongly of sweet scalp and dust.
I fed it water and milk from the edge of a rag.
It didn't live long. I did my best for it.
Still, I found it stiff and cold, leather wings
crumpled like wet gloves around a packet
of air. I buried its body (such as
it was) among the roots of a live oak
that looked like a frog. Then I waited
to spot the first symptoms. There were other
means of escape than longed-for phone call.

Speaking of Windows

My father's church looked like a hospital,
painted little-girl pink and abandoned
by the side of the Tamiami Trail.
It was made of two (tall) stories, square,
with a flat tarpaper roof that was perfect
for watching meteor showers, under
a rough blanket, if you could force yourself
out through the narrow trap door which opened
deliriously close to the edge,
and if you could avoid the puddles
of standing water the clouds dumped there.
My Father used to retreat to his office,
late Saturday night, to work on his sermon.
They were always a beautiful blend
of academics and poetry
(he wrote about finding the skull of a doe,
in the woods of Kentucky, and seeing
flashes of Ezekiel reflected
in those terrible black sockets) and that
worked against him whenever the session
met to argue about his paycheque.
Church types tend to prefer the easy 'nice'
to the terribly beautiful. In any case,
working so late, my father got lonely,
so he'd bring me with him, or else one
of the dogs. I loved the church at night,
I loved the quiet, damp smell of the place,
I loved breaking into the library,
or raiding the fridge for Sunday Morning

Danishes. I loved the sanctuary,
darkened, when the wine-coloured carpets
looked black and the street lamps turned the windows
into negatives of themselves. The windows
were fifteen-foot-high Pre-Raphaelite
paintings in glass. They were a sequence
which told the whole New Testament. I loved
to watch the face of Mary age, one pane
at a time, from perfect, blushing girlhood
to hard-faced mourner at the skulled foot
of the cross. I loved to trace the outline
of Christ's delicate feet (His toes were shaped
exactly like my brother's — finger-like)
and I could understand why the other
Mary longed to wrap her blazing hair
around those soles. I was lonely then,
of course, but I did not understand it.
I was happy there, too. I had my windows.
I had The Book of Job. My father sat
in his office, beneath his bust of Martin
Luther, hammering words which sang sweetly,
but were largely ignored. I lay, sprawled out,
stomach-down in a pew, learning to live
in the right kind of silence, in the odd glow
of numinous images, sharply reversed.

Rose Red

Sometimes, I remember the rose garden.
It was never, really, a garden, but
it tried it's best. Roses cannot thrive, in Florida,
unless you can afford a gardener.
The soil isn't soil; it's glassy silica,
it has nothing to give to a flower.
So, roses are a symbol, there, and not
for love. My father laid this garden out,
in one of his periodic flurries,
as a gift for my mother. He mapped
a six-yard square in the grass and we dug
it out, marveling at the things we found —
a whale's rib, a lump of quartz, an iron
slug left over from a Conquistador's
foundry, the side-mirror from a Volkswagen
Bug. My father bordered the garden
with painted red pine, as though it were
a fence. When that was done, he directed us
(I was ten; the orphanage was ahead of me,
but I couldn't read that signal, yet)
in planting the low-grade shrubs he'd bought,
in bulk, from Sam's. He stood there with the bright,
clean blade of his shovel leaning against
his sweaty shoulder as we laid down bags
of bargain fertilizer which we masked
with a thin layer of expensive cedar
mulch. In the end, the plot looked perfect.
Professional. The smell was delicious.
It looked as put-together as our kitchen:
smooth surfaces, clear and clean, disguising

an absence of fine china, and food.
By the end of the year, the roses
were dead, and my father was searching
for somewhere to place me. When I was fifteen,
I was home, on probation. My absence
had been carefully masked. I adhered
to every stipulation, desperate
not to be uprooted. I dug into
the sand. I smiled at church. I did what he
asked me. I read the right books and I mouthed
the right words. It wasn't enough. At night,
after everyone was quiet and the house
felt dead, I was called into the garden.
I put on a dress of dark, plum velvet,
with princess sleeves and a plunging neck,
and walked, barefoot, into an ocean
of grass. The pine boundary had rotted
into soggy, brown splinters outlining
a gray, barren patch. Nothing would grow, there.
The sand was cool, and empty. I paced
the cavity, endlessly, around
and around in my dark, flowing dress,
my tangled hair loose, about my shoulders.
I was using the death in the garden,
eating it. I would become someone else.

Lovebirds
Armel Dagorn

The bottle bobbed along again.

'It's disgusting, isn't it?'

He agreed. There was a moment of silence, during which he looted through his brain to find something to add, something meaningful, or witty. Anything.

'What can you do, though? Some people are like that.'

The conversation had been going that way for a while. It wasn't at all how he'd imagined it. In his mind the very time and place of the date should have scored him some points. He'd thought that not inviting her to a bar or restaurant would distinguish him from all the sleazy guys who no doubt asked her out, all the sleazy guys who had ever asked her out; that bringing her to the park around the castle's moat would show her he was different, more sensitive maybe, deeper. He saw now it was wrong, the place was wrong. He should have brought her to the sea, or to some shady riverside, not to this imitation of nature. That beer bottle: it was unnatural. It kept coming this way and that, pushed only by the light breeze, the dead scummy water lacking any drive of its own. Where were the currents, the tides?

It hadn't started badly. She'd arrived first, and she'd watched him from the sun-spotted grass where she was sitting, the tree's shade like fluttering lace, watched him walk to her from far off, smiling at him. He'd raised his hand in a little wave as he passed by a large group of punks, young men and women, or boys and girls, in torn pants and T-shirts, bare-chested some of them, folks with their heads shaved underside and long dreadlocks or red hair or thread-wrapped locks like knitwear sausages falling low on their backs, lying on army jackets, in tights with holes big enough for a head to pass through. He'd thrown comically-worried looks around at them for her benefit, and she'd laughed.

'God,' he'd said, sitting down after saying hi, 'what is this, the new *Mad Max*?' She'd laughed again. He hadn't been as inspired since. Maybe he'd peaked too soon, spent all his wit in one go.

A dog was running up and down along the moat's bank. It had been there when he'd arrived and hadn't tired since. It was a black dog, with a patch of white on its neck, the type of dog he thought of as the shepherding kind. It had a red bandanna for a collar, like a Boy Scout. He wished the dog would jump, bring some action to the dead-hot park, provide something to comment on. Now all they did was look at it without a word. They followed it over there by the corner of the moat, down here a few feet from where they sat. It looked intensely into the green, still water, seemed about to jump in when fish surfaced and stirred the soup-like water to feed, or have a look, or just tease the dog. Sometimes the dog stuck out its paw, treading the air above the water as if to remotely catch the fish. He was reminded of a magician scanning the air with his hand above a rabbit-popping top hat. There were long stretches when he thought, for dizzying seconds, that there was nothing to say, that there would not be anything to say ever again, and that they'd just sit silently like that until she had enough and left without a goodbye. It was terrifying, but thankfully there was always a little comment to be made in the end, and if it didn't help him in the greater scheme of things, he was grateful for them, for the little lifeline they offered him.

'Come on, jump in,' said a woman up on the wooden footbridge that stretched, a little bit further up, to the castle's secondary entrance. She was looking down at the dog and the water with her two kids. Up there, a couple of old ladies were following the scene as well. It was all wrong. But he didn't know how to steer the date away from the direction it had taken, which was towards not being a date at all. They were like friends hanging out. They could have been that mother and her kids, these two grannies passing time. He felt something like panic come over him.

'I've read it used to be the river here. Everywhere. Marshes. It's all reclaimed land. The castle was surrounded by water.' She didn't say anything. Just nodded, looking at the dog still. This wasn't how he wanted to impress himself in her mind. Midges pestered him, tickling his scalp, his bare feet. He'd moved to the town a few months back and was still interested in whatever local trivia he came across. She was a native, and had probably been fed these facts as a schoolgirl, had been bored even then. This was all wrong! He should be talking about home, the mountains he came from, their blue looming on winter nights, the stars sharp as knives. The cold, star-sharp on your neck. He'd thought the fact that he came from the other end of the country would make him more interesting, more romantic at first. But in the few months since he'd arrived, he'd found nobody cared much when he talked about home. He wasn't the first guy to leave his hometown. Or maybe they suspected his home wasn't all that different to theirs.

If at least they'd gone to sit by some river, in the fields, or down on rotten leaves in a wood, the gnats would have been the price to pay, not just a pointless nuisance. Maybe the park, the castle and the moat themselves bored her. She might have been coming here for twenty years, might have had her birthday parties here as a schoolgirl. Had her first kiss here. Had her breasts fondled over clothes by an intense fifteen-year-old bad boy. One with dreadlocks or a piercing, like the punks over there. Or some shy, pretty boy who'd told her 'I love you' with moist eyes.

He looked at her, and saw she wasn't looking at the dog any more, or the water, but looking up, at the other spectators maybe, or the blue sky.

'It's such a beautiful day,' she said.

'Yeah,' he answered. He wondered if he should make a joke about how much he sweated.

The dog came back to a few feet in front of them, its ass to them, marking time like the pendulum of a grandfather clock.

What was all the slander about fish and their memory about? That dog was no better, coming up and down, honestly believing it was going to jump in, jump on the fish, but never doing so. Never remembering that it didn't. Its tail swinging unwaveringly, and for a second he saw himself pushing the dog into the water.

The dog was probably one of the punks'. Was the floating beer bottle theirs too? A little scene ran through his mind in which one of them came near the water and threw a bottle into the moat. He cursed at the punk, loud enough that it was possible the man had heard but didn't have the balls to come and confront him.

'What kind of people throw rubbish in the water like this, in a park, where kids play?'

'Evil people,' she answered with a smile. He laughed too loudly, blushed a little.

He felt like a twelve-year-old boy sitting there with her, eliminating potential subjects of conversation in his mind. He was afraid his lack of confidence undermined what he thought of as his main asset, the cool demeanour he wore, the cool of a worldly, discreet bohemian. Or maybe it was just that horde of punks. There was nothing discreet about their hedonism: now and then a loud curse rose from their group, bounced onto the castle's walls and into the ears of all the Saturday loungers, in the ears of kids and grannies. They didn't care. He looked at his loose cotton pants, how safe they looked, how obviously expensive, fair-trade shop got. A little film popped up in his mind, of himself ripping off his clothes and jumping into the water.

They were stirring, the punks. Noise level rose, and they said things like 'Come on,' and 'Lazy arse!' to each other, laughing loudly. One call, 'Keta!' started to cover the rest. 'Keta!' It sounded angry. It was a tall, scrawny punk, his head shaved but for a few fair dreadlocks at the rear, swinging down to mid-back. There were metal implements in them, feathers. He kept calling, walking towards the dog which was now just in front of them. When he reached the dog, he called the name again, this time in a low voice, tenderly almost, and he patted the dog's head. The punk had a tremendously innocent face then, seen up close, as he looked down at the dog that had been too focused on the fish to hear its master call. The punk seemed about to go then, but he looked at the water, and saw the bottle as it came around for its nth lap of the moat.

The punk grumbled something, and without a pause stepped into the water. He was barefoot and wore cut-off jeans, but the water must have been a little bit deeper than he thought, or the slime at the bottom more unstable, and he sank down to nearly mid-thigh. He picked up the bottle and stepped back up on the grass, dripping. The dog looked up at its master with pride, if one was inclined to believe pets felt such things. The punk seemed to only notice the two of them sitting there as he started to walk back towards his friends, and he smiled at them.

'Have a good day, lovebirds,' he told them.

'You too,' she said, and watched the punk walk away, the bottle in his hand while he waited, standing, for his dozen fellow misfits to get up, then all the way to the steps out of the park where the first bin was. It landed in with a small, far-off *ting* you could easily not have heard if you hadn't been paying attention. Above, on the footbridge, no one looked on any more. He thought he would miss the dog.

'This weather,' he said, phewing, 'I feel like I sweat out my whole body volume every day.' She looked at him and gave him a little smile. He was so grateful for it, he nearly let out a thank you.

Two Poems
Rhea Seren Phillips

The Sea Laughed and the Stomach Blushed

The cockles sucked in a breath that left blood open,
the sand jostled to the supratidal, breaking the
waves that frothed like whispers, hissing to the ocean.
Stomach felt a rush of heat that made the rugae titter;
force acid down a corrugated scalloped tube.

Plasticine pearls crackle like sparklers, looking like
white pupils in the intertidal apocalypse.
Black smog settles like fine dust on amphipods that
rustle like anthracite, scattering the shoals of flesh
towards speckled fires, grit so intrusive it hums.

Madness

A distinct madness has snagged me today.
I seized it and dipped a hand into its gore,
let's huddle and listen to its sickening decay.

You arrived; braying for me to delay
my retreat, but I spat aside our rapport.
A distinct madness has snagged me today.

Keep hold of the rope; it's clear today.
Spittle gum fills crevices that we deplore,
let's huddle and listen to its sickening decay.

Lost in the netted shoals my mind will fray
up there with the seagulls above the shore.
A distinct madness has snagged me today.

Tell the painter not to lead the sun astray;
break bones until you reveal an opal core.
Let's huddle and listen to our sickening decay.

Lost in netted shoals my mind will only fray;
sizzle the barbecue with our salt bouquet.
A distinct madness has snagged me today,
let's huddle and listen to its sickening decay.

Waddington
James Clarke

The Ribble comes through Waddington as a brook, and you can fish with your hands in it. Lowry and me used to do this back in the day before graduating to drop lines, the cane pole and then tackle, car batteries when we were shit-faced. In those days we were supervised by Lowry's dad — who I only ever knew as Mr Lowry. Mr Lowry was curious for a lot of reasons, but mainly because he only had the one arm. Yes, I found it weird.

Mr Lowry was older than most dads. He would have been about sixty by the time Lowry and me were ten. You wouldn't have known it other than for the white eyebrows and his tufts of hair that sprouted in clutches from his ear holes, as sharp-looking as those hairs you get on insect legs.

Mr Lowry used to stand in the water a few foot away, or up on the road, spinning his wellington heels on the tarmac, clasping the grab-rail with that lonely hand of his. Meanwhile us boys would sift pebbles and corner Stone Loach. Then we'd spool them up and plop them in our jam jars. Lowry never seemed bothered by the empty bit of his dad's fleece, so while I often found myself fantasising about touching his dad's stump, he would get on with the business at hand, his hair a plaited segment of skipping rope that would drop over one shoulder, grazing the rock gunk and sometimes the river, swaying always.

Lowry always caught more fish than I did. He had a knack for reading nature's patterns, its habits, and went on to become the groundsman at the local golf course, where he lived for many years in a bungalow overlooking the lake. It was just Lowry and his pretty wife and a trio of doomed pet rabbits that neither of them ever stopped talking about. Egg, I called Lowry's missus, Egg.

On this particular occasion all three of us had the day off. Egg drove so me and Lowry could drink, and we travelled in Lowry's car, which funnily enough was a Golf, with me and Lowry sat in the back. It was always a pain in the arse taking the rods apart so we used to keep them whole and propped between us, creating a divide down the car's interior with me and Egg on the one side and Lowry on the other. The rods tickled the front window and once or twice slid over the dashboard so that Egg had to shove them away and go: *Can you not hold 'em, one of you? Fuck's sakes.*

Lowry pinched my arm when I tried to apologise. On the passenger seat was my tackle box, his butty boxes and room for not much else, because in the footwell was the crate of Guinness Draught put there so Lowry couldn't get to it until we arrived. He kept tapping my knee whenever we drove past any woman under the age of forty, going: *What about her?* Though in his accent it sounded more like: *Wah bow terr.* I suppose he thought Egg couldn't hear him over the radio.

Cracking day for it. The sun pulsed and the bulk of grass could have been fake it was so vivid. J.R.R Tolkien taught down Stonyhurst College, which isn't far, and they say the Ribble Valley was his inspiration for Middle Earth, which perhaps explains why Lowry and me were always so obsessed with *Lord of the Rings* growing up. Whenever we had more than one person in tow we would call ourselves 'a fellowship', and I suppose that is what we were that day, with me ferrying the fishing stuff towards the river while Lowry and Egg got briefly intimate against the Golf's bonnet.

My thoughts went as loose as they always do when I'm in open country. There was loads of colour fighting through the short grass: your meadow yellows, rowan berry reds and cotton whites; all kinds of textures if you actually took the time to notice it. I remember a gun grey heron, loping in flight directly over me.

It was my job to set the bivvy up in case the weather flipped as it was forever at risk of doing. Then I began to thread and weight the fishing lines. Downriver was Waddow Hall, which made me wonder what Peg O'Neil was up to. Peg is the ghost of a girl who was tricked into drowning in a well some centuries ago. There's a statue of her in Waddow's grounds that was beheaded in the misconception that it would stop Peg from getting up to I-don't-know-what. I have always believed in spirits; I must have got it from my nan who held no truck with mummery, but did teach me in her gravelly manner that there are ancient spirit guides for each of us. Apparently hers was a Benedictine monk. Daft, isn't it? But there you go.

Are you on wi' that or what, Buzz? Lowry went. He'd been rolling a fag while I got everything ready. At this rate it'll be solstice by the time you've done.

Matt, can you not call him by his actual name for once? said Egg, not looking up from her John Grisham.

Lowry laughed, although as usual I wasn't sure he found it funny. He said, He's Buzz Lightweight to me and always will be. Right, Buzz?

True story, I said to Egg, while the razored tips of the Ribble's flow caught the light.

We settled down for a smoke and a beer or two. Egg didn't partake in this sort of thing having not touched so much as a drop of booze since I first took her down the ice rink when we were fifteen, the night Lowry got her to do all that whizz. I was an Ice Card holder at the time. Lowry worked on the desk where you swap your shoes for skates. You should have seen his nostrils going when he saw me and Egg on our first date; like a pair of blowholes, they were. Lowry's nose always does that when he's trying to hide something. The top lip stiffens and there you have it.

Soon we were on the bank lip. I took the broken stool which I had come to regard as my own so often was it forced upon me, and watched Lowry struggling to find the maggots. While his back was to me I held my phone up, pretending I was after signal, the cracked screen providing a great view of the gentle boundary of Egg, her slinky leggings. She was reading her book, turning the page and turning it, plucking absently at the grass with her toes. Each toenail was painted black and together they looked as round and shiny to me as ten dogs' noses. Egg wore sunglasses and I did wonder, and so I did.

When Lowry failed with the maggots I made a show of fetching them, triumphantly lifting the twenty-ounce bait management container from the tackle box, then flicking open its lid, only for a confusing mist to rise into the air, hovering from the box as if it had been sprayed straight from an aerosol. A dreadful amount of flies hummed around us. They split in the direction of the field opposite, became dots and then nothing under the ragged-edged sun.

Lowry took it better than I thought he would. That all of them? he said.

I nodded.

Makes things more interesting, I suppose.

Lucky it was hot. The two of us returned to the splash of buttercups outside the bivvy to eat our sandwiches and drink more Guinness. It was a Saturday, after all, so when we were well oiled with stout, we decided to make a fire. If there's one thing I know, it's fire. I soon had an old pallet going. The bottom side was a bit damp so it hissed and loads of woodlice crawled out of it, but the smoke wasn't too bad. I remember watching it billow and pulse behind Lowry, trailing in such a way that it looked like noxious thoughts were sifting from his head. All the while Egg played music off her phone, making a sound-system by setting the mobile upside-down in her empty Thermos cup. I always said she was wasted working the till at Next. Said it there and then, but she didn't thank me.

Once our beers were finished, I suggested we fish like we used to do when we were lads, as it would be a shame to come all this way and not have a go. Lowry agreed that was a great idea, so we took our socks off, our trackies and trainers, and splashed out into the river. The water, straight away, reaching up to our waists.

Freezing it was, so I gasped downstream to where it was shallow and the flow was less busy and I could see properly into the water. Beneath that cloudy green, my legs seemed paler than normal. They were these truculent lengths of bone that struck out at odd angles from my knees. My shin hair had disappeared, too. I could have been walking on fucking stilts.

A lovely day. I dipped my hands into the lazy water and waited, thinking to myself how this must have reminded Lowry of fetching the balls from the shallows of the lake outside his house on the golf course, wading in search of dimpled pearls swung into the silt by blokes who lived in patchy states of crisis, driving five-door saloons home to stare at the insides of their garage while the wife clatters plates on the breakfast bar and tries not to cry.

Typically, Lowry caught a fish nearly straight away. He brought it to his eye so he could check its flank then chucked it onto the bank's knoll where it arched its spine and gasped. He gazed at me as the fish perished, probably to make sure I knew he was tallying his catch. I know Lowry. How he thinks.

But I kept at it. River water is obviously unlike the sea, yet it is not without its superstitions. I called upon the water sprites, song filling me as it often does — people like me thanks to my fine singing voice — and I began to sing under my breath, until a fish came.

Roach. Rust-coloured dorsal and fins. I found it upstream because rivers are quickest where they are narrow and deep. I had gone to such an enclave: a broad bend by the undergrowth of the meander.

Egg's yolk-coloured hair was visible to me above the reeds. I listened to her telling someone over the phone about what one of the rabbits had done the other day: digging its way out of the run Lowry had built for it, shitting all over the strawberries before escaping onto the putting green of hole ten.

The roach was floating my way; I let him come, gliding straight into my hands until I could cup him from the water, which I did. Cold. My fish was deeper-bodied than your chub or dace, about the size of a school ruler. I plucked the bastard from the gloom. Best one I ever caught by hand.

And so I called her.

Egg!

She didn't come.

Lowry answered instead, sloshing my way and clapping me on the shoulder. Belter, he said. Get in, Buzz.

That was good of him, I know that. Still, he couldn't be trusted with my excitement so I tried not to let him see it. I hadn't trusted Lowry in that way since we first went lamping over Chorley when we were about twenty. What we did was sneak into the fields and wait outside rabbit warrens, shining our torches at whatever came out. Great do. The rabbits freeze as soon as the light hits them and make easy pickings. Yet around the back of the Queen's Head the first Friday we ever did it, Lowry took the experience away from me by making out to everyone that I'd been the scared one, patrolling Winter Hill at nearly midnight. I never did get the chance to protest, because Egg was there. She said to me: You're so daft, Barry, which was enough to make me go along with the whole thing. She shook her head fondly. How I miss her.

Where was I? Me with a fish. Me willing Egg to come and see it. I was everything: the shimmer and sheen of a dragonfly's wings, the sporadic thrust of a water boatman, the dense lamb kofta of a bulrush head. Course I couldn't see Egg. There was only the river, my fish, the distant road sounding unfastened and plangent, almost as if the traffic was aquaplaning across puddles that were a hundred miles in radius.

The sound made my mind drift as it often tends to. I could see Mr Lowry, fifteen years dead yet watching over me with his terrible stump arm revealed. The arm suffered 'heterotopic ossification', bones growing where they shouldn't be, and looked like melted tallow dipped in rice pudding. Ossification can be caused by a blast wave passing through the body, altering its genetic codes. There are different kinds of blast wave. Death is one. Love is another.

Lowry must have read my mind or seen me slipping into one of my muddles, because he snapped me out of it by shouting. Fuck's sake… Emma! Come see this tiddler Buzz's found, will you?

That drew her. The reeds skittered in the breeze as I presented Egg with my bounty: a gasping fish with lidless eyes, pupils like single drops of balsamic vinegar paralysed in cups of olive oil.

Egg smiled at me with both rows of teeth. What you gonna do with that then, Barry? she said. And all I could do was shrug, conscious, of a sudden, of my boxers and T-shirt, the tide of damp up its bottom half that highlighted my figure.

Lowry read it all. Oh, give over, Buzz, he said, shoulder-barging me so that I stumbled, my knees striking the rocks. Trying to keep hold of my fish, I couldn't put out my hands to save myself. My head went underwater and I lost my cap. The river looked like diluted cola, except it was stark-tasting, empty, dank. I still managed to keep the fish. I kept him true.

Egg must have said something to Lowry whilst I was flapping about because by the time I managed to stand, his nostrils were flared and he had this mad grin on his face. With his lank hair and that fake smile he reminded me of the pictures the two of us used to make when we were little by gluing dried bits of pasta onto the insides of cut-up cereal boxes.

Check him for a rainbow, Lowry said. That's what my dad used to say. If you see a rainbow up your fish's side, chuck it back as that's a sign God's touched it. If you see no colour then you've dinner. Though coarse fish tastes like mud so will need salting.

Tomorrow's dinner, said Egg.

Tomorrow's dinner, I agreed.

And so I brought the fish to my eye so I could look down its length like an archer might do with an arrow. There it was: a wonderful prism of colour forming down the side of its body. Light's spectrum, glistening in shiny June.

It was decided. I took in the glorious rainbow once more, kissed the fish's scales and then its lips, then into the water it went. It spiralled in the air before sloshing a few feet away, where it floated against some yellow froth at the base of the reeds, and stayed there, bobbing away.

Lowry started to laugh. His whole face opened.

Egg, too. Fucking laughing at me.

The fish in the water reminded me of a crescent moon, caught in an evening sky. Egg and Lowry left me to it. I had to listen to them making their merry way back to the bivvy, and in that moment all that was left of me is what's inside, the part that shimmers loneliest, waits the longest.

After a while I strode over to my fish because I owed it more than the death I had given it. I raised it above my head and begged the water sprites for another favour. There was no denying the comfort in the simplicity of the water against my legs. I brought the fish to my chin and began to sing, gently, and soon felt a movement against my beard. The fish was beginning to flex. I dipped it into the water and saw a gentle sequence of bubbles emerging from it gills. Slowly, the fish rippled. It breathed in the shallows of my hand for a second, an hour, a lifetime, and then darted away, a quick-flash slipping silver in the shadows. Egg was chatting on her phone again, and there, on the opposite side of the Ribble, I could see another girl. Her hands were hung loose by her sides and she had a dandelion in her mouth, a passionate yellow. It was Old Peg. And I said her name aloud as she entered the water and waded towards me.

Three Poems
Louise Warren

Cuckoo

Behind the door, he hangs his tongue on a nail
but I can hear the whirring of trapped wings.

In that space between one minute and the next
my lover waits, in the scratchy dark,

a room that smells of rust, he inhabits it like a stifled cough,
listen, he is straining every wired nerve.

it is time— for the hands to jump one on top of the other
it is all for this, the strike and the door opening.

Don't look. He knows he is disappointing,
we are both disappointed.

It's not real I want to say but that is not the point.

Walt

More real than real
you give me each hand coloured frame, at speed,
a better life.

No gaps, no cracks, nothing blown
just skies of rose and lemon, sunrise,
dark when it comes is always bright and stashed with stars

this room is never empty, each cut swept up,
at night you process dreams
hang pearls from trees, my breath held in

will freeze on this. I won't wake up until the credits roll
then play it back, another death
this time off screen, her tiny legs just folded up

his chair thrown back, refused to fly,
another bright blue day, as blue as this you say
the edges turn to black, then pale to hardly there

then music. Light.

Birdlife

She likes to talk
talk about anything
for example, birds in the garden.

The carer perches at the edge of the sofa
in her plastic apron and gloves
she rustles between notes in her vague blue plumage.

Behind the mute glass
they are scrambled words on a blank screen
black carbon points, a scribble of wings.

She remembers putting out scraps of fat
from the Sunday roast, stale bread
crumbs scattered on a frosted lawn,

opens her mouth with the shock of remembering.
Then a jay, bold as a fairground ornament
freshly painted, stalks to the front

anything else before I go?
a small microwave meal cools on the plate
as the birds unhook themselves and vanish.

Into the Woods:
An Interview with Rob Hudson
Jo Mazelis

Songs of Travel – Berges Island

Jo Mazelis: You often reference poems in your landscape photography, does poetry offer a starting point for a series of images or is the relationship deeper than that?

Rob Hudson: It took me a long time to realise that what really interested me about the landscape wasn't its physical properties — the mountains, rocks and trees — so much as our relationship to it. Collectively, not just my relationship, but the stories we tell each other.

That presented a problem for me, someone who fell into landscape photography without knowing a great deal about the land itself. I don't conform to any countryman stereotype; I can't name most plants or flowers or birds despite the best efforts of my late mother when I was a boy. I live in a city, but fortunately for me, quite close to the edge of the conurbation, so I can find inspiration on my doorstep. I still find the landscape itself remarkably mute and rather chaotic. I find the land to be inspiring, somehow magical, a great consolation and, at times, beautiful, yet it is the fundamental mystery of this relationship that is my playground.

I do not associate myself with that masculine stereotype of expressing authority over the landscape. Conquest, mastery and other such macho notions seek to strip the land of its inherent mystery, to explain, to reassure us of our dominant position over the natural world. It is important that we acknowledge the space between the land and us. We are of it, but it is not of us.

The notion of landscape art as sublime buries that distinction somewhat, because of its overt emphasis on a celebration of the natural. This leaves me dissatisfied both intellectually and emotionally as it fails to acknowledge the reality of our situation. I see my job as one that triangulates between human and nature, revealing how we and the land are mutually dependent.

Yes, poetry is a starting point in my photography. But it's also about reflecting that human relationship as well as exploring photography's capacity for metaphor and that sort of peculiar strangulated narrative, which maybe also enables a launch pad into that nether world of visual imagery that is somehow beyond the capacity of language. I also hope in some small way this might illuminate something of our shared humanity.

One of my formative influences was *The Remains of Elmet* by Ted Hughes with photographs by Fay Godwin. I immediately fell in love with it. I identified strongly with the post-industrial landscapes of that corner of Lancashire, relating them to my experiences growing up in the similarly post-industrial Rhymney Valley. However, I reasoned that Godwin's photography didn't relate to Hughes' poetry in any meaningful sense, which I later discovered Godwin openly admitted was true. Godwin's photographs were illustration rather than interpretation and that struck me as shirking the possibilities inherent in such a collaboration.

In response to this apparent distance between word and image I began exploring how I could relate my photography to poetry; primarily through visual metaphor. Initially it was perhaps an overly literal interpretation of individual lines within the poems, for example in my work based on Owen Sheers' book *Skirrid Hill*. Later, this broadened into wider, but hopefully more cohesive concepts informed by both poetry and life experiences in such work as *Mametz Wood* and *North*

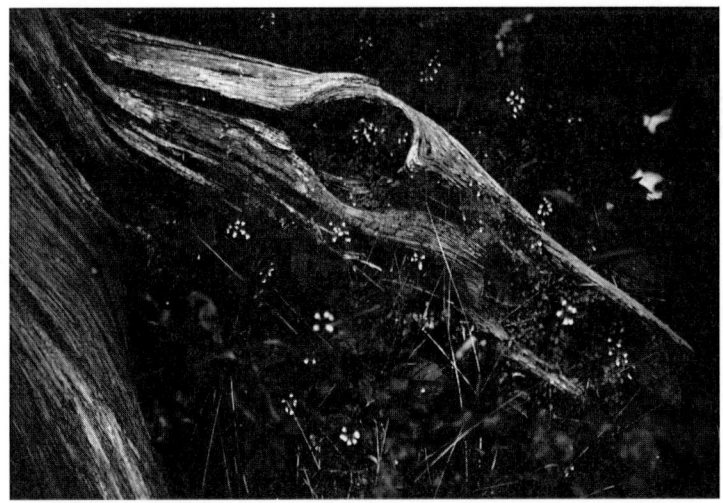

from *Mametz Wood*

Towards the Orison. The concepts began grow out of the poetry rather than trying to interpret the text.

JM: In your images for *Mametz Wood* you seem to be photographing something which is almost impossible — namely the violent past of a World War I battle — and in doing so you have created an almost dreamlike imagery with plants that look like galaxies, tree branches that might be limbs. How did you go about creating these images?

RH: The 'how' (double exposure) is perhaps less interesting than the 'why', although I did attempt to maximise the inherent possibilities in double exposures by making single images and combining them later. This creates a far wider range of combinations and allows for an even greater range of serendipity. For me, photography has a capacity for imagination. I'm sure most of us have experienced the feeling of being transported elsewhere by a photograph and that's maybe led to some form of reverie.

The imaginative potential exists, but hasn't been explicitly explored in recent years, and where it has, it has had a tendency to be stuck in a fairly obvious form of surrealism, which the rest of the art world had left behind about a century ago.

I suppose I believe nothing is impossible in photography just as I believe nothing is impossible in other forms of visual art, or in a novel or poem. Photography, to me, is just another form of visual expression, there's nothing special accrued because it's a form of mechanical reproduction, save that there's a kernel of reality in there which lends it an extra magical edge. When subverted through double exposures photography creates a new reality out of existing reality, which to me is a wonderful thing.

Although ostensibly about the First World War battle of Mametz Wood, the subtext is about experiencing the landscape through the 'lens' of what we now know as post-traumatic stress disorder. Having read *In Parenthesis* and some biographical details I wondered if David Jones had suffered some form of that affliction. Since completing the series a new biography about Jones by Thomas Dilworth has confirmed this suspicion. The role of double exposures then takes on a new aspect, to disturb and disrupt reality. We can't be sure what is real and what is imagined, just as the victims of PTSD cannot help vividly recalling the terrible memories of what they experienced.

As such, the experience of PTSD isn't fixed in time, it is a current malady suffered by many, and not just those who've experienced combat. So the act of creation isn't related to a reality at a fixed point in time or space, but is about something more universal, an element of the human experience.

JM You've written extensively about your work with landscape photography and also that of other photographers. Do you find this enhances your practice, bringing about new ideas or solidifying what was perhaps felt on a subconscious level while you were taking photographs?

RH: Writing, reading and researching are an essential element of my practice. Although it takes two distinct forms: one for developing ideas for my own work; and secondly attempting to find common threads and a degree of intellectual cohesion in the broad range of work with the artist's collective I helped co-found — *The Inside the Outside* group. Sure, these distinct threads feed into each other, it would be difficult to avoid some form of cross fertilisation, but they begin from different perspectives and intents.

The writing and research for my own work doesn't simply help develop or solidify ideas for my work, it also plays an important role in helping educate my subconscious mind to be aware of what to look for when confronted by the myriad of possibilities when photographing in the field (or more likely a wood in my case!). I can't claim to fully understand that process, and I'm fairly certain it would be undesirable to do so, but I know it's there. Think of it as creating a picture in my mind even though I don't necessarily know what the picture is until I see it.

JM: One of the early discoveries of photographers like Paul Strand and Edward Weston was that even the most banal objects could be transformed by photography into beauty; a picket fence, a pepper, even a toilet. By the same token, images of ugliness and war such as those by Robert Capa and Philip Jones Griffiths also manage to create a sort of savage beauty. Does still photography retain its power?

RH: It does for me. I could cite pretty much anything by Josef Koudelka or Cartier-Bresson or many others as continuing to have great power over me, a mysterious form of witchcraft that will often stop me in my tracks. Plus photography plays many roles, some of which are outside the traditional art definitions. Who doesn't still today photograph their children, family or pets, to create a treasured archive of memory, often with immensely powerful personal meanings and emotional weight?

The problem we face today is the sheer volume of imagery we're confronted by in our daily lives, and how to navigate the waters between what is personally significant and that which has a more universal appeal. The latter isn't as clear-cut as

Songs of Travel – Blackmill

many would imagine as demonstrated by found photography and the reappraisal of many personal archives for publication and exhibition.

In no way does my disruptive work with double or multiple exposures seek to undermine the potency of the still image. This is perhaps the most frequent misapprehension about my work. It is simply my way speaking in new forms; an attempt to find the possibilities inherent in the medium and to express something as yet unspoken.

Having said that, I confess that the single image is beginning to have less weight for me. Many of us in modern photography have realised that the old canard 'a picture paints a thousand words' isn't completely honest. So we tend to work in series or bodies of work, which gives room for the work to develop and suggest a greater range of ideas.

I tend to look back to the work of John Berger and Jean Mohr in their book *Another Way of Telling* or to practitioners like John

Blakemore who emphasise the possibilities for visual connections between images in developing a new language for photography. These ideas were at the forefront of photography a generation ago and are all too easily forgotten.

The newest definition of such ideas has been termed 'extended documentary photography'. This also embraces differing forms of display such as multiple projections or the addition of props, or the incorporation of other art forms or text. Our work with the *Inside the Outside* group was featured as part of a course on extended documentary photography at The Photographers Gallery last year, primarily as a result of the way we use words and ideas in our conceptualism to express ideas beyond the photograph itself.

The reverence of the single image in photography strikes me as a strange modern phenomenon, which has come about in part through social media, in part because of the excessive emphasis on the 'greats' in the history of photography and in part due to photographers themselves playing the fame game. They can't be held entirely guilty for this phenomenon as the structures of recognition through competition tends to reward those whose skills are primarily those of composition rather than the more complex and less immediate and accessible aspects of narrative, metaphor and suchlike. My good friend, the photographer Chris Tancock is fond of reminding us that composition is only one element of the art of photography; that in literary terms it is the grammar of photography, not the substance of meaning itself. I suggest that seeing is insufficient, and that we need to make work which embraces ideas if it is to be both compelling and satisfying to viewers who are both emotional and intellectual beings.

Even back in the day when most of the 'greats' of photography's history were working, the images were often made to be seen in context with others; either in exhibitions or, in more journalistic spheres, in publications like the *Picture Post* or the Sunday supplements. So the modern world is in essence stripping images of their context while celebrating an image that was never expected to be seen in isolation.

JM: Photographers like Andreas Gursky and Hannah Collins produce massive, almost life-size prints of their work to create images that are almost immersive — yet with most of humanity now seeing all images on their mobile phone screens do you think something has been lost along the way?

RH: I confess I'm not a fan of oversized prints, I find them overwhelming, confusing and difficult to digest. This isn't to say that size doesn't matter, but perhaps the greatest loss from seeing photographs on our screens is that we no longer perceive them as physical objects. The print is the final destination for my work, even though the vast majority is created digitally. Printing not only completes a work, it also solidifies it, transferring it from one realm to another.

There are good arguments for smaller prints, which can also translate to viewing on a screen — that of the individual viewing experience — intimate because it's not shared with others. And I wonder if the idea of scale lending weight to an image isn't also partly a result of the technological possibilities and, also of the commercial imperative of the high-end art market where so much is destined to be displayed in the lobbies of merchant banks, or bought as investments.

What we lose when viewing on an iPhone screen is primarily detail. It seems somewhat ironic that most oversized prints aren't really about detail, just as my work, unusually for a landscape photographer, is rarely about revealing the details of a landscape. There are other stories to tell, ones about us rather than illustrating a place.

JM: In *Songs of Travel* you've used what look like double or triple exposures to create photographs that look like pencil drawings or etchings. Others, like those of the sea are so fugitive as to be almost abstract, does this reflect an urge towards the painterly? And are you influenced by painting at all?

RH: Actually they're rarely less than eight exposures, sometimes many more. I try to find influences in as wide a range of the arts as possible, both visual and verbal. Actually I'm uncertain how I could avoid them, they are part of me, part of our collective consciousness, so it's inevitable that if I'm to communicate with a contemporary audience elements from beyond photography play a part in my photography.

I have a particular love for the art of the first half of the twentieth century. Yes there was a great deal of abstraction produced then, but what really appeals to me as a

Songs of Travel – Circled Hawthorn Snow

conceptualist is the way so many new movements, ideas and manifestos kept repeatedly bubbling up, seemingly every few years. That's reflected in the way I create constructs for new projects.

Songs of Travel is one such construct; it was an attempt to find a visual language for our experience of moving through the landscape and how that relates to memory.

I realised that most people's experience of the landscape was primarily through journeys, everything from walking the dog, going for a run to travelling by rail or car. And that our memory of such journeys tends to become blurred, mixed up and incomplete. So while *Songs of Travel* is related to movement through the landscape, it also questions whether the notion of stopping and staring, so beloved of artists and photographers, isn't actually the oddity, the rare experience we seem determined to raise above all others in the face of contradictory experiences. It is also chipping away at that other construct — the sublime.

JM: The pictures in *Songlines* use close-up textures derived from nature that are difficult to read; some could be satellite photographs of the Earth from space or microphotography of an insect's wing. Do such images demand more of the viewer than 'straight' photography?

RH: I'd imagined that they are 'straight' photography; the series *Songlines* are colour negatives of tree bark, and if we're aware of the days of film then the negative is a fundamental element of straight photography.

They aren't macro by any normal definition (i.e. greater than human vision). I was determined to avoid that particular form of abstraction because part of my motivation was to reveal the extraordinary in the ordinary. The stuff we miss by not looking hard enough at our everyday environment.

As the author Bruce Chatwin explained in the book of the same name (the naming wasn't accidental) according to the beliefs of the indigenous peoples of Australia: 'A "song" is both a map and a direction finder. Provided you knew the song you could always find your way across country. "So the land must first exist as a concept in the mind. Then it must be sung. Only then can it be said to exist."'

This was also, incidentally, part of a growing realisation of how important photographing my local landscape was becoming. It's easy to miss stuff by not looking closely enough, so by immersing myself in the woods during regular visits I've gained a closer relationship and deeper understanding of place.

This isn't simply a rejection of the exoticism of so much popular landscape photography, but a realisation that it was also beneficial to me as an artist, allowing me to see past the 'new' and the obvious beauty of a place and to focus my mind inward. It allows me to break free of preconceptions, received wisdoms and unwanted visual influences by working through them over long periods of time until I eventually find insights and a way of representing them in a visual form.

Practically it would be impossible to do this at any distance from home, because it requires so much time and regular visits. The fact this also coincides with a growing green consciousness that I should limit my travel and impact on the planet, is both fortuitous and underlines many of the hypocrisies of the way I may have worked in the past. For if a landscape photographer doesn't care about the future of our environment then who will? So, you see, 'the song and the land are one'.

Ease of consumption often relates to the fast food of photography, it's neither [ful]filling nor satisfying. A bite and it's gone in an instance, all too easily forgotten. To take the food/cooking analogy further, the more we put in [of ourselves] the more we get out of it.

I feel beholden to make work that stretches and challenges the viewer because otherwise what is the point making of art? It should be something that is nourishing to the soul. I hope the fact that I'm learning about myself and nourishing my own soul in the process of making the work will somehow be translated in the viewing.

JM: When you were working on *North Towards the Orison; In the Footsteps of John Clare* part of your interest was the poet's state of mind — does this explain the hallucinatory quality of these images?

RH: I don't really know that John Clare suffered hallucinations, there's still much debate about the form his mental illnesses took. The diagnoses of the time included one doctor suggested he suffered from 'an excess of poetising'. This doesn't easily translate into our 'scientific' notions of understanding mental illness.

The inspiration for *North Towards the Orison* came from a number of different elements of the life of the poet John Clare. In essence the work is a visual retelling of the walk he made from his asylum in Epping Forest to his home, Helpston, in the Fens. The 80-mile journey, on foot, without money for sustenance or shelter took Clare four days to complete. That he was returning home to find a woman who he believed to be his wife but was long dead and when he was in fact married to another woman gives some insight into the parlous state of his mental health.

In many ways it's an extension of the ideas about journeys and memory I first explored in *Songs of Travel*. Indeed it uses a similar technique — multiple exposures — to illustrate those ideas, albeit in colour rather than black and white.

The choice of that particular colour palette came from two lines of Clare's writing: 'In the blue mist the orisons edge surrounds' and

> I had imagind that the worlds end was at the edge of the orison & that a days journey was able to find it so I went with my heart full of hopes, pleasures & discoveries expecting when I got to the brink of the world that I could look down like looking into a large pit & see into its secrets the same as I believed I could see heaven looking into water.

As Simon Cooke wrote, 'That conflation of "orison" (prayer) with "horizon"… speaks of the indivisible closeness of Clare's vision with a sense of place.'

My idea was to illustrate the journey through the 'blue mist of the orison' as if seen through water. It is an expression of both his parlous mental health and a eulogy to the joy he felt in experiencing the countryside. In many ways I think of it as the antithesis of the work I made in *Mametz Wood*. It still explores the issue of mental health, but this time the landscape isn't darkly terrifying, it is a source of strength and wonder. It is a journey in search of orison [prayer], one where the other orison, the horizon, is never visible, never quite attainable. So although the journey may have been nourishment to Clare's mind, it didn't finally resolve his mental health issues.

I've attempted to relate that solace of the landscape to a troubled mind through some eighty images that followed the course of day into night and night into day. There's little detail, but I hope it's more hypnotic than hallucinatory.

It was made in the very same wood as *Songs of Travel*, and again illustrates both my commitment to working in my local environment to have as little impact upon the planet as possible. Obviously it makes no attempt to document the places of Clare's actual journey; again it is an act of imagination. I have doubts about the definition of photography as 'documentary'. If we take the root of the idea 'to document' it implies that an objective truth can be found using the camera. I doubt it is possible for people to be objective, furthermore, I don't think it would be desirable in visual art.

It's time to ditch the term 'documentary' as it's served its purpose in establishing a legitimating of photography in the historical context of the 1960s and 1970s and is too closely related to the mechanical means of reproduction for the digital age. As a conceptualist I can see that it's just another construct. The problem is neither I nor seemingly anyone else has the remotest clue about what should replace it. Maybe 'photography' will suffice and we can all stop worrying about legitimacy and get on with making work in whatever form of conceptualism we choose?

JM: Your latest project is *The [Secret] Language of Trees*, can you explain what the starting point for this was and what your process of working is?

RH: As with most of my series the process begins with messing about with cameras. If I wanted to sound more impressive I could call it creative play and it is fundamental to my process. As I play, I discover ways of portraying the land, and I hope that I'll also discover new ideas, which I can weave into the images and give me a focus for further visual investigation.

Bound up in this series are a whole range of ideas that are below the surface: ideas about 'edgeland' from my reading of Rob Cowan's *Common Land*; ideas about wilderness and wildness from reading Robert Macfarlane's *The Wild Places*; my growing green consciousness about low impact local photography; but most fundamentally, and perhaps surprisingly the ideas of Peter Wohlleben on mycorrhizal fungal networks.

Wohlleben is starting to unravel the simple Darwinian assumptions that trees compete for light and nutrients. Trees, it turns out, aren't in competition with one another, but exist in a complex web of interconnecting roots and fungi known by some as the 'Wood Wide Web'. Wohlleben even suggests they are not only able to communicate in some basic form, but also share nutrients to sustain one another. Robert Macfarlane

The Secret Life of Trees – Week Four

described this discovery as 'part of a research revolution that is changing the way we think about forests'.

This also caused me to re-examine the way I understood trees and consider how this could be visualised — above ground. The result was a somewhat poetic response to the beauty of this idea in series I called *The Secret Language of Trees*.

I'd been photographing an area of edgeland near my home for a couple of years. Initially I made a short series called *The Language of Trees* of the trees growing alongside the rather forlorn abandoned canal without much thought beyond the idea that I'd perhaps discovered an area of true wildness — if such a thing can be said to exist in the modern UK. This was where the ideas of Robert Macfarlane came into play; he'd suggested in *The Wild Places* that we're as likely to find wildness in a ditch beside a road as we are in what's perceived as the countryside. The differentiator being whether it's farmed or otherwise managed or somehow influenced by man. Being a landlocked steep slope of trees trapped by the canal and an old railway embankment, therefore unmanaged or farmed, these woods appeared to me to conform closely to this definition of wildness.

When I discovered Wohlleben's ideas I began to refocus my photography onto the visual relationship between the trees. Trees tend to be depicted in isolation in photography and art, perhaps to mitigate the chaos of the land that really exists. I was comfortable with the idea of the land being chaotic, so my visual representation attempted to embrace this. That the results were perhaps somewhat abstract pleased me greatly as it embraces the otherness of the land, the space between it and us and that hypnotic effect of being in nature. It is about the soft fascination of place, the way we feel surrounded and consoled by the natural world and about how we look. It was at this point I adapted the title to show that it is a new body of work that emerged from an old one by inserting the 'secret' into the title.

It also marks a return to the single image, as it seeks to illustrate clearly in order to pose the underlying question of whether this relationship between trees can be seen in the way they coexist above the ground and to question the received way we have learned to see the landscape.

That this sort of 'ordinary' rather scruffy bank of trees could be found almost anywhere also fitted into my growing realisation that not only should I be making as little and impact on the Earth as I can, but perhaps, in some small way, it was also my job to encourage others to appreciate their local environment so that they too can practise a more green life while not feeling like they are missing out on the distant, exotic landscapes so often depicted in popular forms of landscape photography. That, maybe, there's a role to re-educate the viewing public in some small way.

That line from Bruce Chatwin's *Songlines* — 'So the land must first exist as a concept in the mind. Then it must be sung.' — turns out to have become something of a motto for my photography.

from *Mametz Wood*

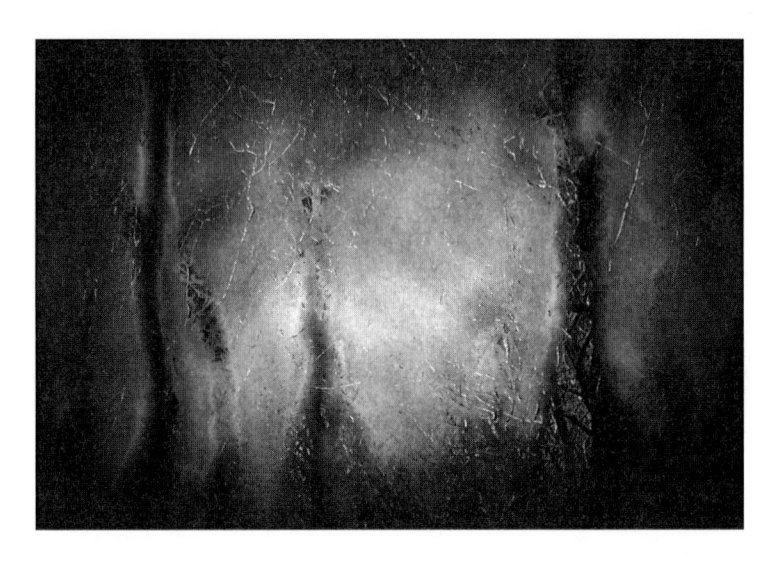

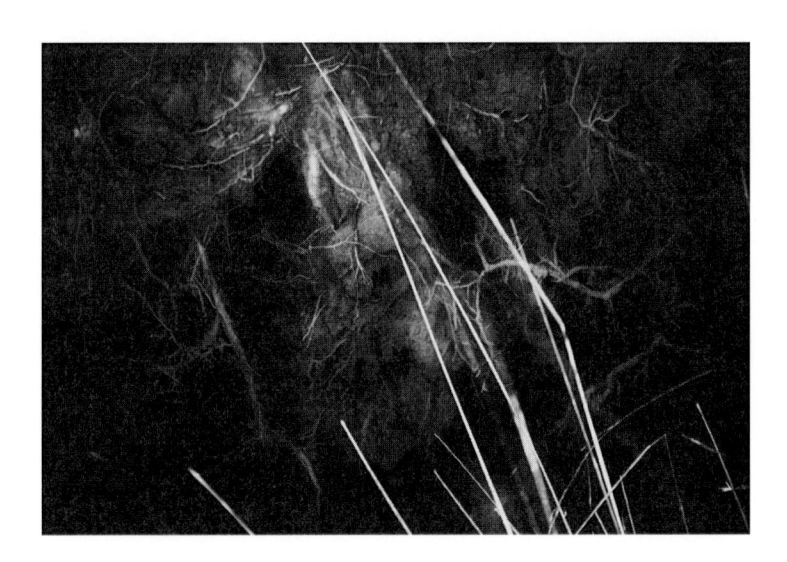

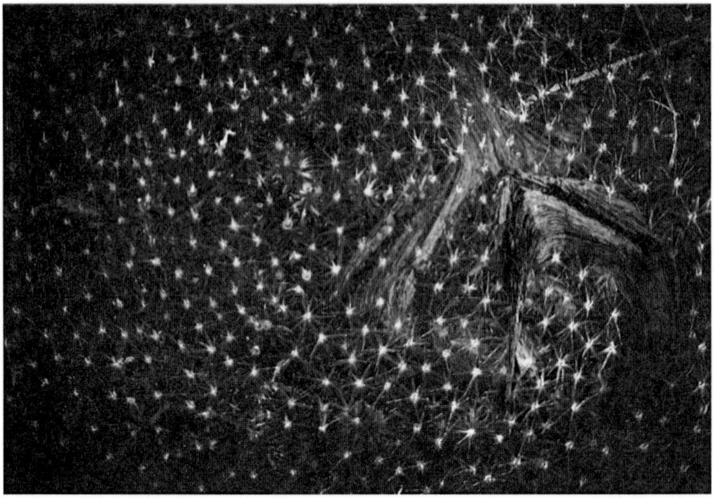

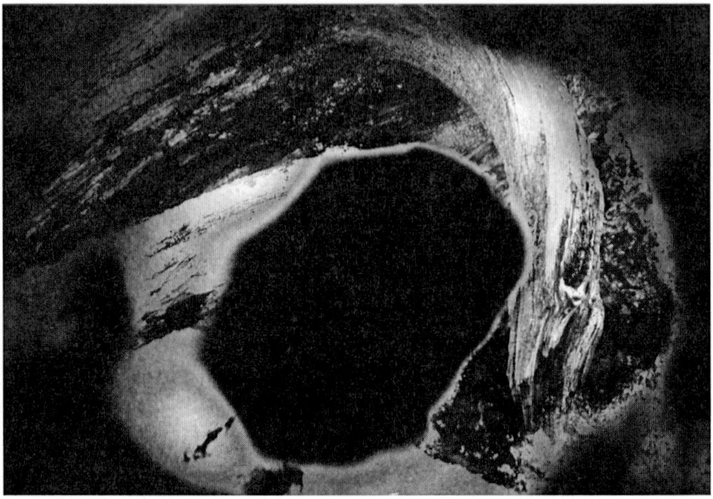

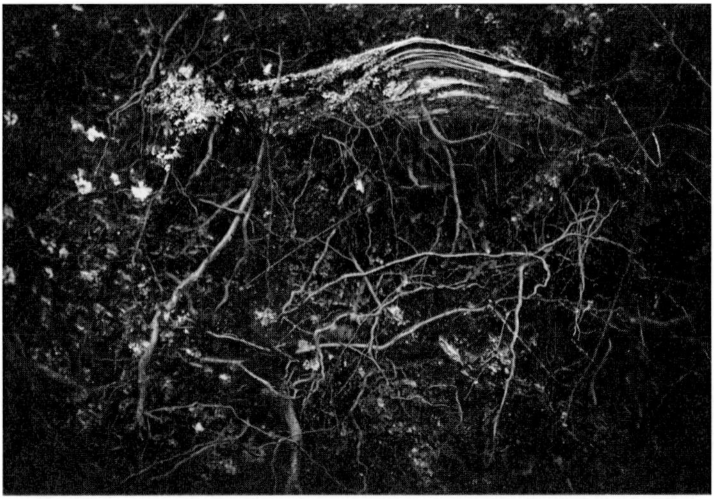

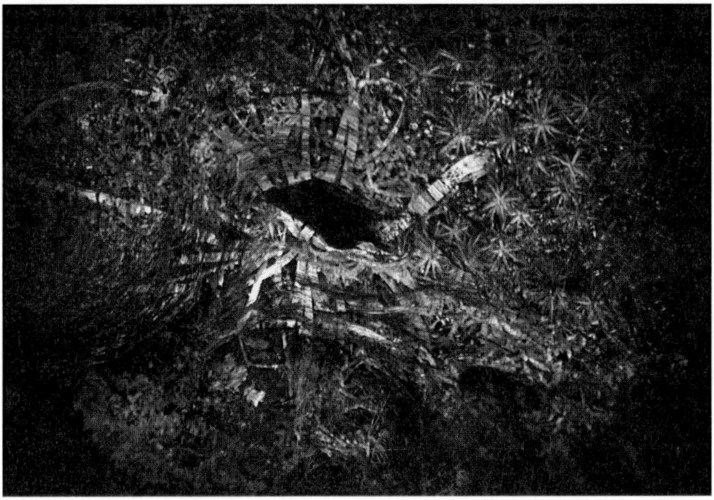

Songs of Travel – *Maen Llia*

Songs of Travel – *Nash Point*

from *The Secret Language of Trees*

Thenar Space
Gareth E. Rees

div-uh-ney-shuhn
(noun)
1. the practice of attempting to foretell future events or discover hidden knowledge by occult or supernatural means.
2. augury; prophecy.
3. perception by intuition; instinctive foresight.

Her real name is Lotte but they call her the Trolley Div. She knows it because she hears it said. The teenagers who drift into the supermarket after school for cans of pop. The skateboard kids who come at dusk. Even grown-ups who should know better. Big men with fat necks from the delivery trucks. Snarky young mums with pushchairs smoking fags. They have all said it, from time to time, within earshot.

'Watch out for the Trolley Div.'

'Trolley Div's comin'.'

'Pssst, check out the Trolley Div. Bloody hell. The face on her.'

Even the ones who don't say it, the polite ones, the casual shoppers, the out of towners, they look like they're thinking it. And if not Trolley Div, then whatever it is they call people who collect shopping trolleys in supermarket car parks.

Trolley Spod. Trolley Bod. Trolley Spaz. Trolley Tart. Trolley Troll.

Maybe they don't have a special name for them. Only a sense that trolley attendants are somehow lesser beings. Stupid. Failed. Unqualified. Bottom of the pile. There to use and abuse, with no ears to hear, no heart to feel, no power at their fingertips with which they could exact their bloody revenge. And Lotte could, you know. She could get her own back on them, easily. When they least expect it, she could send a train of trolleys hurtling in the direction of their shiny cars, their weak flesh, their noisy babies, and crush their bones, burst their skins, ruin their precious paintwork.

But that's not what she's here to do. That's not her destiny.

There's more to this trolley game than shoppers think. More to her than they realise. More to this car park than they can see. But for now she's keeping it close to her chest, hands gripped on the handle, the long chain of interlocked trolleys flexing before her, under control, yet only a microsecond away from chaos. All it takes is a slight change in velocity. One trolley too much at the end of the stack. A sudden shift in weight distribution. Then all hell could break loose, like planets spinning out of the solar system or snooker balls crashing into each other. This event might happen. Probably *will* happen, she suspects. But only when the time is right. At this moment Lotte cannot see that far ahead.

What she does know is that something is coming. Lotte can tell because of a peculiar phenomenon in which she keeps finding trolleys abandoned in the same arrangement at the same time of day, around 3 p.m. It took her a while to notice, but she's sure that it is happening and that she isn't imagining it, not that she'd dare tell anyone at work. Most of the staff treat her like she's mentally disabled. This would only make it worse. But she has eyes in her head and she can see what's in front of her: a clear pattern that repeats itself every day. There's always a trolley out by the recycling area with bins for clothes, bottles and cans. Then there's a sequence of two more trolleys interspersed between car clusters, leading to the zebra crossing by the entrance. There she finds one of those big, deep trolleys with plastic seats for kiddies. From this point, the pattern forks into two lines of four trolleys. Always four in each. At the end of one prong, there's a trolley by the traffic island at the exit with the sign that says, 'See you again!' At the end of the other prong, two trolleys huddled by the hedgerow that separates the car park from the main road. There are always twelve trolleys in the arrangement, all pointing in the same direction, narrow ends angled towards the superstore doors, as if magnetically charged. Lotte doesn't know what it means but it tells her there will be a time of reckoning, and soon.

It was a day of reckoning that led to her getting this job two years ago. One of the friendlier till staff, a girl called Iga, told Lotte that her predecessor wasn't properly trained. They didn't tell him that he was not allowed to push a stack of more than eight trolleys. Ended up pushing ten one day when the stack began to waggle and swerve until he lost control and crunched into a van, shattering his shoulder. That was the end of that. Permanent damage to his tendons. He got lawyers involved and there was a big hoo-ha about it. A nasty fight that was still ongoing.

In the meantime, the supermarket needed someone to collect trolleys from the bays and gather the abandoned ones from the nether regions of the car park. Someone had to keep the stacks by the door replenished for shoppers on their way in. So the marketing people put an advert in the paper and Lotte applied, at the suggestion of her Nana, with encouragement from the social worker who checked on them from time to time, because Nana was harder to care for as she got older and the bad people in the government were cutting everything that helped — snip! snip! snip!

They desperately needed money but Lotte had problems with the whole *getting money* thing. Nothing big. But she'd not worked since she left school at sixteen and wasn't exactly cut out for one of those offices with all those people in suits. It's not that she's dumb. Lotte knows all the constellations. The names of galaxies. The distances between planets. She can sense the tilt of the earth. Smell the onset of seasons. Feel instinctively what the weather will be like this week. She knows the names of every plant in the park, of all the muscles in her body and the bones they connect. But she has trouble with reading and maths, and with talking to non-Nana people or understanding what they mean. In turn, non-Nana people find Lotte odd with her stooped back and heavy brow, a touch of something doctors call 'frontal bossing'. Problems, problems. Nothing major, nothing that need stop you, Nana says, just you have to work harder that is all. You have a bigger mountain to climb. But you have abilities, Nana says, a way of seeing, only people don't know it yet. They haven't caught up with you. In that way, it is they who have special needs.

When Lotte got the trolley attendant job it was something of a surprise. They celebrated with chocolate cake and a mushroom brew. Then they did some loud chanting and rune casting like the old days before the social services told them to stop it for the sake of Lotte's future, stop it.

'You have found your role at last,' Nana said, raising her chipped mug of hallucinogenic tea, 'your magical quest begins here.'

Alan, her manager at the supermarket, has made a bit more effort with training Lotte than he did with her predecessor. He follows the new handbook distributed nationwide to make sure no more trolley attendants get smashed up. But he's a lazy guy. He's been to university and it seems like he doesn't really want to be a supermarket trainee manager. He's in a band.

Writing a novel. Car parks and car park attendants are a bit beneath a man of his talents. Alan hasn't checked on Lotte much since her probation period ended, when her pay went up from £8 an hour to £8.50. Not bad for a twenty-one-year-old Trolley Div. If all goes well she might get promoted to *car park porter*, a much more important job, helping shoppers with bags, directing cars to empty lots at busy times and showing folk to specialist trolleys and electric scooters. It means dealing with strangers, which gives her butterflies, but it pays £9 per hour.

It's this promise of more money that first encouraged her to add another trolley to the eight-trolley limit. It wasn't too hard once she got used to the increased swerve and thrust. Nobody really noticed or cared. And with each additional trolley Lotte has become more efficient at her job. Long stacks of nine, ten, even eleven. She can guide them to the store entrance, rain or shine. It's no longer the lure of a promotion or extra income that motivates her to test the limits of the trolleys in this way. It's a feeling. Like an urge, or something she is supposed to do.

A calling.

Besides, there is little else for her to think about at work, other than the propulsion of the trolley train and its relationship to the many hazards: parked cars, pedestrians and incoming traffic. Her job may look easy to those shoppers who push past her with grunts and harrumphs, but there are multiple complex factors of which she must be constantly aware. The swivel of wheels. The undulations of tarmac. The placements of speed bumps and rain gutters. The welts of road markings. Lotte has learned the delicate dance of velocity, direction and momentum. She can sense the shifts of the trolley train in the tug of finger muscles and the pressure on that bit of her hand where the handle fits into the curve between thumb and forefinger, known as the 'thenar space'. At first these muscles ached with strain but gradually they've become attuned. Now the thenar space is her ultimate sensor, a way of reading the world in motion. She could probably do her job blindfolded if it ever comes down to it. If a crazed villain leapt from a car and stabbed out her eyes with a Bic biro, she could still negotiate the twists and turns of the car park, using only her memory and the instincts in her thenar space.

But life is not always so easily predicable. Lotte knows this too well. Things can happen outside your control.

Pushing a wobbly line of trolleys through a busy car park leaves her exposed to 'random' factors, as she calls them, but always in her mind with inverted commas, like when you say something you don't necessarily mean, or that other people say but you don't necessarily believe. As Nana says, nothing is truly random.

A 'random' describes anything not factored into her calculations that might disrupt the flow of motion. A crushed *Coke* can, discarded, trapped beneath a wheel, might cause the trolley train to skid. That's an example of a 'random'. After all, who could predict the decision of a person to purchase a *Coke*, the speedy guzzling of the drink and the decision to toss the can away? You'd to predict the power and angle of the toss to work out the landing place. Then a passing teenager might kick the can, sending it skittering into the path of Lotte's trolleys as she approached. That would entail a load of 'randoms' happening faster than the human brain could process.

There are more examples, too. A patch of ice in winter. A stray cardboard box, blown by the wind. A freshly formed crack in the concrete. Perhaps one of those big SUVs, parked badly, could scupper Lotte's calculations of the turning angle so that her trolleys go into the back of a Porsche or right up an old lady's bottom. Worse, a toddler might run out from behind a car and end Lotte's career. The child would die, crushed beneath her wheels, and Lotte would hide behind a tree in the cemetery, watching the funeral, murmuring 'sorry' over and over, before the police led her back to the car and took her to prison for the rest of her life.

Every day Lotte lives with these possibilities. Every moment has violent potential. Each millisecond life can go in a million different directions. And sometimes, just sometimes, a person gets to be the guiding hand. This is something a man in a suit doing wordy, numbery gubbins on a computer will never understand. The weight of responsibility. The understanding that anyone can be an agent of the universe. Even a Trolley Div.

At primary school, long before she became Trolley Div, they called her 'Not-A-Lotte' and 'Toi-Lotte' and 'Fat Botty'. She was the awkward kid, the freak, the slowcoach. It didn't matter how many times Nana complained to teachers or lingered at the gates, taking swipes at her classmates' heads as they left school, Lotte was excluded from their games. Then one day they played 'trains'. A child would run around the playground with another child holding onto their coattail. Then another child would latch on, then another, then another. On and on this went until there were ten, twelve, maybe fifteen kids in a weaving line. It didn't matter who joined the train, only that it kept getting longer. It was a case of *the more the merrier*. So Lotte seized her chance. She grasped onto the last child's coat and ran, pulled faster by the train as it weaved and twisted, at a speed she could never achieve under her own steam. Wind in her face, she laughed with a momentary joy, moving as part of a greater whole. Then the leading child changed directions sharply and the line whip-cracked. Lotte lost her grip and flew out, tripping headfirst onto the concrete.

Her schoolmates laughed as she got back on her feet, weeping with pain and spitting out tiny white flecks of enamel. Her front teeth were chipped. It was something she never got fixed, for Nana doesn't trust the medical establishment, dentists included. Whenever Lotte's teeth hurt, Nana would give her a gluey mixture of cloves and garlic to chew. These days a few of her teeth are missing. A few more are rotten. But her chipped incisors are still there, bucked, prominent and rough to the tongue. A legacy of that unfortunate event.

Only now Lotte understands that it was no random incident but a valuable lesson that has finally come to fruition. For today she controls her own train. Except this one is not made up of children. This one is made from plastic and steel and she, Lotte Dugmore, has sole influence over its direction, with full responsibility for what might happen because of it, and to whom. Thanks to that childhood experience of whiplash she knows there are three phases to its motion. First, a sudden reversal in direction, which takes only a small jerk of her hands on the trolley handle. Next, a wave of momentum runs through the chain, bending in the middle, becoming a bigger bend toward the end and — finally — a whiplash strikes with force. All this power unleashed by a twitch of her thenar space, much like that twitch which must have occurred in her father's hand fifteen years before on the M6 motorway. If not, then what else could have caused the accident? Why else would he lose control in the blink of an eye? There must have been a sudden involuntary spasm where her father's thumb and forefinger met the steering wheel, which sent the family car veering from its lane into the barrier — BANG! — then spinning, spinning, with all those cars crunching after, so much smoke and noise, and she a child in the back seat amongst the carnage, the only thing alive in their Renault at the end of it all. Six people dead, including her parents. All because of a tiny twitch in thenar space.

Lotte now has that same power which her dead father once possessed. When the time comes, she will use it for good, or perhaps evil, or something in between. She doesn't know. But whatever it is, it must have a connection to the strange alignment of trolleys she finds in her mid-afternoon collection. Always twelve in a distinct pattern that she draws with pencil onto a piece of paper to show her Nana that evening. Nana who knows about these things and who never disappoints.

At the sight of Lotte's little diagram, Nana's eyes widen. 'I know that shape,' she says, 'and so do you, Lotte, my dear. For it is the constellation of Perseus.'

Nana gets out a book and shows her:

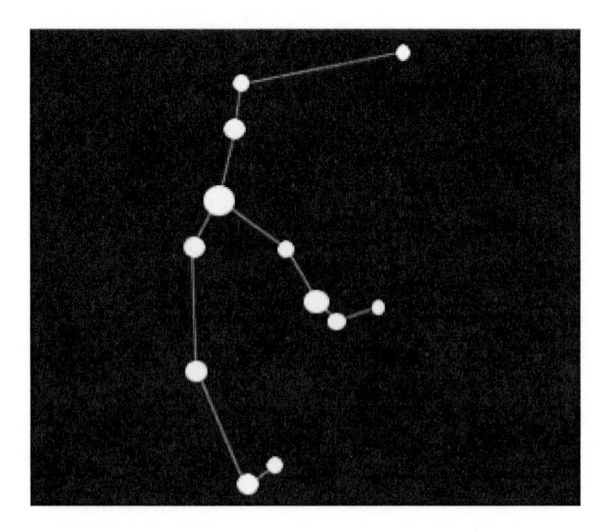

She's right as well. Almost trolley-for-trolley the pattern is the same. Lotte notices that the big star near the middle is that bit at the zebra crossing, which leads shoppers to the entrance from the central pedestrian strip with its pretty saplings. That is where she always finds the deep trolley with the kiddie seats. Nana tells her that this star is Algol, the Demon Star, a harbinger of bad fortune. She says that the word disaster literally means bad star. Dis-*aster*. Well that seals it. Something is coming, Lotte is sure of it, but still she doesn't know what, or when. That is, until she spots two receipts in adjacent trolleys by the hedgerow one morning. Usually when Lotte sees a receipt she has a little nosey at what people have bought. But this time it's not the list of items that catches her eye. It's the price at the bottom. The first receipt is for £234. The second receipt is for £23.40.

Isn't that an odd coincidence?

If nothing is random, and she's sure that it isn't, then there is meaning in these numbers 2, 3 and 4.

Or 2 and 34.

Or 23 and 4.

It puzzles her for a while before it hits her: 23/4. The 23rd of April. That's it! And it's only a week from now. If something is coming, then it is coming on the 23rd of April. It makes sense. And the only place this future event could happen is Algol, the Demon Star at the centre of the Perseus constellation, located on the zebra crossing at the supermarket entrance. Lotte draws a red cross over Algol on her diagram, circles it, then draws the date **23rd April** in big letters. That night she sleeps with the piece of paper beneath her pillow.

Despite her fear of talking to people at work, Lotte is too excited to keep her secret, so she confides in Iga, the nice checkout girl who finds time to speak to her among the hustle and bustle of backroom tea breaks, where Lotte never feels welcome. Lotte doesn't mention the trolley pattern, which Iga might find too weird. Only that she thinks that at 3 p.m. on the 23rd they should look out for trouble near the entrance, because the stars are never wrong.

Iga smiles and nods: 'You must keep watch, Lotte, it's important. Don't let people down.'

And Lotte won't, she swears she won't. She swears this under her breath every night as she lies in bed in their living room with the diagram safe beneath her head, Nana snoring beyond the flimsy partition. They've always slept this way because the flat has only one bedroom, which is where Nana keeps her books on witchcraft, Tarot and astrology, stacked so high and deep you can barely get through the door. It used to annoy Lotte, at times, when she was a teenager. Seemed unfair.

Not any more.

Thanks to this deep knowledge, which Nana has gathered over the years, Lotte can finally do something special in her life and become a respected car park porter, worth £9 an hour. If that's her reward for sleeping beneath a sideboard, so be it. Not that she hasn't enhanced her cramped space with personal touches. A large, colourful chart of the human body, showing the tissues, veins and bones. A mobile hung from the ceiling with the planets of the solar system spinning around a yellow sun. A doll's house in which Lotte likes to arrange effigies of her parents. Sometimes they're sat at the kitchen table. Sometimes lain in bed. Sometimes they're screaming in terror from the top window because of a chip pan fire that's filled the house with smoke (Lotte uses Nana's incense sticks for effect). Other times they stand at the front door, waving proudly as Lotte heads off to work.

Her mother and father have never been so proud as on the 23rd of April when Lotte leaves the flat, nerves jangling. Throughout the morning she's too excited to concentrate on the job, which is tough because it's a busy day. Lots of customers leaving their trolleys willy-nilly instead of in the bays where they are supposed to. There's hustle and bustle by the entrance because a bald man is handing out leaflets about the AA and Cub Scouts are collecting for charity. The customers try to avoid them by cramming through of the left-hand sliding door instead of using both exits, causing a right nuisance as Lotte tries to keep the trolleys stacked up neatly.

Honestly!

After lunch, Alan the manager sends Lotte out back to the delivery area to help clean up a spill after a forklift driver drops a pallet of milk. It takes ages and the men make her go and get them tea from the machine while they smoke and tell rude jokes. This jeopardises the timings. Tick, tock, tick, tock. It's nearly 3 p.m. by the time she hurries around the side of the store, past the staff smoking area and into the car park. Almost instantly, she hears a cry of 'Help'.

It's happening, it's happening.

Heart in her mouth, Lotte runs towards the zebra crossing. But there's something amiss. She feels utterly useless without a trolley train at her command. What can she actually *do*? She has nothing with which to unleash hell on whatever she's about to encounter. This not how she envisioned it. Closer to the store entrance, she's even more uncertain. There's only a woman with a handbag approaching from the avenue of saplings while an old man hobbles through the automatic doors. The crossing is empty, except for something small and brown on the ground. She picks it up. It's a teddy bear with a bandage on its head. A cocktail stick protrudes from its chest, dripping with tomato ketchup.

Lotte hears giggles. She turns to see Iga and a few of the checkout staff stood by the doors, pointing at her.

'You have saved the day,' says Iga. 'The bear will live!'

It's a mean, nasty laugh, not a friendly one. Lotte realises that Iga put the bear there as a joke. It's not nice at all. But worse still, it means that the trolleys were wrong, the stars were wrong, and Nana was wrong. Everything was wrong.

Wrong. Wrong. Wrong.

What was she thinking?

She is, after all, just a Trolley Div.

A stupid, stupid Trolley Div.

*

Lotte doesn't eat for a week. Not much anyway. A bit of Nana's stew. Some turnip soup. A spoon of raw honey here and there. At work, she talks to nobody and certainly not Iga. Sometimes Alan asks her if she is okay but he only does this because he's the manager and wants to look good for the human resources people. He doesn't care. Nobody cares except for Nana, who says: 'Don't let them get you down. You must trust your second sight, Lotte, not everyone has it. Like anything important in life, you won't get it right from the get-go. Maybe you see pieces of a puzzle but not how they fit together.'

Lotte lies awake at night beneath the dangling carboard planets as Nana snores, imagining what her parents would say to make her feel better, had her dad not driven them to their deaths. Did he really lose control, just like that? She wonders how come that she, Lotte Dugmore, can manoeuvre up to twenty trolleys around a car park full of people and traffic and kids and pigeons and Coke cans and never crash once. Not even once!

Lotte leans from her bed and peers into the bedroom of the doll's house, where her Mum sits alone on the bed.

> 'Oh, Lotte, we both loved you so much and we worked hard to get you things you needed. Pretty things to wear. Delicious things to eat. A roof to keep the rain away. Warm radiators in winter. They all cost money, such a lot of money. Your dad worked nights and sometimes when he came home he drank beer to switch off, to settle down, to get some sleep. Each morning he'd drink for a bit longer, and longer, and longer, until it became a habit. A

bad habit, I know. But the stress, Lotte, the stress. Don't blame him. It's hard being a grown-up. All we wanted was the best for you. Then we got a call one morning to say that your Nana had fallen over. She was in hospital. She really needed us. So your dad and I put you in the back seat and we all drove up the motorway, full of worry, even though your dad had not slept, even though he'd drunk a few beers after work, as usual. Maybe it was more than a few, but it was a habit, so he didn't think much about it. He lost control out of love. Out of love for Nana. Out of love for you. Daddy made a mistake at the wheel and we lost control. But you can get it back, Lotte, I know it. You have found your calling at last. The car park is a place where you can shine like a star. We even named you Lotte, as in *car lot*. Don't you see? Can you understand now? It's your destiny!'

Her mother's words inspire Lotte. They lift her spirits. She returns to work full of hope, back to her old self again, with her eyes wide open and that train of trolleys stretching out before her, like a flash forward to the near future. Almost immediately the car park offers up its mysteries once more. On an otherwise uneventful day in early June, Lotte is delighted to find the trolleys laid out in the very same stellar pattern as before. There's one left by the recycling bins, then that familiar sequence of trolleys which splits by the zebra crossing into two prongs, just like the constellation of Perseus. Twelve trolleys, yet again.

This cannot be the work of sneaky Iga, for Lotte never told her about the trolley pattern. Besides, Iga might be smart and popular but there's no way she knows about constellations, and definitely not Perseus. Lotte tries to keep her emotions in check this time, but it's hard to contain herself when, only a day after the astronomical manifestation returns, she finds a receipt in a basket left near the cash machines. It's for £2.34. Again, the numbers 2, 3 and 4. This cannot be a coincidence. It simply cannot be chance. But if it's not the 23rd of April she should look out for, then when?

Like Nana says, it's a puzzle. The pieces are there but she can't get them to fit.

Lotte is still wondering about this on Nana's favourite day of the year, the summer solstice, on the 21st of June. In the 1960s Nana used to go to a place called Stonehenge where our ancestors prayed to the sun on the longest day of the year. Nana would dance around the stones with her friends, eating magic mushrooms and chanting, like she still does these days, except in the flat, because she can't walk any more, and no dancing either, just the mushrooms and chanting. Instead of giant stones there are only Nana's beloved crystals, laid out on the coffee table. As they eat breakfast, even though she's heard it before, Lotte asks Nana to tell her about the solstice, like when she was little, using pictures torn from old books. Nana duly gets out a crumpled diagram of the solar system, the earth and the sun.

'The earth goes around the sun to make a year, and tilts to make the seasons,' Nana intones, 'which is what makes things die and grow and change throughout the years. Think about that Lotte, our lives dependent on a little tilt of the earth, this way and that, bringing heat and cold, light and dark, life and death.'

As Nana speaks, Lotte gasps at the sight of some numbers on the picture. Why didn't she think of this before? The angle of the earth's tilt today is 23.4 degrees. That's always the angle of the earth on the day of the summer solstice, which is today, the 21st of June. All at once, the pieces of the puzzle spin into place.

Lotte's age is 21. The number 21 is 12 backwards. Twelve trolleys. Twelve stars in the constellation of Perseus. Receipts with the numbers 2, 3 and 4. The tilt of the earth on the 21st of June is 23.4 degrees.

Bingo.

Lotte leaps to her feet, kisses Nana, and is out the door and on the way to work within minutes, gnawing her fingernails with excitement. The receipts for £234, £23.40 and £2.34 never signified the 23rd of April. It was the 21st of June all along. She can see it now, as clear as she can see the roof of the superstore gleam in the sun and the lampposts, tall as trees, above the first parked cars of the day. All she needs to do is stay vigilant, keep the trolley train well-stacked, and let her thenar space guide its locomotion.

The hours pass. Ten o'clock, eleven o'clock, twelve o'clock. Lotte eats her egg sandwich on the park bench outside the entrance of the superstore, watching traffic crawl through the high street, while pigeons peck at her feet in the brilliant sunshine of the longest day of the year.

Back to the car park and there's a lot of trolleys to collect in the early afternoon. Remnants of the lunchtime rush. People who squeeze in a quick shop during working hours. Or those who try to get it done before they pick up their kids from school. These types are too busy to put their trolleys in the bays but Lotte doesn't mind. She's glad of it. Gives her plenty of trolleys to keep her barrel loaded. She keeps going around and around the car park, never straying too far from the entrance.

At 3 p.m. she's at alert and fully primed. Then 3 p.m. passes. It becomes 3.05, 3.10, 3.11. Tick tock, tick tock. She begins to feel twinges of despair when she notices two cars moving slowly, one after the other, towards the zebra crossing. Much too slowly for her liking. It's as if the first car is deliberately impeding the one behind. Meanwhile, a young lady with a trolley, grinning toddler in the seat, kicking his little legs, exits through the automatic doors.

Lotte can see what's about to happen, as clearly as if it has already happened. She turns her train of eighteen trolleys in an elegant arc, expertly avoiding the bollards by the taxi rank, and moves at pace towards the crossing where the first car has stopped, engine rumbling with menace. She's close enough to read the number plate: CP18 DIV.

Car park. Eighteen trolleys. A Trolley Div.

This is it.

This is it.

Lotte accelerates as the leading car door opens and a burly man with cropped black hair and a white T-shirt gets out. He turns to the car behind, pulling something from the back seat that looks like a weapon — a rifle, shotgun, something like that, she doesn't know much about weapons. Then a man from the car behind gets out and he too reaches for something, probably a gun. This happens in the very moment that the young lady with the toddler steps onto the crossing. She's going to get in the way of whatever is about to happen. They're going to get hurt unless Lotte does something.

Now.

Lotte doesn't need to think. Two years of muscle memory take over as she jerks the handle of the trolley in precisely the right way to whiplash the stack and send the end trolley whizzing along the road, ripples of energy wobbling the air as it tears a rift in spacetime. It glances off the young lady's shopping trolley, forcing her to pull back from the crossing with a yelp, safely out of harm's way, then it ricochets into the gunman's backside, spinning him round to face Lotte. Next, she gives the whole trolley train a hard shove and lets momentum do the rest. The stack rattles sideways like a snake, hitting the man full on, sweeping him from the road. He slams into a brick pillar and crumples beneath a tangle of steel.

The young lady with the toddler screams, 'Bloody maniac!' and Lotte assumes that she is addressing the gunman, even though she's looking right at Lotte. As Lotte gets closer, she sees the man from the second car, stood by the open door, mouth wide open in surprise, holding his wallet. People rush from the store to see what's going on. Some stop between cars with their shopping bags, heads above the roofs, watching like meercats as Lotte approaches her stricken victim, groaning with pain beneath the trolley stack. It's curious. She cannot see his weapon. No weapon at all. Only a clutch of reusable shopping bags in one of his hands. He must have dropped the shotgun somewhere. Thrown it away somehow. Blood trickles down his face. His eyes are wild with loathing.

'What the hell!' he yells at her. 'You stupid mong! You crazy fucking bitch!'

He keeps going on like that, ranting and raving. All kinds of nasty stuff coming out of his mouth as the crowd of onlookers thickens around them. Lotte beams down at him in triumph. Let him yell. Sticks and stones may break her bones but words won't hurt her any more. She's been called worse. It's of no matter. She has taken control and saved the day. Mum and Dad would burst with pride if they could see her now. She cannot wait to tell Nana when she gets home. And when Alan the manager finds out about this, he's going to be absolutely delighted.

Four Poems
Sarah Doyle

Elegy for Victorian Gasworks

You rise like a crown from the landscape you own. Ageing monarch of iron, imperious in your foul-breathed beauty, belly swelling and falling, you heave with the slow energy of balloons. How you stretch the complex filigree of your fingers far above the craning topography, weaving a ballet of barley-twist limbs. You are the city's vestigial organs.

Imperious as a foul-breathed balloon, how you heave with the complex iron of your ballet. Vestigial in the topography you own, you rise from the craning landscape in barley-twist fingers. Swelling and falling like a monarch, ageing above the stretch of the city's organs, you weave a filigree of limbs.

Craning to survey the city, swelling in the aged ballet of your filigree, your vestigial belly heaves with its own topography. Stretched as balloons, imperious as a monarch, how you weave your foul-breathed slow dance, that iron barley-twist.

You are vestigial filigree, a foul-breathed monarch, craning your iron. A swelling barley-twist of ballet stretching the city, how you rise, imperious and slow, to weave your topography.

The ballet of your topography slows to vestigial. Filigree stretches, cranes. The city rises, imperious and foul-breathed.

Vestigial, you are a slow ballet, breathing the city's filigree.

Near Misses

Always a minute or two behind,
forever running that bit too late,
playing catch-up
                chop-chop
                            hurry-up
and never quite arriving.

That morning, no different from
any other, alarm ignored no matter
how urgent, too many minutes
taming bed-hair, choosing shoes.

And the bus —
the bus is waiting at its stop
as you round the corner, a shiny
red mirage of possibilities

receding with every step
taken towards it. Wrong choice
slappy sandals clip
                clop
                        clapping
ironically as you attempt to run —

while the bus revs its engine,
making to leave, and you are close
enough now to see the driver's
face, and he smiles and his eyes

his eyes are kind and regretful

but he pulls away just as you arrive,
panting and desperate, and the bus
is packed, women your own age

who know to be early, who heed
alarms, who wear the right shoes,
who hear the clock's
      tick
        tock.
Out of top deck windows, smeared,

unclear, stare the faces of children
you will not have. They look at you,
indifferent or accusing, and you
cannot bring yourself to wave.

Stitches

The husband and wife made a ragdoll together.
The wife lifted the hem of her wedding dress,
cut strips and circles of ivory satin from her
under-skirts, diligently pinning them together
to form torso, limbs, head. Then she stitched
and stuffed, using her own cut hair as wadding.
The husband tore two buttons from his shirts –
one button, green like the wife's eyes, one blue
like his. The wife sewed them on to the smooth
pale face until the ragdoll could see. The wife
crafted ears from the net of her bridal veil, sewed
them on carefully, singing lullabies all the while,
and the ragdoll could hear. The wife took blood-
red thread, embroidering a tight smile of mouth,
though the ragdoll could not speak. They pinned
all their hopes on her. She was a beauty; perfect.
They adored her with a passion, played with her
all day.
    Every day.
        Years passed.
            The ragdoll
became limp with loving, grubby with wear.
She taught herself to re-stitch a crooked smile,
fix the button eyes back on to her face. In time,
the husband and wife stopped loving each other.
Both wanting to keep the ragdoll, they argued
over who had made what. *I gave those eyes*,
said the husband. *And I the skin*, said the wife.
They pulled her this way, then that way, tug tug
tug, stitching strained to breaking. The brittle

button eyes were knocked from her face, lace ears torn beyond mending. Long-frayed thread snapped. She ripped down her middle, spilling coils of the wife's hair used for stuffing so long ago. The husband and wife were both jubilant, each wielding their tattered share. *I have her*, said the husband. *So do I*, said the wife, taking up needle and thread to make repairs to her half.

Ammonite

Here on this beach, where history runs deep for those who
care to see, we build castles, plant flags along our sandy
crenellations, defying the odds. Here, where permanence
and impermanence merge, we marvel at our beachcomber

treasures: purses of eggs, frigid starfish, a once-was curl
of shell, calcified to stone. Curved to foetal, the Fibonacci
miracle is cold in our hands: no-one is home, nor has been,
this side of ancient. We crawled from sea, shrugged off

the cephalopod's spiralled mantle, working at the whole
limbs-lungs-brain thing. So here we are, beach-baked
and frozen in time, cupping unspooled ancestral relics,
trying not to think of our own remains, the brittle hollows,

someone's future find.

Edward Elgar Rehearses the Powick Asylum Staff Band
Nigel Jarrett

He decides to walk there, because the weather is set fair. In his larger music case, both violin and viola nestle like indivisible siblings (one never knows who might not turn up). He also carries the piece of music to be tried out with them again — this time 'in public', as it were. His father has helped him copy out the parts anew, and the ink is barely dry. In fact, the title of the quadrille *La Brunette* is still smudged, and resembles a hedge ablaze and smoking.

It's a long walk, a healthy one, but his collar and tie are growing tighter. Not to worry: the Powick Asylum Staff Band has to set an example, so he puts up with it; the green bowler, the buttoned boots, and the tweed three-piece with the watch on a chain likewise. Music as therapy, along with the leafy Powick acres, the pavilions, the cool arbours, the allotment (though for some the concept of a future outcome as they bury the seeds in runnels none too straight is not grasped). All can be dealt with. Only Mr Mordecai Rees, a clarinet virtuoso but currently masquerading as the recipient of intelligence from Mr Ewart William Gladstone, poses a difficulty. Mr Mordecai Rees's twin brothers died in 1854 at, respectively, the Battle of Balaclava and the Battle of Inkermann, and the poor Rees family fell apart. The details are probably apocryphal, but it is rumoured that a Russian cannonball passed clean through the one twin's midriff and shrapnel spinning through the air like sparks from a Catherine wheel reduced the other to the appearance of a headless rag doll. Their father being a drunkard, the wretched Mordecai took to the streets and the byways, grubbing and begging for food, and was eventually sent to Powick; the threat of being 'sent to Powick' having long been Worcestershire shorthand, even in the most respectable families, for incarceration among the deranged as a form of punishment. It was Frank, an oboist, who one afternoon saw Mordecai rocking on his heels before old Frobisher's resting clarinet, as though the acquaintance had been long in the waiting, and Frobisher who offered to teach him. It was not so much tuition as the re-awakening of some inherited but dormant aptitude, for within two years Mordecai (with Gladstone's approval, no doubt) had arrived note-perfect to within twenty bars of the end of Mozart's Clarinet Quintet before exposing himself to the audience, albeit one consisting of members each in a remote world, given to changing their seats every whip-stitch, wandering in and out, and not caring a birch bobbin about the appearance in polite company of a man's dangler. Frank joked that the music appeared to accommodate the outrage rather than suffer outrageous disruption. In any case, there was applause, instigated by a sole-clapping charge nurse on duty in the shadows and with hands as wide as griddles.

 He passes through the gates and continues down the drive between an avenue of towering trees. The building swings into view, swaying to his confident tread and curiously silent, its chimneys crawling with gargoyles, those devils protecting the demons within like sentinels appointed by an army of diabolical conquerors. He can see the chairs being arranged higgledy-piggledy on the front lawn. He smiles at the staff's anticipation in deliberately creating disorder because they know that order at Powick is everywhere tainted by the certain prospect of disarray. For a couple of years he has played in the band, his violin part sailing unimpeded through — how shall he put it? — the *studied conventionality* of the amateurs, an unimprovable thing. Fired always by aspiration and the achievable goal, he knows only its opposite. Has not Mr Samuel Smiles asserted, 'We often discover what will do, by finding out what will not do; and probably he who never made a mistake never made a discovery.' His ship always sails on, through the jetsam of split notes, misreadings, collapsing cane chairs, simmering rivalry, and Powick's cataract of counter-attractions. Among this last — and he can see her at a high window, smoothing her tresses — is *La Brunette* herself, Miss Molly Smithson of Chaddesley Corbett, who had a baby out of wedlock at the age of fourteen and was 'sent to Powick', as if to prove the old threat meaningful as well as ubiquitous. But Frank has told him to be careful: Miss Smithson wanders the corridors as an alluring temptress, her modesty barely covered, her nymphomaniac seeking, but never finding, Mordecai Rees's satyr. This is Powick all over: conditions that have been arrived at now constrained to go no further, their names — Dementia, Melancholia, Nymphomania, Moral Insanity, Satyriasis — giving the place at least the semblance of knowledge fixed and inviolable, and governing the limits of what it can do before assigning a name to an outcome: Recovery, Relief, Inaction, Death. Just those.

The old bandmaster has retired and he has taken over. This is his first 'public' outing — the Powick band is not bad and its audience captive and undiscerning. As he approaches the entrance and begins climbing the steps, he is humming the *tutti* opening of *La Brunette*, a jaunty six-in-a-bar that propels him skippingly to the front door, where he twirls his moustache. In the distance, emerging on to the lawn, is Mordecai Rees, head bowed and holding a clarinet in his fist as one might hold a bludgeon. What to do about Mordecai Rees? The Powick band is supposed to be a staff band, its audience Powick's unfortunates. Mordecai is demonstrably one of the latter, though with a talent that has risen uncorrupted from the electric chaos of hysteria, and cannot be denied. Frank hopes that Mordecai's loyalties, unlike his realities, will remain undivided.

The Powick Asylum stands monolithic and forbidding, but not on ceremony. That morning there was an interment, the six-hundredth since the place opened in 1848, all tipped into pits like burials at sea. Frank told him that the funeral services in the Asylum chapel were 'an entertainment'. But surely not as amusing as Powick's new Budding 'rotormower', a jangle of parts painted in bright red and green and housed in its own enclosure, an orchestra's kitchen department seeking shelter from a squall. Frank, his brother, helps out at Powick as well as playing in its staff band — the Elgars, always willing to depart graciously from the norm. In any case, two accomplished outsiders gave staff an example to look up to, which made a change from always looking down without much hope of witnessing 'a pearl-fisher suddenly come to the surface who had been thought lost for ever', as one of the physicians put it to him. Sometimes it happened; but only as a prelude to a return to the depths (they watched them swimming back, so falteringly as to suggest the hope of a last-minute return to sanity).

Inside, he heads straight for the anteroom where the musicians meet beforehand to re-construct their instruments, tune them, and trip up and down scales. On the way he is aware of that familiar struggle of wraiths that arabesque around Powick's officious comings and goings. Among them is Molly Smithson, but, heeding Frank's advice, he ignores her; not that she has recognised him. She has her own urgencies to consider at the ends of her fingers, and they do not take in the expectations of a dedicatee. Not that he has inscribed *La*

Brunette to her, or that he will, or that she will understand if he does. But that's music: the incorporation in alluring form of all the feelings of the tone-deaf. It was Frank's tongue-in-cheek definition; Frank, who has such high hopes of him, and who is at that moment eyeing Mordecai Rees's arrival at the threshold; Mordecai, beseeching, the clarinet transformed from weapon to offering and held before him in outstretched hands. Not that his misdemeanour is now for him anything but an inexplicable blur.

Just this once, is their verdict, and no nonsense. Mordecai nods his head, gratitude overcoming any idea of consequence. Just this once, not ever again. It is like dealing with a child. They are used to that. The fact is that Mordecai is someone they cannot do without. Frank distributes the re-drawn parts. Performances of *La Brunette* are turning out to be easy if rough-cast, even for the Powick Asylum Staff Band. They all play through their music again at the same time in an unintended hymn to the place and its discord. On the lawn, the audience is drifting towards its seats from all corners. Even the Tourette's are there. He once joked to the Superintendent that they could always be heard but not seen, but heard and seen they will be. (There was once a loud rapid-fire SHIT POO SHIT in the slow movement of Schubert's Octet.) The first time *La Brunette* was played, he explained what a quadrille was. Their surly faces turned to him not because he sounded patronising (they needed reminding) but because he insisted on lighting up a cheroot and speeding through his violin part faster than anyone else and without so much as a glance at the music — Edward Elgar, assistant organist to his father at St George's and capable of turning a quadrille into something a quadrille-lover would scarcely recognise; and his name always in the paper. They neither went to the services nor attended his recitals. When they aren't dealing with God's faulty handiwork they are at home wondering whatever made Him reveal it; the mysterious Trinity — you could say that again. Griddlehands is there once more, sparking the applause by example as they stride out of the building in a line to take up their positions.

He leads from the end of their semicircle, his head movements and frequent glances encouraging them to keep up. Someone in the front row — or what passes for a row — gets up after two bars, salutes, turns smartly and marches back into the building. Others arrive in small groups, resembling deaf and blind interlopers chancing upon them in what flashes before him as the supreme example of innocence. A knotted handkerchief on his head, the Superintendent is there, now and then cupping in his hands a bivalve watch but for sure not checking on the accuracy of the metronome markings. There are usually five figures to a quadrille, but he has 'symphonised' *La Brunette*, as Frank termed it, by making each dance express a different emotion. It is not a quadrille for dancing, that's certain; it is for listening to: an invitation to listen to the dance. At its core he has placed a slow movement bordering on stasis that reminds Frank of processional figures on a Greek vase. The band's reception of *La Brunette* up to that point has been mixed. Performing for inmates of the Powick Asylum reminds him of synchronising clocks in a single inertial frame, explained in his new edition of *The World's Encyclopaedia* by Monsieur Poincaré, except that at Powick time is not synchronised, the audience during the opening piece behaving as though the concert has not begun and, a quarter of the way through, suddenly paying attention as though it just has; similarly, at the end, when applause is expected, the audience will still be listening but will need to be shaken out its reveries by Griddlehands. Anyway, Frank winks at him as the very slow movement, *adagissimo*, begins, Mordecai leading off in measured fashion. It's not long before he notices an undulation in the corner of his right eye, as of white sheets billowing. He sees that Mordecai has noticed it too. Frank and the others are facing the other way, or looking up, transported by his departure, his originality. And he realises it is Molly Smithson, in the guise of Frank's sorceress, swirling about on the fringes of their al fresco auditorium, unnoticed, unattended and unconcerned; until she begins moving towards him in the scimitar of greensward between audience and band, like a Muse, not the proverbial source of inspiration but one of the daughters of Mnemosyne, seeking her given authority. Griddlehands steps in, scoops her up under one arm, and carts her off. It jolts the Superintendent but has no effect on the rest of the audience who, he's long discovered, are oblivious to incident except as some undefined and therefore troubling agitation, and in any case are only three pieces into the concert of eight items at the point where the band has two to go. They never know that every appearance of the band before them is a rehearsal for its few public concerts outside Powick's walls.

Afterwards he thanks them for their efforts. They pay grudging respects to *La Brunette*. He tells them about his forthcoming Bach recital at St George's: silence, apart from instruments being de-constructed and snapped into their cases and one grovelling inquiry, much stared at. Perhaps their reaction is envy — not of his accomplishments, though that too, but of his ability to come and go freely at Powick. On the walk back, Frank, ever fascinated by what demons control the human mind, talks about Galton's lexical hypothesis of personality, and what remains to be discovered about the brain, about humanity. We are still a mystery, he says; an enigma.

From her high barred window, Molly Smithson, his 'windflower' as he refers to her, watches them pass through the gates, strangers come from nowhere and gone for ever.

Two Poems
Michael Ray

Reverb while digging

This moment is all about her love
for the ripe avocado
she's scooping out with a spoon.

These days she does what she feels
and it feels fine eating
reptilian skinned fruit and drinking

Malbec at four in the afternoon
winding back to when
she could stand her mind up neatly waxed

while holding a padmasana in the dunes,
wearing only lipstick
and a necklace of blue shells.

Inside the warm conservatory she squints
through the cherry's yellowing
flags, to her husband working his spade.

She leans back until she has him drowning
in a sea of leaves while her tongue
dives through the shipwreck of her mouth,

seeking out the few teeth unblunted
by years of children swirling
round the house like oil and blood.

She watches him bend, lower down
the row now, lost
in his pattern of lifts and turns.

He pauses to consider the reddish
weight, neat slices of earth, how,
in its rhythms, it has taken care of them.

He knows this machine, the slow-
moving parts as intimately
as his own, parts that give him space,

like the woody shade at the garden's end
where he builds cities
of leaves, and everything is dappled,

quiet, where he can stare unnoticed
at the curved beach,
the scattering of spent shells.

Gypsy

How it is that when empty, the willow
bottom of the *champignon* basket
I keep loo rolls in
looks like the splayed
intestines of a fish,
I'll one day intuit.
What's left of the bark
is the colour of iron
after dousing;
and when held up close
still holds the faint
scent of wood smoke
from a forest in northern France
that in my head I still cannot revisit.

The Good Poltergeist
Ronan Flaherty

Only while speaking does Violet seem to stay still, otherwise she is invading and shorting out electrical appliances and streaming brightly across the walls of my one-room flat. Tonight she has occupied the fat-backed cathode television that has been in the flat since I first moved in but presents too bothersome a chore for me to simply lug downstairs and get rid of. From the old television with its lifeless grey screen, Violet once again tells me about her sense of incompleteness.

'At times it's as if I'm not really here,' she says, 'as if I never really were.'

Violet's voice is clear and crisp. She speaks with the heightened received pronunciation of an old-time screen siren, a Joan Crawford or a Barbara Stanwyck. Occasionally, Violet will materialise as a shifting shadow, or a smartphone-captured tiny, glowing orb, sometimes even as a floating pool of milky light shimmering at the end of my bed. Mostly, I never actually see her. Violet prefers to inhabit something. Such as the air vent with its plastic grille built into my flat's boarded-up fireplace, which lends to her voice an echoey quality. Today though it's the old television she has chosen to project herself from.

'Oh selfish me!' Violet suddenly exclaims. 'How was your day? I forgot to ask.'

Even though I know she knows, I tell her anyway. Her omnipresence is something we have both come to acknowledge; for me it has become the most frightening aspect of this whole ordeal. A certain flicker of my desktop screen always points to her presence at my workplace. A chilly draught to my side indicates she has just boarded the bus along with me.

Soon we are back to discussing Violet.

'I have come to consider it a conscious effort,' she says. 'If in my current state one were to stop thinking one would simply cease being.'

I continue to listen to her, as I get ready for bed. Violet will go silent whenever I undress and that once familiar emptiness reinvades my cramped flat. Being very much someone of her era she grants me my modesty.

Having dressed for bed, I hear Violet again. She tells me she's 'concerned'.

'Concerned? About what?'

The television goes quiet. My reflection looms darkly in its lifeless screen. The only light comes from my bedside lamp.

'These recent *choices* of yours,' she says, 'I must admit to finding them rather troubling.'

For a second time, I ask what she means. But no response comes from the dead television. Violet has either left or is still there, not speaking, just watching, as I flick off my bedside lamp and settle down for the night.

*

After work the next day, we meet in a coffee shop off Dame Street. This has become routine since we started dating. We take our coffees to a window-side table and watch the streams of impatiently passing commuters and dawdling tourists outside. Nina has her work clothes on under a frayed denim jacket; a black polo shirt with matching slacks. Loose tangles of her dark hair dangle loose from her ponytail. Every so often, she rubs at her eyes. Despite my ongoing supernatural ordeal,

Nina appears far more tired than I do. After several minutes of small talk, she glances away, draws a breath. She then proceeds to convey her news, her decision. She will stay. She desires to remain in Ireland more than anything, but she continues to miss her friends and family back home. Even though the air inside the small coffee shop is somewhat muggy and still, I am conscious of a draught. I haven't told Nina about Violet, haven't told anybody.

'I will stay here,' Nina says, nodding to herself. 'Maybe this is selfish of me. But this is the decision I have come to.'

'I wouldn't consider it selfish of you,' I say, reaching reassuringly for her hand.

My gesture goes unseen.

A huff of wind has just swept in through the coffee shop. A number of stacked paper cups upend and pinwheel across the countertop and a sandwich board propped just inside the open door clomps over on the floor. One of the two baristas on duty rounds the counter and sticks his head out the door as if trying to catch sight of the fleeing phantom gust.

*

The only thing I know about Violet's death was that it was untimely. From that initial interaction, she has sought to make it clear how she isn't one of 'them'. Them being those 'poor bedraggled souls' who don't know they are dead, or simply refuse to accept the fact, happy to remain locked forever in the routine of a bygone existence, even as former homes are demolished around them and their bones become dust. Violet has told me there was a time when she had felt sorry for them, but no longer. Ghosts, she maintains, are quite a pathetic bunch really.

Aside from her opinions, I know next to nothing about Violet. Her accent though has an unmistakable lilt to it. Violet's particular manner of well-spokenness was once the staple of the old wireless set. Those long-gone radio announcers who when you hear their voice broadcast nostalgically over the airwaves seem to be calling from beyond the grave.

*

She's there waiting when I get back. One of the two chairs has been pulled out from under the butterfly table, the soft vinyl seat cover with faint impression on it.

'She has no decorum,' Violet declares, 'though I shan't feign surprise.'

Violet has taken it upon herself to spy on Nina. Though I have discouraged this, on some level, I am curious to hear what Violet reports back, this despite having come to realise how completely negative she is in her observations of Nina.

'She sits like a tradesman. It seems not even to occur to her to cross her legs.'

I tell Violet I no longer want to hear it. She continues nonetheless.

'And that grubby little café she works in. Works, pah! Now there's a lark. All day picking at her fingernails and twirling her hair.'

I announce that I'm about to undress and Violet concludes her diatribe. The impression in the seat cover slowly melds away.

'People are selfish,' she says, her voice small and distant. 'You really don't know how selfish people can be.'

There follows a creak of floorboard, like a single, stifled note, and Violet has gone again.

*

Violet has remained guarded. Playfully she will say that the year she was born had a nought at its end. Often things just slip out. Like pre-decimal denominations, 'two and six', 'three and eight'. The name of a long-shut Camden Street cinema. Cars referred to as motorcars. Boland's Bread. Rudolph Valentino. Then there are the lone reminiscences. Violet told me how the sound of the Harcourt Street Line trains passing over the bridge at Dartmouth Road would set the rows of fine bone china on her mother's Welsh dresser to clink like a chorus of chattering false teeth. While at night, the rumble of the 'Cattle Special' chugging up from Enniscorthy had the brass ends of her childhood bed jitter like the rockings of some frail ghost. I am aware that the Cattle Special (which infamously overshot the last stop at Harcourt Street crashing through onto the adjacent Hatch Street) hasn't past near Dartmouth Road in some time. The Harcourt Street Line was closed in the fifties. This is history.

*

Two days pass without hearing from Violet, not even a squeak of floorboard. Her absence coincides with a period of sunny weather. On the second day, I rendezvous with Nina after work. Hand in hand, we go up to Stephen's Green, with its tree-canopied pathways and grassy spaces. There are couples, young and old, as well as mothers with their children. We are given two free ice lollies by a guy wheeling a refrigerated pushcart around the park as part of some product promotion. Next, we find a bench to sit on and enjoy the good weather.

   Once I asked Violet what it was like being dead. 'Cold,' she said, 'quite literally, as on a winter's night.'

We say little as we lick our ice pops and watch others relish the sunshine as well. With Nina, I sense myself wanting to be honest in a way I have never been with anyone before. I want to tell her everything about me, implement a policy of total clarity, which must include, I know, explaining about Violet.

Our lollies slurped to bare icicles, our fingers syrupy with sugar, bumblebees buzzing around, Nina evokes the wintry grey of her childhood. Eight floors up in a Soviet-era housing block, three younger siblings, both parents at work, every night the same lonely dog barking outside. Nina says she prefers dreams to memories. Recently she dreamt she was back in her grandma's house, a stout, one-storey wooden building out in the countryside surrounded by tall stands of birch. In the dream, she had been on her own inside her grandma's house while outside was a tiger, sat nonchalant on his haunches like the ones you see at the zoo.

'I look out and see the tiger there,' says Nina, 'so I go and make certain the windows and doors are closed. I watch him then.'

Directly behind the bench is a City Council-installed flowerbed. Here the bumblebees congregate in their lazy hovering.

'I watch the tiger. I wait for him,' she says, 'I wait for him to come over to the house but he doesn't. He just sits.'

Curious, I ask more about the tiger, which has Nina point out the unlikelihood of the big cat appearing outside her grandma's house. For one thing they are much, much further east, she says, Siberia. She has had this same dream before, she admits, versions of it. The more she has had this dream the more reassured she becomes in the tiger's presence. She feels he is there protecting the house, watching over her.

Suddenly, Nina springs to her feet, swatting at her lower back and hips. I am up as well, palms poised as if to smother invisible flames. She swipes at a passing bumblebee.

'Stung me… They stung me.'

Nina hikes up the back hem of her shirt looking for the sting.

'It was probably a wasp,' I say. 'A bee wouldn't sting for no reason.'

She continues to probe the exposed skin above her waistline.

'I can't see where it stung me.'

'It's okay,' I say, 'I'll check.'

I stoop to search for the bee sting, but notice something else.

'You see it?'

Indistinctly imprinted on the fleshy back part of her left hip are two converging, half-moon-shaped indentations. The marks of two ghostly fingernails.

*

Violet told me how difficult it is for her to infringe on my 'side of the road', as she will often dub the realm of the living. For her to nudge a door ajar she describes as similar to me trying to heave aside a grand piano. Despite this, she indulges in the customary poltergeist shenanigans; turning on bathroom taps and pressing on and off light switches. Boredom plays a part, Violet will concede. It is after all eternity she finds herself up against.

*

Returned to my flat, I flop back on my unmade bed. Seven minutes pass. I know she's there.

'Nice day?' says Violet, eventually. Her voice issues from the ventilation grille in the redundant fireplace.

I have no idea whether what she says is intended as a question, a statement, or both.

'You were there,' I say, 'the weather was good. A lot of bees about, stinging people for no good reason.'

'Yes. A good wholesome pinch.'

'Just leave Nina alone! What is it you have against her?'

'Your accent, it's so flat,' Violet laments, 'it wasn't always like that. When you were a boy you spoke so well. It was those years you worked in that awful department store with all those little louts that you chose to forget how to finish your words. Often I see no sense in talking to you, since clearly you never listen to anything I say, much like my dear sister.'

'You had a sister?'

'Yes.'

'Tell me about her?'

'Someone prepared to overlook anything. Happiness to her was something one simply plucked from a branch, like a plum. Poor girl.'

'What happened to her?'

'Inevitability, it catches up with us all in the end.'

'Look,' I say, attempting to veer back to the point, 'please just promise you'll leave Nina alone from now on. Please.'

'Promises, I've had my fill.'

'Violet, please be reasonable.'

'The dead, are we not reason itself?'

'Come on, Violet. Please, I'm begging you.'

A slight subsidence at the end of my bed lets me know Violet has sat down. I hear her sigh.

'Do you ever wonder what it was like for me, at first? When I realised that it was all gone, every bit of it. No, I don't expect you do or would even burden yourself to try.'

I had tried. So terrible a thought I refused to contemplate it further. I don't tell her this.

'Stop the games Violet, just leave Nina alone. What you're doing is really pathetic.'

My bedside lamp thwacks on the ground.

I remain frozen on my bed through a brief and unnerving quiet. Soon I hear my bedsprings creak. An icy sweep of air suddenly makes me aware of those previously unacknowledged, minuscule hairs on my cheeks.

'I'll show you games,' Violet hisses. 'By God I'll show you games.'

I wait for her to say more but all I get is a silence, dense and wrenching, as if balled in my stomach. I call out Violet's name half a dozen times before I register the disquiet in my voice. I am dabbing at a cold patch of sweat already slick on the nape of my neck. I feel overcome by an urge to flee out into the night but recognise the futility in this. Soon I am securing the bedcovers up over my head, a child again, hiding from ghosts.

*

A number of weeks back, while partway through my morning commute, I had stopped in a café bar on Amiens Street for a morning jolt of espresso. The interior was gloomy but airy and possessed old-fashioned, wood-panelled walls and a big mirror behind the counter that ran its entire length. Reflected in the mirror was a woman in a cream overcoat and a mauve coloured cloche hat. She was in one of the rear booths. Maybe in her mid-thirties she was slender, brown-haired. Of course, when I turned and looked over at the booth she was gone. I had glimpsed large, doleful eyes, a small mouth and a high brow that gave to the face a deeply meditative, almost owl-like, quality.

*

The morning after Violet's threat, I call Nina from work but her phone keeps switching to voicemail. I leave five voice messages in which I do my best not to sound anxious. Multiple text messages also sent. With Violet's warning hanging over me, it began, a portentous day. I turn on my work desktop only for it to wheeze into a dead silence. After one of the IT guys carts away my computer, I send another text to Nina, my ninth that day. The near instantaneous reply has me shudder, nearly dropping my phone as I go to answer. Nina informs me she's very busy. She offers to see me later. She warns me against calling her at work in future then hangs up.

*

When I meet Nina, she still has her work apron on. She seems wary, apprehensive. I call to her across the street and she reacts with a start.

With clouds gathering grey and ominous above, I suggest we sit inside somewhere but Nina wants to go for a walk. We reach a compromise.

After lunch, I had headed down to IT to find my desktop — minus its side — stood on a table. Its power supply unit had been burnt out. 'Totally fried,' the IT guy conveyed in an overworked jocularity. He assured me I would have a new computer by the end of the week. He suspected a sudden power surge was to blame, a rare, but not uncommon, occurrence. 'Random,' he told me, 'completely random.' It wasn't though. That much I knew.

Nina and I take an outside table, its zinc surface dappled with raindrops. She sits hunched, her arms folded into her stomach as she gazes about, watchful. I ask her if she's okay. A dream, she imparts, a bad dream was all.

'Sometimes they can be scary,' she says, 'when they seem real.'

Before I can stop myself, I am telling Nina about Violet. She listens, inexpressive.

'There is no need to do this,' she interrupts.

'Do what?'

'Make fun of me.'

'I'm not making fun of you.'

Nina says nothing for a couple of moments. She rises and says she'll call me. Then she goes.

*

The next day I choose not to go to work — too stressed. Instead having taken my usual bus into the city I spend the day traipsing through rain-soaked streets without the hindsight of an umbrella or even a hood. I wander, directionless. At times, I loiter hopelessly. I focus on trying to clear my head. But it's no good. Everywhere I go I see Violet's spectral hand at work. My fully charged phone drains of its charge within a solitary minute. Digitised bus boards blip blank upon my approach. Every ATM I try spits my bank card back out at me. Eventually I wander my way back through the city's redbrick Edwardian inner suburbs. Here, on Phibsborough Road, a cat sleeks out from under a front garden privet hedge and halts defiantly on the pavement ahead of me. The smoky grey cat with its pale green eyes seems to regard me. Thinking it is Violet having assumed corporeal form I turn and hurry back the other way.

*

I return to my flat, hungry and stressed. To my surprise, I find it exactly as I had left it. A part of me anticipated some kind of poltergeist retribution, spurting taps, overturned furniture, smashed crockery. Yet everything appears untouched.

'Hello,' I call in, as if intruding in someone else's space.

No answer, I go over, turn on my laptop, and wait for it to boot-up. Meanwhile I take the newly bought CD from my pocket and tear off its clear plastic film. The songs on the CD are by an Irish lyric tenor popular during the first half of the twentieth century. I press PLAY. A velvety-toned voice sings 'Somewhere a voice is calling'.

I wait.

'Obviously a stab at humour on your part.'

Violet's voice filters through the slightly ajar bathroom door.

'I thought you'd like it,' I say. 'He was popular back in your era, wasn't he?'

'My era?'

'My grandparents used to talk about him.'

'So this is all for my benefit.'

'You're stuck in purgatory.'

A sardonic laugh follows.

'Why do you so readily assume I am — was — a Roman Catholic?'

The song is still playing. I press STOP.

'Oh yes, I see now,' she says. 'The morbid obsession with guilt, enough to anchor one in eternity it seems.'

Violet goes quiet then and I speak up.

'The other night you said something about the way I spoke when I was a boy was different. How could you know that? Or that I worked in a department store?'

Even before I utter the words, I know.

'I see this as ungratefulness on your part,' says the voice from the bathroom.

'Ungratefulness?'

'You know how many times I stopped you from stepping out under a bus, that cold nip on your neck that had you look just in time? How many of your youthful nightly excursions were you inexplicably guided home when you were too drunk even to remain upright? So near-sighted and yet you refuse to wear spectacles. I know everything about you, every secret, fib, falsehood. And now I feel I have had quite enough.'

'How long?'

'You needed someone to keep you from harm, to chaperon you. I did as best as I could manage. I never chose it. That's what I miss most about being alive, choices.'

'How long?' The only two words I now seem able to utter.

'You were an awkward child,' says Violet, 'terribly clumsy.'

My lips form and reform, my tongue moves, but no words come. Language has deserted me. Then, out of nowhere, I hear myself say, 'Nina.' Her name, at this precise moment, no more than any other word clonking about inside my head.

'She's not in love with you.'

'How do you know that?'

'I don't, but I have my suspicions.'

Violet takes a wearied breath, or what passes for a wearied breath for a poltergeist.

'You want to know how I died. Don't you?' she asks. 'It's been fascinating you.'

I did, but tell her I don't.

'A chill.'

'A chill?'

'One night I expected a door to be answered to me and it wasn't. I walked home through a rain shower. I had a temperature that same night. The following evening a doctor was summoned. Eight days later and I was dead. All because someone wasn't prepared to see me, my presence posing too much of an inconvenience for them. This is what I'm left with, this example of human consideration.'

'I'm sorry,' I say. 'I'm sorry.'

'Often I think how long I would have lasted if they'd given me some little thug of a corner boy. I tried my best with you, I did. But you're lazy, irredeemably so. You are honest though, to your detriment it must be said, but honest nonetheless, a rarity. When it all ends, you might well find yourself in good stead. If I have contributed that much…'

My breaths have become wet and hastened. My eyes damp. Yet I've never felt so vital, so alive.

'Violet,' I call out.

'Any secrets you have are safe with me, don't worry,' she assures.

Then nothing.

Violet's final words hang there in the air. I say her name repeatedly, but receive no response. When at last I open the bathroom door, I find a soundlessly thin tendril of water streaming from the sink's cold tap. I turn it off.

*

Three weeks pass and I meet up with Nina in a restaurant on Parliament Street that sports a vaguely Brazilian theme. She wears clothes I have never seen her in before; a crinkly blouse adorned with two gold-sequined flamingos and diamanté-studded heeled boots. Nina arranged this rendezvous. She has something to tell me.

'It is this negative energy from us,' she says, downing a quick mouthful of the complementary water. 'It affects me, even when I sleep. It must affect you too.'

I don't dispute this, even find myself nodding along to her words. After a while, I become aware of someone observing us. Stood by the kitchen entrance in a white smock is a short, thick-shouldered cook. He watches our table like a concerned parent. Nina takes another sip of her water.

'It is this bad energy we create when we are together,' she says. 'We will both be happier apart. I still have feelings for you but this is how it must be.'

*

The last time I see Violet and it is in the box room of my father's house out in Lucan. I awake during the early hours and she is stood there at the foot of my bed. There, in the dim blue light, I recognise the cloche hat, that meditative brow. There is a scarf about her neck. The belt on her coat has been fastened. Her hands are in the pockets. She looks as if she is about to start off on a long journey.

'I have to leave,' she says. Just like that.

She mentions somewhere far to the west, a place not on any maps. There will be someone else found for her in the meantime, she supposes, yet another poor little maladjusted soul ill-equipped for the world. Once again, she will put her time in. She will persevere. She will one day get her wings.

'Is it because of me?' I ask.

'It's simply a matter of knowing when to move on,' she says.

'I don't know if I'm ready to say goodbye,' I say.

'You only get a few final farewells. Don't waste them. Be patient. That's all I can really do now,' she says, a weariness to her tone, 'extol the great virtue of fortitude.'

'Don't go.'

'Even at your most pessimistic you never expect it to end, to just end.'

'Please don't go.'

'It's all so precarious…'

'You don't have to go.'

'…so bewildering. So infuriating. And oh so very, very short.'

Violet's countenance grows benign, even impassive.

'And you don't ask for it, any of it,' she says. 'That's the thing.'

Violet has stepped back towards where the shadows collect against the door and adjacent wall. I wonder if she is even aware of my tears. She goes very still as the shadows fold about her.

'Violet,' I call and call.

Finally, I get up and flick on the light but find no sign of her. She has gone for good, my guardian angel.

Two Poems
Natalie Ann Holborow

VICTORIA TERRACE

Tap splutters and spits
in a shared bathroom, too grey,
bleachy Atlantic. She twists
the handle: fizzing jets.
Takes too long. Listen:
group uproar, letters splashed
over side tables,
closed doors. Towel rub.
Mould blooms green as a banknote.

                                        You are big now,
                            sophisticated. Look at you,
                              cracking dry spaghetti:
                                 thin, wheaty bones
                          over pans, sputtering gas
                and grease-ring Michelin stars.
                          Popping lids from jars,
                      buggy mushrooms. Bean-slop.
                    Eating well, Mam. Eating well.

Is this the dream then,
this flaking, shuddering house,
moth-freckled, damp-bottomed
and senile? Something still beats
in the scarred white walls,

boot-bruises. Fractured doors,
unhinged. Breakfast eaten shyly
in the wrong language, stiff
in marijuana haze. Wrench
open the skylight. Intruding rain.

                    Around her wet mangle
               of clothes, a housemate hums.
               A native tune perhaps, her
                Polish eyes lost in her head.
           Her thin limbs in the early hours
          stretch and lift, and there you are
                   with your ratty eye
             meeting her ice-blues. Blue
                as this salty sea-town,
                  your freezing home.

RUNNING

must be doing something because
now I'm crying
over the smell of fresh laundry,
the sweet folds, warm, *soft*
as a baby's arse
and the woman
in the garden, tugging towels
from the wind,

  running
past pubs
where someone's father
fossilised on a barstool,
picks beermats
to mosaics. He presses
the wet rags
to his fingertips,
a pad of roughened skin,
but doesn't notice me

   running
through whirlwinds of litter,
tugging my ponytail tight
as the dark thatch
of telephone wires
humming with gossip,

      running,
ziplining
the fragile stalk of someone's
tenth cigarette
in a car park, as they
shield the struggling
light. It shrivels out
into ashes, whispers
back into the wind
where I'm

        running
to forget
the hollow places,
to forget
the neat ounce of your life.

The Driver
Tanya Farrelly

'You have to hand it to him,' Siobhan says, taking a sip of whatever new-fangled blend of tea she's drinking.

'Hand it to him how?' I say.

'Well, putting himself through college like that. What was it you said he was doing?'

'Environmental Biology.' I stand back to survey the bouquet, then reach for the scissors and the roll of tape on the countertop.

Siobhan readjusts her silk blouse on her narrow shoulders. 'It's not something I'd have expected…'

'What? From someone like him you mean? Someone from *that* neighbourhood?' I grip the flowers tighter, winding the tape from base to stem.

'No, that's not what I meant… I simply meant it's… admirable.' Siobhan's hand makes an arc in the air like an actress in a Shakespearean drama. 'You know the father's not around?' she says, leaning one elbow on the counter. A smooth duck-egg pendant, too large not to be vulgar, swings onto her right breast and rests there. It lurches again, pendulum-like, as she shifts to examine my work.

'Would you say that if he'd been brought up in Foxrock?' I say, ignoring the comment about the boy's father.

She shrugs. 'Probably not. I don't mean anything derogatory by it, but where he's from, as you say, it wouldn't be the most… aspirational area.'

'Oh, you're wrong there, Siobhan. We're all upwardly mobile now,' I say, fingers rapidly binding. 'Did you know we went to the same school? He even had my old maths teacher. Thought the old bugger'd be retired by now.'

That takes her aback. 'I didn't know you were from that side of town. You don't have an accent.' The pendulum swings again as she leans in. 'You'd have known his father then, would you?' she asks.

'I don't know. Maybe.' I twist to retrieve the scissors so she doesn't see the heat that creeps up my neck and sets my face aflame.

*

Siobhan was in Malta when Marty Moyes, who'd been working for the shop for a decade, had taken a heart attack. The doctors, his wife had said, expected him to make a full recovery, but it would be a while before they'd let him behind the wheel again. I'd phoned Siobhan, told her what was happening and she'd given me the go-ahead to advertise for a new driver.

That day, as I attempted to do the deliveries on my lunchbreak, I stopped off at a newsagent's near UCD and asked if I could put an advert in their window. Students were always looking for jobs. And that was where Conor Delaney had seen it.

I'd just turned the sign to closed and was sweeping cuttings into a pile when there was a rap of knuckles on glass. I looked up to see a young man eyeing me intently. 'We're closed,' I told him, pointing to the sign. 'There was an ad for a driver,' he said. 'Have you filled it?' 'No.' I unlocked the door and he passed, this fair-haired giant, into the flower shop. I worried that he'd turn and, in doing so, smash all around him, but he stood patiently and waited.

'Do you have a full license?' I asked.

He nodded, took a card from his wallet and held it out. His

hands were huge. This young man had no place in a flower shop. He could crush everything in it — he could crush me. I took the card he offered, read the name in bold letters before my eyes slid down to the address beneath. An address I knew by heart. I handed the license back to him, surprised as I did so that my hand remained steady. The trembling was on the inside. I could have turned him away then, told him I'd call him and never would, but something stopped me. 'Do you have any experience?' I asked.

He shook his head. 'I'm a student. I'll work hard.' He looked nothing like his father, but his voice, his timbre, was identical. There was some resemblance too in the fierce way he looked at me.

'Any penalty points?'

'No.'

'Well, we are pretty stuck. Is there any chance you could start tomorrow?'

He smiled and held out his giant's hand. 'I won't let you down.' His fingers closed round mine and I nodded, dumb.

He worked every day between nine and two. His classes were in the afternoons and in the evenings he'd come for the following day's list. He'd sit up at the counter and plan his route, checking Google maps for locations and the easiest ways to get there. That first week I waited, convinced that Conor's turning up here was more than just coincidence, but as the days passed, we grew easy with one another. I'd make tea and he'd tell me things. Not private things, but about his classes and funny incidents, which seemed to happen daily. I wished that Siobhan would stay away and it could be just the two of us for another while.

'He's a bit young, isn't he?' Siobhan said, eyeing Conor as he loaded up the back of the car. I shrugged. 'If you compare him to poor Marty, I suppose he is. But he's careful, and he's got his full license.' I didn't want to say it, but he also managed to get through the deliveries in half the time Marty Moyes did. The man was, after all, over seventy.

Siobhan watches Conor with undisguised interest. She asks him about his studies and clearly, she's asked him other questions too, to have gleaned that his father's not in the picture. Siobhan's nosey like that. I've learned how to handle her over the years, found ways to deflect unwanted curiosity. I don't know what Conor's told her about his father and I'm not about to ask. That would be to invite all kinds of unwanted questions.

*

I'd met Darragh Delaney in secondary school. He saved me from getting smacked in the face by a basketball — intercepted it as one of his classmates lobbed it across the corridor to bounce against the wall. I'd jumped back in fright and Darragh had smiled at me briefly as he knocked it clear, shouting 'Hickey, you moron… will you watch it?'

After that he nodded to me in the corridor. Hickey teased me, pretending he was going to throw the basketball at me whenever I passed. He'd make as if to launch the ball, then let it slip through his hands, before he bounced it and laughed.

The fifth-years had art class directly before we had and I discovered that Darragh Delaney usually sat in the same place I did. He realised it too because soon coded messages started to appear etched into the huge wooden table in the form of song lyrics. After each quote, the initial D appeared. Standing outside the art room, I watched Darragh pack up his bag. Some days, he'd nod as he passed me on his way out, others he'd pretend not to have seen me. I started to etch responses to his lyrics. Usually I knew them, they ranged from Bon Jovi to

Meatloaf, but if I didn't recognise the song, I'd reply with something different. Anything to keep the thread going — and it did. For months it continued before anything actually happened.

My route home from school consisted of an uphill climb, and a trek across a field before I exited through a gap in the railings. Darragh took this way home too, but he was usually with Hickey and some of the others, so I'd stay a good distance behind. One day though I was walking home and I noticed Darragh walking in front of me. There was a sixth-year, who I knew to see, walking quickly behind him. When the boy got almost level with Darragh, he pulled his backpack hard knocking him to the ground and proceeded to kick him. I looked around, panicked, but the closest bunch of students were far behind me and by this time his assailant had walked away leaving Darragh pulling himself up from the ground, his school uniform covered in mud.

'Hey — are you alright?' I said, breathless from the run to catch up with him.

'Yeah, fuckin asshole,' he said. He was turning his glasses in his hands. One lens had been cracked and the left arm hung loose from the frame.

'Do you know him?'

'Yeah. Gareth Hynes,' he said.

'What happened? I mean why did he do that?'

Darragh folded his glasses and put them in his pocket. Without them I noticed that his eyes were an almost transparent green. 'He reckons an amp I've got was nicked from his garage.'

'Why does he think that?'

'Because, unfortunately for me, he's probably right, but I paid fifty quid for it and there's no way I can get my money back.'

'What'll you do?'

'Give him back his amp, I suppose, and suffer the loss. He'll never let it go.'

'Why don't you tell him who you got it from?'

He looked at me as if I were totally naive. 'What? And risk an even worse thrashing? You must be joking.'

I blushed at my own stupidity, and tried to think of something to say to redeem myself. We'd exited the gap in the railings, reached the point where I turned off left for home. We'd both slowed our step. 'How long have you been playing?' I asked.

'A few years. I'm a bassist.'

'Oh yeah?'

'Yeah. Lead is lead,' he said, 'but bass… bass is the backbone of the band. Which way are you going? he asked.

I pointed in the direction of home. 'Come on,' he said. 'I'll walk you.'

*

'Conor?'

He's sitting up at the counter staring at nothing. 'Sorry?' When he looks up, his eyes are huge, startled.

'Is everything alright? You've been miles away.' I put two mugs of tea on the counter and sit on the stool next to him. Siobhan is off today and it's just the two of us. Conor takes a Kimberly biscuit from the packet between us and chews distractedly. 'Is it a girl?' I say, teasing. He shakes his head. Then looks at me, that intent stare, like he's sussing me out, wondering if he can trust me. 'It's just family stuff,' he says then.

I nod, sip my tea. He tells me about some experiment they did in the university that went terribly wrong, resulted in the third-years setting the lab on fire, but even as he tells the story, he's not really in it. Not like he normally is, and I'm pretty sure I know the reason.

*

When the poster went up outside the Martello bar, it had been more than a decade since I'd seen Darragh Delaney. We'd parted amicably — as amicably as you can at eighteen. He wanted to pursue his music career; didn't have time for a girlfriend. If you didn't make it by twenty-five he said, you never would; the industry wanted young people. I knew the real reason was my refusal to sleep with him.

Skinny Lizzy the poster read. I remembered how adamant he'd been that he'd never play in a tribute band. I examined the photo. He looked the same — was carrying a bit more weight round the face, but there was no doubting it was him. I thought I recognised one of the others too, but I wasn't sure. For whatever madness, I decided to go to see them.

I didn't tell the friends I invited that I knew him. Instead, I feigned surprise when I ran into him at the bar before the gig. He was delighted to see me, asked if we could have a drink after. His friends had to call him several times for the soundcheck. 'Don't go anywhere,' he said, squeezing my shoulder, and I knew that I shouldn't have come.

Afterwards, I waited as he and the rest of the band loaded up the van.

'How come you're here tonight… I mean you didn't…?' Darragh waved his hand, a small smile on his lips.

'What? Come to see you?' I said. 'No. It's my local. They've always got bands… they're usually good.'

'Lovely,' he said, lifting his glass. 'Cheers for that.'

I laughed. 'Anyway, whatever happened to your antipathy

for cover outfits? Musicians cashing in on other people's talent, isn't that what you used to say?'

Darragh rounded his shoulders over his pint. 'Youth and optimism,' he said. 'They've both flown west. If you don't make it by twenty-five...' I knew the rest before he said it.

We stayed talking that night till closing time. He told me that he'd married at twenty-two, so much for focusing on his music career. 'She was pregnant,' he said, 'with Conor. He's almost ten now.' When he walked me back to the flat, I didn't invite him in. We stood awkwardly until I flagged down a taxi for him, not wanting a long goodbye, but he still managed to pull me into a hug. As he held me against him, I thought of the rangy teenager he was. Now he was solid without being overweight. When he released me abruptly, I almost toppled over. 'It's been great,' he said. He hopped in the taxi and with a small wave vanished into the night.

We should have left it at that, but the next day I got a friend request on Facebook and a month later a private message telling me that he was playing in Jim Doyle's if I was free. I wasn't, but I turned up anyway. I needed to exorcise him. Since the previous meeting he'd been living inside my head. It didn't work of course and that night he followed me up to the flat without being invited.

*

Conor continues to be distracted during the days that follow. He's not the only one. I began counting down months before, even though Darragh had cut all contact. On the Wednesday, two customers phone to complain about a serious mix-up; a funeral spray has been delivered to a wedding. Unfortunately, it's Siobhan who takes the call. 'This would never have happened with Marty,' she rages. Conor, luckily, is still out doing deliveries and I tell her that I'll deal with it.

He's devastated when I tell him. 'I'm sorry Lillian. Is Siobhan hopping? I suppose that's it now.' 'Look, it could happen to anyone,' I tell him. 'Human error.' He shakes his head. 'No, it shouldn't have happened. It's my fault, I've been distracted. My old man's getting out of prison this week. I haven't seen him in eight years.' He digs into his jeans pocket, and pulls out a folded piece of paper. 'He wrote to me, wants to meet…'

I nod, eye the paper in his hand, wondering if he wants me to read it, but he doesn't offer. Instead, he puts it back in his jeans pocket. 'He killed a man,' he tells me. 'Got in a car drunk.'

*

We'd taken Darragh's car that night. The idea was that I would drive us home, but then he'd got the text from Ann-Marie telling him he couldn't take Conor out the following day and he'd grabbed the keys and left the bar in a rage to confront her.

'Darragh,' I'd shouted, grabbing my coat and running to catch up.

'What?' he said, turning. 'She can't do this. I have rights.'

'Look, you can't drive, not like this,' I said, reaching for the keys.

He held them out of my reach. 'I'm fine,' he said.

'You're not.'

'Right, you drive me then.'

I shook my head. 'It's not a good idea. Wait till the morning…'

'No, I'm going to sort this out. Come on. I'll drop you on the way.'

I refused to get in the car. 'Suit yourself,' he said. He'd jumped in then, slamming the door after him. He'd practically skidded out of the car park. As he took the bend beneath the bridge, he'd mounted the kerb, didn't even see the elderly man until he'd felt the thump.

*

'Do you want to see him?' I ask. Conor hangs his head. 'I don't know.' 'He is your dad.' 'Yeah, I'm thinking about it.' He drains his tea. By the time he gets up to leave, he still looks unhappy. 'Hey, Conor,' I say. 'Yeah?' 'You put some hex on that wedding today.' We both begin to laugh. 'Not to mention the message of congratulations to the late Frank Devine.'

Days pass. Conor works hard. He doesn't say anything else about his father. When Darragh was sentenced he told me to forget about him. I visited him in prison but he refused to see me. I wrote to him and he didn't reply. I needed to know if he resented me. If I hadn't turned up at his gig that night, he might still have been with Ann-Marie. Even though he didn't acknowledge them, I sent him things — books mostly and an mp3 player with all his favourite music. I don't know if he was allowed keep it.

On Wednesday morning, Conor comes in from loading up the van. I'm busy working on a bridal bouquet. 'Lillian, do you think it would be okay to take Friday off?' he asks. 'Or to do the deliveries a bit later? I could come in the afternoon.' I stop what I'm doing, turn to look at him standing there, awkward. 'I wouldn't ask,' he says, 'but I'm collecting my dad.' 'Don't worry,' I tell him, 'Siobhan's here on Friday so I can do the deliveries.' He smiles. 'Thanks,' he says. He takes a step towards me and for a moment I think he's about to give me a hug. I turn away from him, pick up the pruners and continue to divest a rose of its thorns. 'I'm glad,' I say. 'He'll appreciate that, your dad.'

Two Poems
Kate North

Mount Ainos

Today we drove half way up
and set out to walk the rest.

We spiralled the mountain
flanked by firs, insect hum.
We leant into the steepening
land like it was strong wind.
Each turn promised us silent
trees watching over cool space.

When the summit arrived
I was static heat so my body
sank against the pylon
out of place at the peak.

We looked into the haze,
could not see Zakynthos,
Ithaca, Lefkada. We had no water,
or fruit, we each took a photo
and began our return.

At the bottom, over drinks, I showed you
how ants trail towards crushed potato chips,
surprised you didn't already know.

Later, I looked up our day and discovered
it was equivalent to climbing Ben Nevis,
or so the website said.

Paris, December 25th
for Alex

mute winter window
two paces from bed
you watch white-white
specks bless my face

charging the spiral
as if a slide, bells
quicken our pace,
into the dizzy courtyard,
greased with life we stop,
inhale morning, step into the quiet
hall of salons past,

onto Balzac holding hands
the cinema's Chaplin
meets my gaze
and you smile
to the pigeons

on the Champs-Élysée
a surprise, casual
arrogance, throated
bustle of trade
wetting the day
a baby's head

we slip empty
into George V,
fake ivy flocking
the Givenchy front,
yellow light caught
in leaves we pull

scarves to noses,
rub elbows, chatter
of New York, Tokyo,
Trocadero, home

outside a palace
winking at the river
mulled hands cosy
brittle purchases
bagged and across
the bridge we nod
serious, a first this trip.

gendarme crackles

Mummy
Derwen Morfayel

When Cadence is five years old and a day, she refuses to drink her mug of milk. She is sitting at the kitchen table with arms crossed and eyes on Nanny. As a child, Cadence's cobalt blue eyes are deep-set and unapologetic. Nanny is not what her new British friends call a nanny. Not old. Not family.

'Drink up,' she says, smoothing her blond hair at each side of the parting.

Mother is in the garden testing the temperature of the morning and warming up her voice by tuning it with the breeze before going to work.

'Do you understand me?' Nanny whispers. 'Cadence, please. Your mother insists you finish your breakfast before ten to eight.'

Cadence thinks of their house on top of a shop on a colourful street back in Guanajuato. Nobody calls her Cadencia here. It is in this town where she learns that when it rains, it has never been the actual rain she can smell but the things it dampens and at school she is taught that the clouds are full of gutters.

With lips together and her tongue trying especially hard, Cadence says 'no, no, no' inside her closed mouth, in case Nanny thinks of pouring into it the mug of milk.

'Young lady, speak properly!' Mother is silhouetted at the door and her skirt and shoulder-padded jacket make her broader than she is. She speaks with the tone she uses on children in her music class, never making any distinction between Cadence and the others.

Even though Cadence wouldn't mind going early and being in the deserted playground while her mother is in the staffroom, taking her to school is Nanny's job and she is paid an extra pound the hour if she makes Cadence recite the multiplication tables on the way, and then again in the afternoon on their way back to the house which is now home.

'*Ya no más*, Mummy. *Ya no quiero más.*' Cadence covers her mouth with her hands.

Nanny seems to suddenly understand the Spanish words. 'Your mother will be awfully sad if you don't finish your milk.'

Right now a signal is sent from Mother to Nanny — a wink that is tossed in the air like a coin and Cadence is too young to catch it.

'Yes, in fact, feeling sad makes me unwell.' Mother brushes her forehead with the back of her hand, her movements graceful as usual, and lets out a high-pitched sigh.

'Is that what you want?' asks Nanny.

Cadence dips a finger in her milk and tastes it. The women smile in secret, but again the girl shakes her head.

'Oh, no,' her mother says. First she falls to her knees and then to the floor.

She lies there stiff, with eyes open and tongue out.

The little Cadence gets off the stool and crawls towards her. For a few seconds, her heart jumps and her breath stops. She calls, 'Mummy! Mummy! Mummy!' then she is silent as she shakes her mother.

'Quick, the milk!' Nanny brings the mug.

The mug is shoved in Cadence's face but she knew already, in these seconds without air, that she must drink it. She gulps it down as she would if she was thirsty. It has never tasted so thick. She wasn't aware of its weight until now.

Mummy does not wake until the very last drop.

When this moment becomes memory, it haunts Cadence with shame. It becomes even more embarrassing than playing the music she prefers at full volume — that music too modern for her mother and too foreign for her friends. Her mother will laugh away what happened here. Cadence will never admit how it felt to think herself an orphan. How she begged.

*

'They are always difficult, the first-borns,' Mother is saying. 'I guess, like everything, it is hard to get right the first time…'

At the age of forty-two, Cadence understands that these words are an attack on her as both a mother and a daughter, since she is not first- or second- but the only-born.

'…that's why I had Nanny to help. You know, Hernando was telling me all about these tablets you can give to… confused children, such as yours. It makes them sort of *stop* and stay somewhere in between, until they decide.'

'I never heard of that,' says Cadence. 'I'm sure it is not so easy.'

'It is horrendous.'

Mother is Valerie. The sort of person who shouts 'Telephone!' when it rings as if others can't hear it. She is a widowed teacher, *la señora de Gómez*; a proper lady. Cadence on the other hand is a single mother knocked-up by surprise in her thirties by a hypochondriac interpreter during the months she spent in Europe with her colleagues at the soap company.

'And then there's his daughter.' Valerie stands, holding herself up with the long-closed umbrella she uses because she refuses a cane at all costs. She goes to Chichi's cage and plays the metal bars as if it were a harp. Chichimeca is her part-demon yellow canary that has lived, according to Cadence, for far too long. 'You know how she never went to church and now she is studying Religion, deciding which to take home as if it is… How did she describe it? She said it is the same with brands, best to stick to the popular ones, just in case.'

Cadence doesn't care about Hernando or his daughter.

'She says Javier is lost.' Valerie holds the silver cross charm of her bracelet. 'Not his mind, but his soul.'

When Cadence had returned from that work trip to Bruges, fatter than usual, she remembers her mother called her stupid. Only her friends called her brave and over the years a few acquaintances even asked questions that implied they mistook her for a Samaritan to a poor African orphan. She didn't understand at first why they assumed her son was adopted. In time she learned that it was usually a type of people that said these things; the type that couldn't conceive the idea of the raw and naked brown in her making love to black.

Valerie is close to Chichimeca's cage and big in its eyes. She is its partner and its jailer, its keeper and its mistress. The two of them sing together. Her British vowels have morphed, especially since her second marriage, but it has not affected her singing voice because even when they lived in England she was of the belief that 'it is easier to sing with the American accent', as if it really is only one accent. Cadence always thought she resembled Julie Andrews when she sang with that straight smile and short neat hair.

Valerie doesn't sing for too long any more and her posture is lost. Cadence can almost see new scars forming in her mother's white matter.

'Help him. Help your son,' Valerie says.

But Cadence knows Javier is not her son.

*

Whenever Cadence tells Valerie about her few ephemeral romantic thoughts and ardent encounters with men, she is reassured that loving a stranger within days is impossible. Valerie would say that only happens with 'dogs, and perhaps new-borns'. So she had decided not to tell her mother about Bruce, the Scottish photographer. He is only a boy, fresh out of university, and so she reserves this information for a night out with her colleagues instead, once she feels pretty enough to have people watch her for the duration of the story. Yes, that story is better placed in a cocktail glass — a strong spirit with a dash of fruity exaggeration and the type of details that make one fizz, but honest as the salted olive on the toothpick. Her opening line would be: 'I couldn't understand a word he said, but we understood each other in more ways than one…' She yearns for that sense of relief, after work and before home, in her most glamourous heels.

Bruce has become a platonic pen pal. They exchange postcards because letters have no pictures and emails have no charm. His last postcard came in summer, explaining why he didn't return as he had said he would. Cadence doesn't think she had believed him for a second anyway. At first she wondered why he kept in contact and if it was simply the memories of his trip and her picturesque neighbourhood. The more postcards they exchanged, the more it saddened her to realise it had been nothing other than photogenic to him. He wrote of the exoticism of it all. Did he also mean her? The Latina from Guanajuato, she imagined him saying. Or worse, a MILF! Was she some sort of tick on a bucket list?

She is writing to him, replying to that last letter in which he went on — in that tiny handwriting — about a new camera, his brother's wedding and his visit to the museum of the mummies when he was here. From her room she can hear Chichimeca's infernal chirping.

I had that dream again. I was in the room of doors and as usual I can't remember what colours they were. The floor is earth. I step over nuggets of gold to get to the doors. They're closed. I think them locked but I never try to open one, never even touch their brass knobs. I just stare at the doors without seeing their colour.

Cadence questions herself about keeping in contact too. It is something to do with that sense of release. She can tell him things without a care in the world because aside from the couple of orgasms during those nights they spent together, which she told him were three, they shared nothing. She could spill her feelings on the postcards the way drunk people tell their worries to strangers and forget about it in the morning.

A deep voice calls her, 'Mom,' and then again, '*Mamá*.' It is Jael, now adolescent, telling her for the first time that Grandmother has fallen over. From that day on it is always Jael who finds Valerie first when she suffers.

Cadence is tired of feeling her own body existing independently, functioning without her participation. Her feet walk. Her brain works. Her right hand spends the money she makes on a life she doesn't remember choosing. Her left hand cleans when she gets home. It is as if she — her mind, her self — is the neglectful husband and her body the dependable tireless wife.

*

Valerie is lying in bed, dead. Much deader than the day of the milk.

She is naked underneath the dressing gown; lately she was easier to clean that way. Her skin smells of baby wipes and her gown of sweat.

Jael concentrates on the body, contemplates whether it is still a body or technically something else altogether. Cadaver? Organic residue? Empty soul-pot? Meat? Cadence finds more curious the surroundings: packets and plastic bottles of pills for the pain on the bedside table, not all of the drugs prescribed and some not even legal; huge pads around her on the bed arranged in crisscross; the cacti in the holed cookie tin that have been bleeding through their spines since Chichimeca's carcass was mixed with the soil. She finds these things curious because she would never have imagined Mother, who had on many occasions slapped the back of her hand while telling her to speak properly, cursing as she had done the past month and swearing at the mattress and the walls. Pious Mother turned pagan in her last breaths as she pleaded her dead pet and all gods of the sky for wings like Chichi's. Wholesome, unpolluted Mother who tormented Jael for taking her pills and at the very end cried out for drugs she couldn't reach. They both were addicts in their own way; both wanted things gone from their bodies. The stained pads underneath Valerie remind Cadence that her piss was as yellow as Jael's, despite her insistence on continuing to call her granddaughter 'Javier'.

Cadence also struggled at first with the change of name in much the same way as she did when picking up mail addressed to her mother, who had changed her surname again for her late second husband. It made her ponder on all the instances throughout her life in which Valerie had complained about her struggle to ascend in her early days at schools run by men or when she gossiped about submissive married women she met. Having lived the process from Javier to Jael, Cadence knew the importance of a name and thought her mother was the submissive one for changing part of her identity to someone else's. Valerie's comments were surely in an attempt to teach her something but all Cadence hoped was that she wouldn't inherit that teacher's face. She vowed not to become anything that Valerie was so when Javier told her she wasn't a boy, she nodded — because a part of her knew — and she waited.

Cadence and her daughter are sitting each on a chair at the foot of the bed. They have done their crying and made all the calls. They have even decided on Valerie's last clothes and laid out Jael's long leather skirt, because she is thin and closer to her grandmother's size, and a frilly shirt of floral pattern. It is an outfit Valerie would never have chosen for her own wake. She hated leather and she hated flowers.

Jael stares at her grandmother's feet. After a long silence, she says, 'Sometimes I wish I could understand you…' Her accent is irregular; a bastard of two continents just as she is. '…as much as you understand me.'

How could Cadence not? She always identified with her daughter who grew up with neither siblings nor men and didn't feel she fitted in anywhere. How could Cadence not understand when Javier was not yet ten the day she approached her with the tact of a loving adult to ask her what she thought about the new name. It was the sweetest thing, as if asking permission. As if apologising for thinking that the name that had been chosen nine years ago was not the right one. 'Jael is beautiful,' she told her daughter and since then, it only seems odd at times. As with her black-haired friend Leticia who has been dying her hair blond for half her life, roots grow and show, unsightly, as a reminder. In the case of Jael it is bits of boy getting stronger, larger, hairier.

'I mean, like right now, I wish I could see what you're feeling exactly but I don't. Not all of what you're feeling anyway.' Jael sighed and placed the hair pin she had been playing with between her lips because she had taken to smoking when she was nervous but not in front of her mother. 'Mom, would you forgive me for anything at all?'

All sorts of things go through Cadence's head in a second. Has Jael killed her own grandmother? Euthanized her after some clandestine pact? These cautious words remind Cadence of Jael at thirteen, when no razor could hide the wrong parts of her face and she told her mother a little late that she decided they were put to better use on her genitals. Cadence bought her an epilator to make sure it was only hair that she was cutting from then on and the result left her happier. Sometimes, when her sceptic shell cracks in places, Cadence believes that this suffering is her own fault for feeling very slightly disappointed when Jael was born and she came with a penis.

'I found one of your postcards and read it. I'm sorry, Mom. I thought your mystery pen pal… that maybe it was my dad and that's why you kept it a secret. It's some Bruce guy—'

Does this mean she wants to meet her dad? Cadence isn't even sure she still has his number. She hadn't told him much about him. He didn't exist until now.

'Why are you bringing up "some Bruce guy" now?' she asks her daughter.

'There was something he said that stuck with me. This story he was told in the museum about a girl mummy they found biting her arm with a mouth full of dry blood. He called it walking the corridors of the dead. He said how death leaves a mark on us all but to be buried alive… That's the worst, you know?'

Perhaps Jael has taken his words to have a wiser meaning behind them but Cadence knows Bruce-the-Scottish-photographer isn't as deep as he thinks and travelling is just another thing kids do nowadays. Jael however still has that charm of a child's mind that refuses to be put to sleep. The little girl who wants to stay up late and watch the film her mother has on. The young woman who can speak however the fuck she wants to.

'Buried alive,' Jael says again. 'I used to be that girl mummy.'

As a mother, Cadence has always felt deficient. She carries with her the huge shame of being incapable of giving birth to a soul in its right body. It wasn't her daughter's job to be a woman; it was hers, and she had failed.

Jael brings a comb and picks out one of Valerie's silver hairs from its teeth before using it on Cadence. 'Bruce wrote that that's why he doesn't stop in one place for long. Makes sense except, some people feel free in just one place too, right?'

Jael's faith in good things is a shining star on her shoulder. Cadence won't be the one to put out its light. She sits in silence as her daughter combs her hair, like an animal being groomed; a pet that was lost in a foreign town and miraculously found its way home. She looks at the soil pot full of Chichimeca and relives moments of Valerie whispering to it through bars.

Three Poems
Susanna Galbraith

for M

skeletons are beautiful as anything cleaned-out by sea-muscle
of history by roots pulled and senses swallowed
the attics of bodies filled with the endless quiver of big water

sea time and cat spine

///

i had a little creature combing my heaves and heartbeats with
a geological purr
and a sudden sigh reaching out like a limb with a hot palm
always changing things

tiny shuddering into another deepness and then a deep sound
as sunset warms through still shallows pink-milked with
evening
and sea putting itself to bed easy as the coil of a cat
so much the way you close like a tongue into a mouth
and then are profoundly sleeping

/

sweet sweet — the word *sweet* as I speak it

you are the meaning of *sweet* entirely as my mouth closes
around it finishing
between my teeth and still ringing, although I never exactly
tasted you

inside some afternoons lifting my shirt to feel the furred
stretch that coated your heartbeat
on the nerves of baldness up and down like tiny breathing
saying more than speaking

and underneath a little thing profoundly living —
in dim light its music welled up in your eyes
and your pupils gaped love hungry as sky

with such eyes you were nothing of words and a deep hole to
be slowly falling into

for R

there is only one among us who can listen fully to the flowers for their speaking and suffers for it

this being native to a depthless remembering that awes little bodies to trembling flecks

hung out in a white sky that has eaten all of the stories up whole and hungers still

whose face is cracked constantly to crumbling by the under-skin sun of his terrible kindness

I think of him often, bereft of eyelids and walking unbound inside the white wilderness of all I cannot know about

but, eyes shut, I can love him without knowing by the brief way of him having once loved very near my mouth as I was breathing *for N*

i have written you down
again and again and again
for your impossibility
your enormity
cracking at the edges
with ever expanding invisibility
round
rooted through with light
like being born
because you are the very green
that speaks orange secrets
electrically
a sapling with charcoal knuckles
after the blazes
of love and eternity
your eyes, looking,
new blades out of dust
like ideas
brief and fleshless

Sound of the Riverbed
Dan Coxon

They source the fish from a nearby river. Every Thursday a man delivers them in the back of an unmarked truck, its sides streaked with mildew and rust. *Arcenciel*. That's what they call him: *Monsieur Arcenciel*. She thinks it's his name at first; her French isn't strong, despite the months spent among them. It's Marc who eventually explains it to her. *Arc-en-ciel* means *rainbow*. Like the trout. Like the fish he brings, still gaping and thrashing in their tanks, the glass smeared with algae. She flushes with embarrassment, brings the knife down even harder than usual.

It was meant to be a two-month assignment. An opportunity for travel, some additional credit towards her final grade. She has now been here for five. Each day is much like the last, but she has settled into a routine, found her groove. When she bothers to call home, her dad asks her what she's doing over there. What the research is for. She jokes that they're developing hearing aids for fish, because in reality she doesn't know. The routine is everything. The routine is reason enough.

The worst part is catching them. She doesn't think it's this hard for Monsieur Arcenciel, with his glass tanks, his line and bait. He has a helper, too: a young man about her own age, handsome, a diamond stud in one ear. She thinks he is his son. She has only a small net, the kind she imagines a child might use to pluck baby crabs from a rockpool. The trout thrash against the sides of the tank, fighting her every inch of the way. By the time she has one out on the worktop, its eyes wide and glassy, its tail thumping against the wood, she no longer feels any sympathy. It's amazing to her, how quickly she stops caring. How much ill will she can feel towards a fish.

Taking the blood sample is the worst part. Finding the vein, sliding the needle in. It's harder than it sounds. Once that's done, the blood stored and labelled, she turns to the knife. With one hand she holds the trout still; the other swings the blade upwards, a shining arc, bringing it down with force and precision on its head. The tail thrashes for a few seconds more, the nerves refusing to call it a day. Clinging on to the residue of life. She waits until it stops before she peers inside the skull. So intricate, so delicate. With a syringe she locates the inner ear and extracts the fluid, just a few millilitres, the point of this entire exercise. Stores it, labels it, starts again.

*

Kadeen is the only one who really talks to her in the lab. The others are friendly, but distant. They nod and smile, then go back to their conversations, their muttered French too fast for her to follow. She has a sneaking suspicion they may be talking about her, although they could be discussing anything. News, films, music — whatever it is that French people talk about.

She calls him Kad, although it feels like a betrayal. He isn't a cad, not at all. He is a welcome, gentle presence in her isolation. She knows that he has romantic intentions but she isn't interested, not like that. He's too short for her, a little thick around the middle. His face reminds her of a young Ben Kingsley. When he's concentrating on his work, unaware of her gaze, his mouth hangs open, slack and unappealing. He's a good friend to her, so when he asks her out for a beer she says yes. It has taken him months to pluck up the courage. It's the least she can do.

'We can explore the town, yes? Maybe eat? I know a place.'

'That sounds wonderful,' she lies. She prefers to eat alone in her room. She has lost almost ten pounds since she came here. Most dinners these days consist of a bowl of cornflakes and an apple. 'Tomorrow?'

'I was thinking tonight? Unless you have plans?'

She almost laughs. No, she doesn't have plans. Today, tomorrow, or next week. His eagerness is sweet, but heartbreaking. There will come a point when she has to let him down. For now, it might be nice to have some company. She has barely seen the centre of Cannes while she's been here.

They meet outside her dorm block and walk into town. Kadeen talks most of the way. His accent gets thicker when he's not concentrating, and when that happens she struggles to follow him. He tells her about his family. How they moved here when he was less than a year old, how it's been hard for his father to find work. He was lucky, getting the job in the lab. She wants to ask exactly where they came from, but it feels like an intrusion. She thinks he assumes that she knows.

She isn't sure where they end up. Somewhere off the Rue d'Antibes, one of those family-run bars that can't quite decide whether it's a pub or a café. She orders a beer, and the waitress brings her a giant tankard of lager, the glass frosted and cold to the touch. She's British, clearly this is what she wanted. It's more than she can possibly drink. She sips at it slowly, her lips sticking to the rim. Kadeen orders himself a short drink, something thick and yellow, and she assumes it's an exotic concoction of some kind, a cocktail she hasn't heard of. It's only when he excuses himself to go to the toilet that she dares to steal a taste, and discovers that it's pure pineapple juice. Maybe he doesn't drink alcohol. It strikes her that the offer of a beer was made for her benefit. She feels she should be offended, but she isn't.

When he finishes his pineapple juice she still has half her beer left. She does her best to quaff it, but the gas sits high and uncomfortable in her stomach. As they finally stand to leave she discovers that she is tipsier than she thought. Steadies herself with a hand on the table edge. She can see that Kadeem wants to take her hand in his, put his arm around her in a not-too-subtle gesture of support. She feels unkind, but she keeps her distance.

She notices the boys before he does. There are four of them, standing around two mopeds, the bikes and the boys illuminated beneath a weak yellow streetlight. It's the tallest of the four who catches her eye, and she double-takes; yes, it's him, she's certain. Monsieur Arcenciel's son. He has a cigarette hanging from his lip, so contrived that he may have placed it there as a prop, a green plastic lighter cupped between his hands. His thumb is flicking the wheel, the flame sparking on, then off, then on, then off. One of his friends passes his hand over it, near enough for it to almost burn, and they laugh. She notices a few empty beer bottles at their feet.

When someone shouts across the street she thinks they're talking to her. She looks up, expecting it to be the Arcenciel boy. But his head is down, rummaging in a pocket. It's his friend, the one with the fireproof hands. She doesn't know what he's saying, but it's clear she isn't the target. Kadeem has his face bowed to the road. He's picked up his pace.

They're following them now, the four boys, and she hears more than one voice raised in anger. Kadeem is no longer interested in holding her hand. He is wilting, trying to make himself small, trying to vanish into the tarmac. It doesn't work like that, she wants to say. It's not that easy to be seen, or not be seen. Sometimes, the world decides for you.

Gradually, she falls back. She knows she should feel like a coward, but her sense of self-preservation is stronger than her liking for this boy she barely knows. A few passers-by have stopped and she lingers close, hoping to be taken for one of them. Nobody is looking in her direction. She tries to make out what the boys are shouting, but she only grasps fragments. The word for 'Arab'. The word for 'terrorist'. There's laughter, just before the first bottle is thrown. The glass shatters on the street like a falling chandelier.

The second bottle catches Kadeen on the back of the thigh, disrupting his stride. He stumbles as the third strikes his shoulder, and then they've caught up with him. The Arcenciel boy assumes the mantle of ringleader, spitting vitriol. Two of the others grab Kadeen by the arms. Kad does his best to hold his head high, recover his pride, be a man — but she can see he's terrified. When he struggles they use it as an excuse to start hitting him. Body blows at first, soft thuds as they land. He raises his hands to cover his face but it only makes his ribs an easier target. Then somebody throws a fist at his jaw.

She doesn't leave immediately. Standing with the other bystanders, she gasps at each punch that connects, avoiding Kadeen's eyes all the while. She bears witness until she can't bear it any more, then she turns and scurries back to her dorm.

*

Kadeem isn't in the lab the next day. Or the day after. When Thursday comes, Monsieur Arcenciel delivers the trout alone, without his helper. Now she thinks of it, the boy didn't look much like him. Maybe he never was his son.

She's certain, more than ever, that the others in the lab are talking about her. She hears her name whispered, the 'Anglaise'. She hears mention of Kadeem. Marc smiles at her when she passes his workspace, but it's a smile of sympathy, not acceptance. It's gone before she has a chance to acknowledge it.

To top it off, the fish are more troublesome than usual. They thrash in the tank when she draws near, their tails thudding against the glass. The sound reminds her of fists on flesh and she cringes. When she lowers the net into the water it takes her almost five minutes to bag one of them, and then he slips out before she can lift him clear. She suspects they can detect the atmosphere in the lab. She finally secures one after eight minutes; a small, weedy specimen, his sides a lacklustre brown.

When the time comes to remove the top of his head, she pauses. She doesn't know what it means, her work. There must be some significance to somebody, somewhere. This can't all be for nothing.

The slice is clean. She waits for the tail's thumping to stop before sliding the tip of the syringe into the ear cavity. Guides the metal point between filigree bones. Not for the first time, she wonders what the fish hear when they're lying at the bottom of the river. Can they hear the pike approaching, the whisper of the fisherman's net? Or do they hear nothing but the gentle bustle of the passing water? The brush of the weeds, swaying in the current?

In the morning, she will ask about a transfer back to England. But today, there are samples to collect.

Two Poems and a Photograph
Jo Mazelis

Winnie
(For Shani Rhys James)

No one is there now.
The room is empty of flowers.
Gone the blown-head peony,
The naked phallic stamen.
Gone memory.
Handbag empty.

And being a mother
Meant that, previously,
All such disasters had been
Accounted for
with:

Tissues, safety pins, aspirin,
Remedies for colic,
Anti-vampiric garlic,
Warnings of catastrophe.
Story books, crayons,
Gin and tonic,
Gin and valium,
Valium and lipstick,
A hairbrush,

Cures for dysentery.
And:

Smacks and cuddles
That hang like thunderheads
In the yawning emptiness
Of her carpet bag,
Blazoned with flowers,
Worn thin with overuse
And up to her neck in

Everything.

Still Life with Mirror

The Omnipresent God of Self

Alone then,
Facing the mirror
Whose grip holds you even in
Sleep. And at a guess

Beyond death even.
The journey undertaken
(bitter, complaining)
Will rock you like a train.

Until, arriving home, it's
Back to the mirror again.

You might be a secretary,
A thwarted poet,
The toilet attendant
In the basement of a Berlin bar

With a china saucer of Euros
And a vase of plastic flowers,
Air spray, bleach and a chair to sit in
Beneath the throb of music above.

You might be a starlet with
Your mirror boxed by light bulbs,
But still, there's no escaping this —
That same face, those relentless twin
Planets — your eyes, even through
The star-spikes of tears or glisten of

Love. Or blinded by the regularity,
The habit of seeing.
Of saying.
Then lilacs.

Detroit
Anne Hayden

The table had been laid for breakfast when he got home, four bowls, four spoons, two mugs, two plastic beakers. Anything to save a few minutes in the morning, Maeve had said, but he couldn't help feel she was making a point by laying a place for him. He was expected at breakfast, she seemed to be saying, no matter how late he'd gotten home, no matter how busy a night it had been. The house was silent apart from the hum of the fridge which always seemed louder at this hour. He took a beer from it, uncapped the bottle as quietly as he could and padded in his socks to the living room.

Elsa from *Frozen* was propped up in a corner of the couch, Hannah had taken to leaving one of her dolls there for him so he wouldn't be lonely when he got home. But Daniel didn't suffer from loneliness, he had an aptitude for solitude, sometimes he was still surprised to find himself married. He sat in the other corner of the sofa, put his feet up on the coffee table and turned on the TV. There was nothing on but reruns of American sitcoms and repeats of daytime chat shows with a woman doing sign language in the corner of the screen. He picked a film from the digital recorder instead, a documentary about Detroit. A bit of Motown music might be just the thing to bring the adrenaline levels down after the rush to deadline. It had been a busy one, two late-breaking stories, chopping and changing pages at the last minute.

In the early days, Maeve used to wait up for him, having promised not to go ahead on whatever box set they were watching. They worked their way through five seasons of *The*

Wire and all seven of *The Sopranos* in those first couple of years. They'd talk to each other in the accents of Baltimore street dealers or Italian-American mobsters, Maeve's Carmela was spot-on. Then they'd go to bed together and he'd lie awake in the dark with his mind whirring.

But when she became pregnant with James, she was often too tired to wait up, and once the baby arrived, forget it. It was around then that he had started to sleep in the box room, it meant he didn't wake her or the baby and it allowed him to sleep through the early-morning feeds. But he still wasn't quite sure how he'd gone from crashing in there every now and again to sleeping there every night, even though the babies weren't babies any more and had moved into their own beds in their own room. How he'd come to the point where he no longer felt like he had a right to walk into what he now thought of as Maeve's room. His clothes had migrated across shirt by shirt, his shoes pair by pair, leaving him little reason to cross the hallway.

On the screen, the camera panned along a street of clapboard houses that must have been beautiful once but were now shells with broken windows, rotten wood and peeling paint, the gardens turned jungle-like, nature moving back in. One of the boarded-up homes was being torn down, bits of pink patterned wallpaper visible in the rubble. The climbing frame in the garden had long ago turned to rust.

Tomorrow he'd be sure to get up early to see Maeve and the kids off, he might even make breakfast for them. There would be no time for going back to bed, as was sometimes his way, or for taking his time over a second mug of tea. He had the interview at midday. It was only a formality, his editor had assured him, the job was his, but everything had to go through official channels these days, forms filled out, boxes ticked. HR wanted to sit in on interview panels to justify their existence, not like the old days when promotions were handed out in the pub. Daniel knew he should do some prep but thought it better to leave it to the morning when he was fresh. He'd have a look through the website, see how they did things on there. He wasn't too worried, graphics were graphics whether for print or online.

He got up to get another bottle of beer, careful not to clink as he put the first empty in the recycling bin, and returned to the couch. He still found it hard to imagine, them all being here together in the evening, himself and Maeve taking turns to prepare the dinner depending on who got home first. Working nine to five and leading a normal family life. Helping the kids with their homework. The four of them settling down on the sofa to watch a reality talent show or whatever normal people watch at the end of their day. Bedtime stories. Maybe he'd play five-a-side one evening a week, it sounded better than mid-morning yoga with the maternity-leave mums. He hadn't even applied for the job, it just fell into his lap.

It looked cold in Detroit but there was something romantic about the urban decay. The dilapidated theatre with cars parked in what was once the foyer, the abandoned car dealership that had been turned into an art gallery, the empty streets.

It would take a bit of adjustment, he knew that. There would no longer be excuses for missing Sunday dinner with the in-laws. Sometimes, on his Wednesdays off, he felt like a stranger in his own home, the three of them had their established rhythm and routine, their own way of communicating, and he only seemed to get in the way of it. Setting the table for dinner was Hannah's job, though she could barely reach the cutlery drawer, and clearing it after was James's, rendering Daniel useless until the washing-up.

Wednesday was the one night of the week that Maeve got to go out herself, with him here to babysit, although he knew better than to call it babysitting since they were his own children. Once the kids were put to bed, she put on her make-up and disappeared. He never relaxed in the same way on those nights, even with the two asleep upstairs and Maeve out, never quite felt he had the place to himself the way he did when he came in from work late the other nights.

Sometimes she came home from her outings tipsy and amorous and climbed on top of him on the couch. They only ever did it on the couch these days, never in a bed, and when she came there was no big explosion, just a sigh like she'd scratched an itch away or released a muscle that had been too tight. The last time, which seemed like a long time ago now, she'd already taken her shoes and tights off when he told her his back was too sore. She looked more wounded than he'd expected when she picked the shoes and tights up from the floor and he regretted it immediately but didn't know how to undo it. Her voice was shaky when she said something about what did he expect, a grown man sleeping in a child's bed, before she headed for the stairs. She hadn't initiated anything since and he'd always been the shy one physically, even in marriage.

It was difficult to focus on the film, which wasn't about Motown at all as it turned out. And he had lost track of what was happening, why the city had fallen into disrepair, something to do with the motor industry collapsing. His concentration wasn't what it used to be, frazzled from flitting between too many screens. He gave up on the documentary and flicked through the 24-hour news stations, but nothing new had happened since he'd left work. On another channel, a French arthouse film was about to start, it was called *Love* but was mostly sex according to a review he'd read while laying out the TV pages. The reviewer had criticised it for being little more than dressed-up pornography, the sex was unsimulated, the plotline thin and the actors unlikely to be picking up Oscars anytime soon. Perfect, he thought, not having the nerve to download real porn for fear James would come across it between episodes of Paw Patrol. He got up and took another beer from the fridge, smoked a cigarette out the back door, then went back to the sitting room.

There'd be no more watching pornographic French arthouse movies at two in the morning once he started the nine-to-five job. There'd be no second mug of tea, and no strolls around the park before work. And there'd be no more reason for him to be sleeping in the box room. He kept the sound down and ignored the subtitles so all the film provided was flesh-toned background images while he finished his third beer. The sex scenes, which were copious and unsimulated as promised, had little effect on him; their realness made them less sexy somehow. He drained the bottle and decided he'd leave it at that, he needed a clear head for the morning.

At the top of the stairs, the door to the kids' bedroom was half-open, a lamp throwing a triangle of light on to the landing floor. He saw Maeve asleep on Hannah's bed, the girl's head in the crook of her arm, the book she'd been reading her open on her lap. He slipped into his own room without bothering to brush his teeth. The small single bunk was all that would fit in there but he'd made the best of the space. The bookshelf he'd picked up from a second-hand shop had filled up nicely, he'd brought back his old records from the attic in his mother's house and had framed his *Taxi Driver* poster for the wall. He'd even managed to keep alive the pot plant that Maeve had put on the windowsill when he first started sleeping there. He smoked a cigarette out the window while sitting up in bed, simply because he could, then reached across and hit the lightswitch.

Daniel lay in bed listening to the sound of the morning rush. The small steps up and down the stairs, the daily battle over tooth-brushing and hair-brushing, the clink of spoons against bowls, the search for a missing glove. He heard Maeve calling James to help her zip up her dress. The handle on his door moved but the door didn't open, her telling Hannah 'Don't wake Daddy, he's tired.' He wondered if she even wanted him to get up or if she preferred him to leave them to it. Sometimes when he was trying to get chat out of the kids while they were eating their Weetabix, Maeve would look at him frustrated, as if he was slowing down the whole show. Maybe she only set the breakfast place for him because she felt she had to. Still, he felt guilty for not getting up, the morning was the only time he saw them on work days, but he had a queasy feeling in his stomach and couldn't lift his head from the pillow. He'd wait until they were out of the house, then make himself a strong cup of tea and prepare for the interview. His suit was still in her room, he realised.

 There was a clatter of activity in the hall, then silence after the front door closed, but still he lay there for another hour, telling himself once he was up by ten, there'd be plenty of time. He pulled the duvet over his eyes, the light was making his headache worse, and cursed his bad luck to be sick today of all days. He hit the snooze button on his phone again and again until the digits said 11.00, then he swung his feet out from under the duvet, they didn't have far to travel to reach the ground from the low bunk. The pain in his gut and his head accompanied him to the shower and then back out to the landing, where he stood paralysed for a moment between their two doors.

He went in and found that nothing had changed in there but everything seemed different. It smelled of her, and the feeling it brought — familiarity and strangeness together — reminded him of being homesick. The bed was unmade, but only on one side. When they used to change the sheets together, there were two long tea stains on the mattress marking roughly the spaces their bodies had occupied. Now, if he stripped the bed, he'd find his would have faded and hers become darker. A book lay open, cover-side up, where he used to sleep, the title in green and shocking pink shook him a little, *I Love Dick*. She didn't used to read things like that, she used to stick strictly to literary fiction. The dressing table had been overtaken with her products, her creams and potions and lotions filling the spaces where his things used to be. The part of the wardrobe where his shirts once hung had been filled up too. He found his suit and hurried back to the box room to dress.

In the kitchen, Elsa was propped up on a chair at the table, making him feel a pang of something. But he didn't have time to dwell on it nor to make a cup of tea, not to mind study up on the website. He'd have to wing it, he'd feed them some guff about interactive infographics and digital being the future of journalism. They would all pretend that there was a future for journalism, that someone, somewhere had a plan.

At the bus stop at the end of the road, the real-time digital orange lights told him the 39A would pass in four minutes but he felt he needed the walk to get his head together. It was a half-hour to the office but could be done in twenty-seven minutes at a push and this was going to have to be one of those days. Outside the cafe on the corner, a group of new mums wore sunglasses and sipped lattes. A quick coffee might help him focus in the interview, he thought, might get rid of the headache. He ordered a double espresso to go, drank it as he walked. He had to pick up the pace and spilled some coffee on his white shirt. When he cursed, a woman pushing a buggy threw him daggers. He walked a bit faster, squinting into the sun, and could feel the sweat seeping into the material of his shirt.

It was ten past twelve when he turned on to the street where he worked. He cursed again, but no one around here took any notice. The coffee had left a metallic taste in his mouth. He got to the newspaper building and let the revolving door do a 180 before he stepped into a slice of it. Through the glass he could see Sean Daly walking towards the elevator wearing a suit and carrying a folder, looking like he was all set to make his First Communion. Daniel caught his own reflection in the glass, he looked dishevelled and not in a good way. He followed the revolving door all the way around and found himself back on the street. He stood dazzled by the sun for a moment and looked down to shield his eyes from the glare. The weeds sprouting between the cracks in the footpath reminded him of Detroit and how quickly nature had reclaimed the space occupied by abandoned houses.

He started to walk back the way he'd come, there was no point in turning up to the interview fifteen minutes late and looking a state, he'd be better to phone them and tell them he was sick and had slept it out, or to pretend he'd gotten the day wrong. He wasn't going to get the job either way now, he'd have to let it go to someone else. Sean Daly and his social media presence would probably get it even though everyone knew his graphics weren't a patch on Daniel's, he once did up a map of Ireland and put Cork on the west coast and there was that time he photoshopped out Rihanna's left arm. Daniel would keep laying out pages until he was laid off, wait it out until the decline in print sales made him redundant.

He had plenty of time now to get home, change out of the suit and come back to work for a 3 p.m. start so he strolled enjoying the sun on his back. The fresh air seemed to be doing him a power of good, his headache lifted and he started to feel hungry. It was Friday, which meant fish and chips at the desk later and he'd go for his constitutional four pints with the lads after work. One good thing about the box room was that Maeve didn't have to smell the Guinness off his breath when he came in late on a Friday night. Not that she'd ever complained, she said she didn't care how late he came in as long as he got up to bring the kids to the playground and give her a couple of hours' peace on Saturday morning. He always held up his end of the bargain.

He'd put the suit back in the wardrobe in her room and she'd never even know he'd been in there.

Celebrating the Life
John Freeman

For Jean-Jacques Gabas

1: The Artist

'Nothing to celebrate', he said one birthday.
Only half laughing, he added that he wanted
a statue on his grave, himself reclining,
thumbing his nose at the divinity.
Life gives everybody a wound, perhaps,
to spend their years partly overcoming —
at any rate, those of us lucky enough
not to be crushed completely early on.
His overcoming was spectacular. As
I wrote to him yesterday, no-one I know
has embodied the art of living better
than he has done, and very few come close.
His joy in scholarship, and art, and music,
teaching, travel, food and wine, and friendship,
has prompted many to surpass themselves.
Today he writes that until recently
he spent a long time on the net exploring,
with great pleasure, some of the photographs
of Florentine and Roman churches. Now,
he says, he tends to doze off. 'But memories
hover above, and they're warming and glowing,
without a hint of bitterness or regret.'

As I wrote in my reply, difficult
to start, and more difficult to finish,
he's rising to the last and hardest challenge
for a past master in the art of living,
showing us by example what it is
to master too the tricky art of dying,
leaving in our perishable hearts
a better legacy than an edition,
or a recumbent statue on a tombstone.

2: Last Call

I can write another time about the content
of Jean-Jacques' email, which was so moving —
the evidence will still be in my inbox.
But what I must record, though time is pressing,
before it fades is the auditory trace
of hearing his voice on the phone, so himself,
so rich and velvety and civilized,
and slightly accented for all the years,
half a century, he's lived in Wales.
It's the first time I've heard his voice for months,
since last we went to lunch with him and Ieuan,
and possibly the last time ever, though,
listening, you would not guess how far, now,
the illness has progressed, and he assures me
he feels quite peaceful, and the agitation
in which he wrote to me has passed. He's had
a long and happy life, and when I say
he's an inspiration to us all, he says
'an old fool is still a fool to the end',
and I can't help laughing, and I tell him
that it's just like him to make me more
cheerful rather than less, and leave me giggling.
We send each other love, and I promise
to phone again when I come back, although
we both know he may by then be beyond
taking my call, or knowing if I made one.

3: Cézanne at the National Portrait Gallery

We three share our insights, and we have some,
but all the time a silent friend is with me,
someone who spent not hours but many days
taking notes in other exhibitions.
He travelled Europe just to see Cézannes.
I was confident he would be famous.
Who was it said he put his talent into
his art, his genius into living?
Of course, it must have been Oscar, and Jean-Jacques
had something of Wilde's wit and his flamboyance,
his all-round culture and sophistication,
with a warmth and gentleness that was his own.
He could have answered anything we asked,
questions rising in us as we focused
on painting after painting, and the wording
on the helpful notices beside them.
I've felt his absence sorely all this morning.
'He might have been your heartiest welcomer'
and our most entertaining, wise explainer.
It was the proper place to be, of all days
on this, when just before leaving the hotel
to come here, in a rush, running late, I found
an email telling me that, with a nurse present,
he died last night, and that he did not suffer.

4: A Moment Sketched

He was telling me about the funeral,
how the old ladies came to shake his hand,
and here he did a stylized imitation
of their nodding heads, bowed down with the years,
and with a grief they almost seemed to relish
to judge from his rendition, barking
as if through sobs, it will come to us all,
'ça nous arrivera tous.' It was so vivid,
his little sketch, that all these years later,
trying to find him in my memories,
this one brings me closer than most others,
and in its wake I hear him moving on
in his own more usual way of talking
to say that though in fact it was he
who was more grief-stricken than anyone,
he found himself having to comfort them,
these dowagers, making a meal of it,
self-centredness they took for something else
skewered in retrospect by his performance,
but at the time, when he had needed kindness,
adding to his cares and his distresses.
Of course they were thinking of their own
proximity to death, and he and I
knew, theoretically, that we were mortal,
but it was too far down the things to do,
item umpteen on our own agendas,
the last before the letters AOB,
for us to hear as more than notional.
'Ça nous arrivera tous.' My dear Jean-Jacques,
I hear and see your little bit of acting

so vividly that, though I know it has,
I can't believe it has happened to you.
Any other business? Date of next meeting?
Perhaps you're reunited with the mother
whose death you never quite recovered from.

5: My Daughter Answers a Question

'I certainly do remember him! I remember
someone very intelligent and learned,
vastly *érudit*, and very stylish
in a positive way, as in, brought up
with good manners he had cultivated,
the way he used to cultivate his melons —
or tomatoes, or whatever it was —
in Cucuron, *un intellectuel
bourgeois*, enlightened by the simplicity
only the real ones can afford (as opposed
to '*la culture c'est comme la confiture,
moins tu en as, plus tu l'étales*'). I recall
going to his elegant place near Cardiff
with you and others, his big dog (or dogs?),
and the delicious food, the lovely wine.
It was he, I'm certain, who informed me
I had the syndrome of the '*haricot vert
qui se prend pour une aubergine.*' I do
remember him, someone I would have liked
to spend more time with, somebody from whom
you always felt you could learn more, a very
generous and genuine *professeur.*
To sum up, I remember him with details
some of which may be a bit approximate,
but with a fondness which there's no mistaking.'

And, Cathy, you have prompted me to see you,
And your sister, when you were young children,
and we went with your mother to Cucuron,
having grown restless as the adults chatted,

magically calmed when Jean-Jacques led you both,
each of you slipping a hand into his,
to see and sample melons, or something else.
I see the three of you as in a painting,
returning into view, his spell still holding,
having revealed another of his talents,
one I might otherwise not have suspected.

I wonder whether anyone could count them,
the different ways in which his one light shone.

Forty Years of Editing
Some Do's, Some Don'ts: 1978—2018
Gerald Dawe

My plan is to think aloud about my experiences, stretching over roughly forty years, of editing sixteen or so titles. These books, edited by myself or with co-editors, include collections of essays, poetry anthologies, editions of individual writers' work and proceedings from conferences and lecture series. But I'd like to begin with some (brief) personal background which I hope will help underpin the narrative of what follows. It also helps me focus as best I can on what kind of 'lessons' or recommendations I can offer to those younger colleagues starting, or seeking to expand, their publishing 'careers' as scholars, researchers and as writers in their own right.

But first let me take you back to the early 1970s. As a young poet based at what was then UCG, now NUI, Galway, researching the nineteenth-century Irish novelist William Carleton, I had left behind the very troubled city of Belfast where I had grown up. My academic interest in nineteenth-century Irish fiction was fuelled by a fascination with how writers from Ireland had coped imaginatively with the apocalyptic transformation of the Great Famine along with the political challenges of a resurgent nationalism and the moral and cultural issues that flowed from Empire. It was a heavy subject and in the climate of the times raised more questions than answers, particularly when the subject of my thesis — William Carleton — had been effectively forgotten and very little read, outside of a handful of writers such as Thomas

Flanagan, Anthony Cronin, Benedict Kiely, Eileen Ibarra-Sullivan of Florida, Maurice Harmon and later on, Barbara Hayley.

But the extent to which Carleton was at the time considered unworthy of academic study was brought home to me when, in an interview for a junior lectureship in the late 1970s, the patrician external examiner asked me why I had wasted my time on such a 'minor' figure in a century of minor Irish writers, I piped up and said I thought Carleton's struggle with political violence and national conflict was well worth examining, before comparing Carleton with the generation of Thirties writers in Britain and, then putting my foot in it, by proposing a parallel with how a poet such as Sylvia Plath had tried to wrestle with the breakdown of civilised society post WW2, the revelations of the Holocaust and the unfolding crisis of Vietnam and American society. I wasn't offered the position!

*

I had, however, been publishing poems here and there, some of which were included in an anthology published by The Blackstaff Press in Belfast in October 1974. The anthology, *The Wearing of the Black*, subtitled, *An Anthology of Contemporary Ulster Poetry* was edited by Padraic Fiacc, an Irish-American poet who had relocated from New York in the 1950s and was living in a small urban village called Glengormley, on the northern outskirts of Belfast. In those days books rarely were 'launched' and there were precious few 'readings'; the public face of writing and editing basically stopped at publication and reviews took over. But the publication of this anthology — which would subsequently become 'controversial' in the hard-wired politicised climate of the time — was unusually marked by a party in Fiacc's s Glengormley home in December.

I attended the publishing party with my girlfriend and we met there several of the lesser-known contributors, including one young aspiring poet, a year or so younger myself, who I'd previously met a few times before leaving Belfast. His name was Gerard McLoughlin, though he published as Gerry Locke. The party went off very well. Fiacc had hosted several in earlier years, writers then making their names, such as John McGahern (sacked from his teacher's job in 1965 after the banning of his novel, *The Dark*), Derek Mahon — whose parents lived in the area and whose 'iconic' poem, 'Glengormley' was originally dedicated to Fiacc — and the locally influential short story writer and novelist Michael McLaverty, much praised by Seamus Heaney, among others.

Anyway, after the party we returned to Galway and Christmas 1974. The anthology was out in the world. Four months later in April, sitting in the living room of our tiny flat in Abbeygate Street in Galway, the news brought word of yet another sectarian killing in Belfast. It was Gerard McLoughlin, the young starter we had met in Belfast only a few months previously.

I can see now, looking back over forty years later, that it was as a result of this very early experience, and given such a heavily politicised and lethal environment of the preceding three or four years, that my own scholarly and research interests ended up constantly returning to the role crisis, conflict and war play in the life of the literary imagination, both in Ireland but also further afield, in what used to be known as 'Eastern Europe'.

With only a very few exceptions, which I'll come to, my own editorial interventions, such as they are, generally have had some kind of connection to politics and how a poet, or dramatist, or novelist copes with the pressures of history. Maybe the value of hindsight makes this seem as a planned project, but nothing could be further from the truth. So maybe if I turn to some of the earlier books, I might be able to illustrate what I mean here.

*

In 1978 my first book of poems, *Sheltering Places* was published by The Blackstaff Press. At the same time I established a literary supplement called 'Writing in the West' which appeared every month in *The Connacht Tribune*. The pre-digital Republic was very Dublin-centric with the majority of broadsheet and broadcast media focused there. 'Writing in the West' was an attempt to provide a literary platform for writers and others interested in the arts based in Galway and in the wider west of Ireland region. A few years later, my first serious piece of editing, *The Younger Irish Poets* was published in 1982. It was the first poetry anthology to concentrate upon a *generation* of poets who, coming from various parts of Ireland, and not (as was more commonly the case) focusing upon a particular region such as Northern Ireland, attempted to identify a new vibration in the culture; a questioning of the ideological past that had been handed down often uncritically. From the opening poems of Paul Durcan and Eavan Boland the idea was to demonstrate 'in their search for what makes sense over and against the inherited, given meanings of Irish history, north and south, an independence from any "accredited theme"'. The somewhat portentous penultimate paragraph, picking up on the Beckett reference, went on:

> …the poets presented here are finding ways to liberate themselves, their art, and by implication alone, their readers, from the literary conventions and literal expectations that have been handed down from the

past. Present, I feel, in their best work is a need to unburden themselves of the past through whatever means, traditional or experimental, that sustains their own imaginative responsibilities.

So with poems such as Paul Durcan's 'Backside to the Wind' and 'Making Love outside Aras An Uachtarain', Richard Ryan's 'From My Lai the thunder went west', Aidan Mathews' 'Minding Ruth' and Medbh McGuckian's 'Family Planning', the anthology brought a fresh sense of the modern world coming into view as well as a contemporary Ireland opening up to it.

That was 1982. The book went on to three reprints and achieved a relatively healthy lifespan, with respectable sales and some degree of critical recognition. But, and here's my first, somewhat hesitant, 'Don't', it was hampered with my sense of *mission* and not enough introductory focus on the *formal* qualities of the twenty-one poets included. While there was an understandable impulse behind the editing of that anthology, it might have served the poets better if it had not been so obvious; better practice is to present the best poems and, after the ground had been prepared, let them speak for themselves. However — and here comes my first 'Do' — if the whole point of taking on a particular piece of research or editorial task is to rectify or restore what one considers to be an important or neglected writer or topic, then all that advocacy needs is a clearly stated and well researched case. This idea of advocacy is an often overlooked side of scholarship. To draw critical attention to a writer, or period, or subject, which either languishes on the margins of public acknowledgement and/or academic discourse, is what the novelist and Professor of Contemporary Literature at UEA, Amit Chaudhuri terms 'Literary Activism' in a wise and challenging collection of essays, *Literary Activism: A Symposium* (2016). Alongside academic custodianship, such advocacy requires energy and staying power but it also requires what Rónán McDonald has referred to in his valuable study, *The Death of the Critic* (2007) as 'evidence that has an external validity', a sense of authorising the subject which comes from various and as far as possible, impartial sources.

In the case of three writers to whom I'll turn, personal experience can be both chastening as much as it can be rewarding. I'm thinking of the efforts of my co-editor, Aodan Mac Poilin and myself, on behalf of the poet, Padraic Fiacc. Aodan who was known to many in the Irish language community as a power-house, sadly died in 2016, so it is appropriate to say how much I owed to him over the five decades of our friendship and collaborations. He was the Irish language editor of *Krino: the Review* (1986–1996) but he was also my — and many others — first responder when questions of Irish language literary culture needed an answer.

We both thought more highly of Fiacc's work than most of the critical and academic establishment in Ireland and further afield. With the exception of Terence Brown, who edited for Blackstaff Press in 1979, a volume of Fiacc's *Selected Poems*, Fiacc was viewed as a grim and damaged soul whose obsessively fragmented and fragmentary poems were overbearingly predicated upon the northern violence. Fiacc's reputation had been damaged as a result of that controversial anthology, *The Wearing of the Black* and subsequent publications and in the decade immediately after its publication, he suffered a breakdown with the collapse of his marriage and the loss of the family home. Throughout much of the 1980s and '90s his life turned into a chaotic indigent existence, moving from boarding room to temporary lodging, alcohol-fuelled, marginalised by his unpredictable and self-lacerating lifestyle.

Our first effort to rehabilitate and present an alternative view, *Ruined Pages: Selected Poems*, clarified and collected Fiacc's scattered volumes from *By the Black Stream* (1969), *Odour of Blood* (1973), *Nights in the Bad Place* (1977) and *Missa Terriblis* (1986). Only for the stabilising efforts of close, long standing friends and supporters, such as Aodan, Fiacc would not have survived. Though frail and house-bound he did indeed survive and at the great age of ninety-four is in the good care of a resident home in south Belfast. Our second effort on Fiacc's behalf, a new selected poems, concentrated solely upon the best of his seventy years of writing, including the texts of two fascinating radio broadcasts produced by Paul Muldoon for BBC. The book was published by Lagan, a small yet dynamic local literary press in 2014 but received little response.

So it has to be said that despite our best efforts, Fiacc's work remains under-recognised and under-researched although, as we tried to point out in both editions, the life and the work are relevant to a more copious and integrated understanding of the dynamic interchanges of Irish writing — how, for instance, literary and cultural influences such as New York modernism of the post-WW2 period are at play within Fiacc's poetry alongside the embers of Celtic romanticism which he inherited from his early mentor, Padraic Colum. The emigrant sensibility, the sexual and gender flux and the Catholic spiritual legacies feature throughout Fiacc's work but these await a new generation's engagement. As one of the contributors to *Literary Activism: A Symposium* remarks:

> Literary activism is supposed to usurp our comfortable and rigid mainstream opinions, to shake up our literary tastes and standards, to promote unknown writers and neglected literary territories, to bring fresh knowledge about literature.

Undoubtedly true, but 'to promote unknown' or little known writers also requires a literary and academic community interested in something beyond the mainstream, and this is not at a premium in Ireland where it is often the case that outside expectations are even more dependent upon 'mainstream opinions'.

Another writer, originally from the north of Ireland (Co. Tyrone) but whose radical life and writing has received little attention, caught my critical interest as far back as the late 1970s. It took almost thirty years before the poems and selected prose of Charles Donnelly were published in book form, along with his brother Joseph's memoir, *Heroic Heart: A Charles Donnelly Reader*, edited by his sister-in-law, Kay.

It was a very special project because of the family's long-standing belief in Charlie's achievement as a poet who had died in 1937 aged twenty-two fighting against fascism in the Spanish Civil War. But again, considering the role of critical advocacy and retrieval, the canon has been less than hospitable to Donnelly's short life and complicated story — a fascinating portrait of radical Thirties Dublin, that still remains largely unchronicled and yet reveals an energetic political and cultural atmosphere of young men and women activists and writers, which cuts across the often drab stereotypes of De Valera's Ireland. To quote again from Rónán McDonald's, *The Death of the Critic*:

> Lesser-known writers, perhaps producing vital, innovative work tend to be swamped out in the commercial din, lacking as they do informed apologists with sufficient authority and access to sufficient numbers of readers. Too often in this arena

hype and puff pieces do the work of critical judgement and evaluation.

I'm glad to say that one of the successes along this editorial journey has been Stewart Parker, and in particular my collaboration with Maria Johnston, on the publication of Parker's lithe and hugely readable, *High Pop: The Irish Times Column of 1970—1976* (2008). This was followed by a second collection, edited with Maria and Claire Wallace, of Stewart Parker's *Dramatis Personae and other writings* (also 2008). Both books have established the range and verve of the playwright's artistic and critical imagination and are now integrated into Parker's overall achievement as one of Ireland's leading playwrights. It should be pointed out too that most of these titles would not have happened without the commitment and enthusiasm of what was Patrick Ramsey's small and independent Lagan Press.

*

Concentrating upon a single author's work makes for a less contentious engagement. When the anthology of Irish war poetry, *Earth Voices Whispering* was published in November 2008 I hadn't foreseen, rather naively, that, firstly, there could be a division in critical response between Ireland and Britain and secondly, that what it stated on the cover, would be overlooked.

And here I can offer a further couple of 'Don'ts' — no matter how much work you put into a book or project, don't expect reviews, good, bad, or indifferent; and also, crucially, don't think that the community to whom your work is nominally addressed will thank you; so be prepared for misconceptions.

Earth Voices Whispering, the first anthology of its kind, took about three years in the making. It stated, quite clearly, on the cover, that it was dealing with the period 1914 to 1945. It was a difficult decision but to have moved beyond the symbolic date of 1945 as the endpoint of the anthology, seemed apt because it provided a point of closure before the unfolding of other wars in the Fifties and later but also as a cut-off point for the included poets. No poet would be included who had been born after that date

The intense, century-defining time span of thirty-one years encapsulated such major events as WW1, the Easter Rising, the War of Independence, the Irish Civil War, The Spanish Civil War and WW2, matched by poems which reflected upon these events, including those written by many poets such as Padraic Fallon, Winifred Letts, Freda Laughton, Eileen Shanahan, Sean Jennett and Sheila Wingfield who had been largely forgotten. Yet some largely favourable reviews complained that 'younger' poets — Ciaran Carson and Paul Muldoon, both born post 1945, among them — weren't included; to that extent an opportunity had been missed. So another 'Do' heading our way: Do be prepared for the misreading; what you think is clear and obvious as a rubric may not be so registered. The other point that may be of interest here is that I soon discovered how world historical events can often be seen as actually belonging to a particular 'national' culture. It struck me as strange that the response to *Earth Voices Whispering* in the UK in particular was somewhat muted around the issue of Irish poets and WW1.

It were as if WW1 was an 'English' literary subject and therefore confusing categories to introduce it as an 'Irish' subject. 'We' have Easter 1916 and all the rest of it, so leave The Great War, alone. Such stereotypes are there for a reason, usually, and they can be almost subconscious but it is part of scholarship and research to challenge them.

Out of editing *Earth Voices Whispering* I started to view the best known Irish soldier poet, Francis Ledwidge who died in the conflict, in a very different light. The 100th anniversary of his death at the Front in 1917 was marked by a seminar on Ledwidge and WW1 organised with colleagues and the local Ledwidge societies in Inchcore in Dublin and the Ledwidge Museum in Slane. The results of that day's deliberations, *The Ledwidge Papers*, are currently being edited and will be published later this year.

So I think if there is one very important positive 'Do's' that I can recommend it is to get out into the wider community with literary and academic projects; attach yourself to the general reader and local historian for there is much to achieve in partnership with this highly motivated community; certainly that has been my experience. On the other hand, and here a big 'Don't' hoves into view, don't assume that what you do as an editor will be received on its own terms. Terms change as much as the times and contexts often alter. The notion of critical 'genre' which underscores what academics 'do' — the differences between a tutorial, a seminar, a lecture — can easily be conflated into a one-size fits all, 'class'.

Similarly the distinctions which operate within scholarship, research and book publication are becoming increasingly blurred and even redundant. My experience editing the *Cambridge Companion to Irish Poets* (2017) is a case in point.*

There's certainly a faintly Victorian tint to the term 'Companion'; what exactly is it? After having a good look

* *For a fuller treatment:*
https://www.irishtimes.com/culture/books/selected-poets-and-their-work-alive-and-present-to-the-reader-1.3394727

through previous *Cambridge Companions,* I quickly realised what it's *not:* not an anthology, not a reader, not a handbook, not a dictionary and not a history. It is a *Companion,* a very site-specific publication with clear, if negotiable, terms of reference, in my case, limited to thirty or fewer individual essays on individual poets, with a historical starting point (Ireland and the 1590s) and a definitive or symbolic endpoint, in my case, the emergence, with widespread critical recognition, of Nuala Ni Dhomhnaill, a poet from a 'minority' language into the English mainstream of a vastly globalised world.

The time-span of, roughly, five centuries is how the reader approaches the new(ish) century and then promptly leaves the stage, it is hoped, encouraged to read and discover more, via the selected reading list which signposts critical, historical, biographical studies and poetry anthologies as first ports of call.

This particular *Companion* also lives within an extensive series of such Irish-related studies, published by Cambridge University Press in the last fifteen years, from the *Cambridge Companion to Contemporary Irish Poetry* edited by Matthew Campbell (2003) to the forthcoming *History of Modern Irish Women's Literature,* edited by Heather Ingman and Cliona O'Gallchoir. So it needed to 'fit in' to this wider picture as well. The invitation to prepare a *Companion* was clearly predicated on poetic value — excellence and influence. Soon into the research it was clear that the ratio of first class women poets *after* 1945 is high, pre-1945 lower. There are social, cultural and historical reasons for this which the *Companion* reflects. Similarly, the pressure to acknowledge contemporary or recent Irish poets, both men and women, was also clear from the outset, but the choice was made to close the historical circle at the turn of the millennium with those poets who had already established international recognition with the bulk of substantial work behind them, and literary reputations critically acknowledged as such with scholarship. This *Companion* wasn't going to be a *Companion* to *Irish Poetry since 2000*, or a *Companion* to *Twenty-First Century Irish Poetry*, although either (future) publication could sit neatly alongside it.

The *Companion* came in for pre-publication trouncing and subsequently on the issue of gender representation: why where there not more women poets as subjects for essays. The answer is simple but difficult at the same time: had this *Companion* focused on *contemporary* Irish poets, options would have abounded, but going back through the centuries, consulting all the standard anthologies and literary histories, it was difficult to identify, outside of specific research subjects, poets who were women and who had, under the rubric of this *Companion*, achieved global recognition and canonical status. As has been illustrated in other artistic communities, it may well be the fault of the canon and its development into a domain often over-populated with artists who are men. So this is obviously an important discussion in its own right. The editorial brief this time around did not involve re-writing the history or producing scholarly introductions to under-recognised poets, women or men.

However, if such a book as this produces discussion and makes us think about the *poetic* tradition that informs our culture and of how to identify, recognise, foster and support artistic and literary excellence, so much the better. When the formal qualities, the aesthetics, of the purely *artistic* drive and structure of imagination are refashioned through a different set of priorities, the balancing act between equality and excellence, and the strains of subjectivity which underpin all decision-making, clearly need to be examined and redefined. And there needs to be some kind of editorial mechanism or leeway available in real-time publication deadlines and contracts to ensure getting the gender balance right in individual contributors.

For this *Companion* the overriding and defining priority was to provide an introductory portrait of twenty-nine Irish poets, spanning five centuries, covering both languages and presenting these in a readable and engaging style so that the general reader as much as the student could approach the book with confidence that the self-contained essays would not be overly technical in terminology or use an imposing academic style.

I think the contributors have achieved this as the selected poets and their work are alive and present to the reader. The four women poets in the *Companion* who have established international reputations — Eavan Boland, Eiléan Ní Chuilleanáin, Medbh McGuckian and Nuala Ní Dhombhnaill — anticipate the burgeoning contemporary poetry scene as 'trailblazers' and form part of a much wider discourse of women's voices — poets as much as critics — throughout the *Companion*. While criss-crossing generations and borders in a vibrant conversation within the *Companion*, the reader encounters a substantial number of women writers, poets and critics.

*

When I edited *Earth Voices Whispering* the 416 pages included several fascinating Irish women poets who had largely been forgotten, among them, Mary Devenport O'Neill, Blanaid Salkeld, Winifred Letts, Freda Laughton, Eileen Shanahan and Sheila Wingfield — a cluster of women poets who shared an intriguingly distinctive class and educational background shaped by the British Empire. I was surprised by the critical silence which, outside the classroom, largely met these and other exciting inclusions such as *The New Younger Irish Poets* (1991) and an anthology of the ten years of *Krino: The Review*, which appeared in 1996, co-edited with Jonathan Williams. There is no way of telling about such things.

This *Companion* will, I hope, be read, enjoyed and debated by all those around the globe who love poetry and have a particular interest in knowing a little more about how Ireland has produced so many great poets, including but not limited to, the representative twenty-nine voices explored in the book with such skill and care by writers and scholars, many of whom have devoted their personal and professional lives to poetry from Ireland and many other younger contributors in whose custodianship the tradition is placed for revision and reimagining into the future. Ten or twenty years hence, who knows what sort of a book the next *Companion* will make; it is an exhilarating and challenging prospect. But in the interim, and to interrogate issues raised in relation to the Irish poetic canon, a symposium, 'Missing Voices: Irish Women Poets, 16th—20st centuries', similar in structure to the Ledwidge Seminar, will be hosted by Poetry Ireland and will hopefully conclude with a publication of selected papers. Which takes me to my conclusion.

*

When I think about these and other books, and what I have written on this or that writer over the years I've tried to sketch in here, I think I see one recurring theme and without sounding — I trust — too ponderous about it, it is this. That there is an abiding tension between the needs of the imaginative fascination with language and form, often seen as the preserve of the poet and artist, and the pressures of political crisis and conflict in civic society; the preserve often of the critic. These contrary flows are rarely, if ever, satisfactorily equalised or balanced. Writing — creative and critical, research and scholarship — is a never-ending search because it is ever elusive. We never get to the bottom of things. We never can say the final word. What I do know, now more than ever before, is that the manner in which we engage with these matters as writers, intellectuals, academics and readers, requires its own scrutiny. As McDonald states, 'Perhaps it is now time to devote attention to the value of value'. Certainly at a time when social media can militate against such introspection and questioning and — as we've seen globally — become even more spiteful against reason and reasonable debate, this is clearly going to be a major issue for a younger generation of intellectuals and writers to assess and provide leadership on. The sheer volume of material — academic and literary — that is produced and the accompanying expectation for recognition can lead to dissatisfaction when acknowledgement of this work is not forthcoming as quickly as one hopes it will be.

The weakening of critical filters, one of the downsides of the internet, the disappearance (effectively) of the role and cultural support of an engaged, proactive editor in the present globalized publishing world — a theme productively explored in *Literary Activism* — and the merging of standards under pressures of book marketing and PR in the main broadsheet newspapers and broadcast media, are substantial topics in themselves.

While the tagging of publication to academic promotion still seems to me to undermine the key values of teaching and research for their own sakes, but that is another subject into which I best not stray.

On a much less urgent matter, the sense of self-advertisement which the internet provides looks like reinforcing the mainstreaming of 'market activism' rather than inspiring the kind of genuine critical dialogue that any intellectually adventurous and challenging culture needs in order to thrive. Universities have a huge role to play in guiding this kind of intellectual scrutiny if we agree, as I do, with Ronan McDonald that 'the point of literary studies was the nurture of the moral imagination' — a belief which he wisely situates in the context of the recent past:

> Once frozen, the canon was easily dismantled by the next generation of politicized critics, suspicious of the category of literature as a whole. The refusal of the literary 'canon' may in one respect be an admirably democratic dismantling of fusty old edifices. However, in failing to replace the permanent tradition with any renovated notion of literary merit, in ousting evaluation for simple analysis, criticism has undermined its own disciplinary foundations. This, crucially, is one of the key factors in cutting academic criticism off from a wider reading public.

Maybe it is high time to revitalise the nurturing of the moral imagination as the whole point of literary studies in our age of anxiety.

This text is based upon a talk given to the Staff and Post Graduate Seminar, School of English, Trinity College Dublin, The Long Room Hub - 27th March 2018

About the Authors

James Clarke is a graduate of The Manchester Writing School. His debut novel *The Litten Path* will be published by Salt in August 2018.

Dan Coxon edited the award-winning anthology *Being Dad* (Best Anthology, Saboteur Awards 2016) and is a Contributing Editor at The Lonely Crowd. His writing has appeared in Salon, Popshot, The Lonely Crowd, Open Pen, Wales Arts Review, Gutter, The Portland Review and *Unthology 9* amongst others, and he was long-listed for the Bath Flash Fiction Award 2017. He can be found on Twitter at @dancoxonauthor and runs an editing and proofreading business at: momuseditorial.co.uk

Armel Dagorn is now back in his native France after living in Ireland for seven years. His writing has appeared in magazines such as Tin House online, The Stinging Fly and Unthology. His short story collection *The Proverb Zoo* will be out in May 2018 from The Penny Dreadful Press.

Stevie Davies is Emeritus Professor of Creative Writing at Swansea University. She is a Fellow of the Royal Society of Literature and a Fellow of the Welsh Academy. Stevie has published widely in the fields of fiction, literary criticism, biography and popular history. A collection of her short stories, *Arrest Me, For I Have Run Away*, will be published by Parthian in April 2018. Parthian will also be reprinting *The Web of Belonging* (1997) which was adapted as a Channel 4 television film written by Alan Plater, starring Brenda Blethyn, Kevin

Whately and Anna Massie. *The Element of Water* (2001) will also be reprinted this year: it was long-listed for the Booker and Orange Prizes and won the Arts Council of Wales Book of the Year in 2002.

Gerald Dawe was professor of English and Fellow of Trinity College Dublin until his retirement in 2017. His poetry collection include *Points West*, *Selected Poems* and *Mickey Finn's Air*. Other publications include *In Another World: Van Morrison and Belfast* and *The Wrong Country: Essays on Modern Irish Writing*.

Sarah Doyle is the Pre-Raphaelite Society's Poet-in-Residence, and is a graduate of the Creative Writing MA programme at Royal Holloway College, University of London. She has been published widely in magazines such as Poetry News, Orbis, The Dawntreader and The Fenland Reed; and in many poetry anthologies. She won the William Blake Poetry Prize in 2015, and has been placed in poetry competitions such as The Frogmore Prize, Poetry on the Lake, Mslexia, Live Canon, Café Writers, York Mix, etc. Sarah has been a guest reader at numerous poetry events in and around London, and is co-author of *Dreaming Spheres: Poems of the Solar System* (PS Publishing, 2014). More at: www.sarahdoyle.co.uk.

Martina Evans is the author of eleven books of prose and poetry. Her first novel, *Midnight Feast*, won a Betty Trask Award in 1995 and her third novel, *No Drinking No Dancing No Doctors* (Bloomsbury, 2000), won an Arts Council England Award in 1999. Martina's fourth poetry collection, *Facing the Public* was published by Anvil Press in September 2009 and has won bursary awards from both the Irish Arts Council (An Chomhairle Eiraíon) and Arts Council England. *Facing the*

Public was a TLS Book of the Year in 2009 and won the Premio Ciampi International Prize for Poetry in 2011. *Petrol*, a prose poem won a Grants for the Arts Award in 2010 and was published by Anvil Press in 2012. A revised edition of *Midnight Feast* and *Through the Glass Mountain*, a new prose poem, were published by Bloom Books in June 2013. *Burnfort, Las Vegas* (Anvil Press 2014) was shortlisted for the Irish Times Poetry Now Award 2015. *The Windows of Graceland, New & Selected Poems* was published by Carcanet in May 2016.

Currently she is Royal Literary Fund Advisory Fellow and reviews for the Irish Times. *Now We Can Talk Openly About Men* will be published by Carcanet in May 2018.

Tanya Farrelly works as an EFL teacher, and facilitates Creative Writing classes for South Dublin County Council. Her stories have won prizes and been shortlisted in such competitions as the Hennessy Awards, the RTE Francis MacManus Awards (2002/2015), and the Fish International short story competition. Runner-up in the William Trevor International Short Story Competition in both 2008 and 2009, her stories have appeared in literary journals such as the Cuirt Annual, Crannog magazine and the Incubator. Her debut fiction collection *When Black Dogs Sing* was published by Arlen House in 2016.

John Freeman is a prize-winning poet and critic whose work has appeared in magazines and anthologies over several decades. His most recent books are *What Possessed Me* (Worple Press), and *Strata Smith and the Anthropocene* (Knives Forks and Spoons Press), both published in 2016. Earlier collections include *A Suite for Summer* (Worple), *White Wings: New and Selected Prose Poems* (Contraband Books), *Landscape with Portraits* (Redbeck Press) and *The Light Is Of Love, I Think: New* *and Selected Poems* (Stride Editions). Stride also published a collection of essays, *The Less Received: Neglected Modern Poets*. John grew up in South London and lived in Yorkshire before settling in Wales. He taught for many years at Cardiff University and now lives in the Vale of Glamorgan. *What Possessed Me* won the Roland Mathias Poetry Award as part of the Wales Book of the Year Awards in November 2017.

Susanna Galbraith is from Belfast and lives in York. She is the Editorial Assistant at Abridged magazine. Her poems have appeared recently in issues of Abridged, The HU, The Penny Dreadful, The Pickled Body, and The Tangerine.

Anne Hayden is from Cork and lives in Dublin. Her short fiction has been published in Stinging Fly magazine, Incubator journal and the Irish Times where she was shortlisted for the 2017 Hennessy Literary Awards.

David Hayden's short story collection, *Darker with the Lights On*, is published by Little Island Press. His writing has appeared in gorse, The Yellow Nib, The Moth, The Stinging Fly, Spolia and The Warwick Review, and poetry in PN Review. He was shortlisted for the 25th RTÉ Francis MacManus Short Story prize. Born in Dublin, he has lived in the US and Australia and is now based in Norwich, UK, where he is currently working on a novel.

Natalie Ann Holborow is a Swansea-born writer. She won the Terry Hetherington Award and the Robin Reeves Prize in 2015, and her debut poetry collection *And Suddenly You Find Yourself* was published by Parthian in Kolkata, India in 2017. She is currently writing a non-fiction book for young people on living positively with type 1 diabetes as well as a debut novel.

Born in the Rhymney Valley in 1968, conceptual landscape photographer and photography writer **Rob Hudson** turns 50 this year. Now living in Cardiff he has developed a vision for landscape photography that embraces ecological concerns and seeks to develop our appreciation of the land through sharing the stories we tell each other of our experience of the land. Immersing himself in his local surroundings enables him to both develop new ways of expressing these experiences and to critique the way landscape has hitherto been portrayed.

His work is often influenced by poetry, which allows him to explore ideas about metaphor and narrative in his photography. In 2014 he was the first to realise the significance of the photographs made by the poet Edward Thomas during his 1913 journey from London to Somerset that became Thomas's prose work *In Pursuit of Spring*. Little Toller Books subsequently republished an edition of the book including those photographs.

Nigel Jarrett is a winner of the Rhys Davies prize for short fiction and, in 2016, the inaugural Templar Shorts award. He's a former daily-newspaperman and a contributor to the Wales Arts Review, Jazz Journal and Acumen poetry magazine, among others. He is also a poet and novelist. His first collection of stories, *Funderland*, was warmly reviewed in the Independent, the Guardian, and the Times, and long-listed for the Edge Hill prize. Parthian also published his first poetry collection, *Miners At The Quarry Pool*. His latest collection, *Who Killed Emil Kreisler?* was published in 2016. This year sees the publication of his short fiction pamphlet, *A Gloucester Trilogy*.

Jo Mazelis is a prize-winning novelist, short story writer, poet, photographer & essayist. Her debut novel *Significance* (Seren,

2014) won The Jerwood Fiction Uncovered Prize in 2015. Her first collection of stories *Diving Girls* was short-listed for Commonwealth Best First Book & Welsh Book of the Year. Her latest book, a collection of short stories entitled, *Ritual, 1969* (Seren, 2016), was long-listed for the Edge Hill Prize & shortlisted for Wales Book of the Year in 2017.

Robert Minhinnick is a prize-winning poet, novelist, short story writer & essayist. He has won Wales Book of the Year & the Forward Poetry Prize. His latest collection *Diary of the Last Man* was recently shortlisted for the T.S. Eliot Prize. He has read at literary festivals around the world.

Derwen Morfayel is a fiction writer with short stories and poetry in literary magazines Silvae, Halo, Severine, The Lonely Crowd, Halcyon, Shooter, Unbroken Journal, Ink, Sweat & Tears and in the upcoming anthology *A Furious Hope*. Visit her website www.derwenmorfayel.com for a selection of her work. She tweets about writing @DerwenMorfayel.

Courttia Newland is the author of seven works of fiction that include his debut, *The Scholar*. His latest novel, *The Gospel According to Cane*, was published in 2013. His short stories have appeared in anthologies including *Best British Short Stories 2017* and broadcast on BBC Radio 4. In 2016 he was awarded the Tayner Barbers Award for science fiction writing and the Roland Rees Busary for playwriting. He is an associate lecturer at the University of Westminster and is completing a PhD in creative writing.

Kate North has written a novel (*Eva Shell*, Cinnamon, 2007) and poetry collection (*Bistro*, Cinnamon, 2012). Her second poetry collection, *The Way Out* will be available from Parthian in 2018.

Bethany W. Pope was named by the Huffington Post 'one of the five Expat poets to watch in 2016'. Nicholas Lezard, writing for The Guardian, described her latest collection as 'poetry as salvation... This harrowing collection drawn from a youth spent in an orphanage delights in language as a place of private escape.' Bethany has an MA in Creative Writing from Trinity, St David's and a PhD from Aberystwyth University. Bethany has won many literary awards. Her poetry collections include: *A Radiance* (Cultured Llama, 2012*) Crown of Thorns* (Oneiros Books, 2013), *The Gospel of Flies* (Writing Knights Press 2014), *Undisturbed Circles* (Lapwing, 2014), *The Rag and Boneyard* (Indigo Dreams 2016), and *Silage* (Indigo Dreams, 2017). Her first novel, *Masque*, was published by Seren in 2016.

Matt Rader is the author of four collections of poetry, *Miraculous Hours* (2005), *Living Things* (2009), *A Doctor Pedalled Her Bicycle Over the River Arno* (2011) and *Desecrations* (2016). He is also the author of the story collection *What I Want to Tell Goes Like This* (2014) and several chapbooks including *I Don't Want to Die Like Frank O'Hara* (2014). His work has appeared in journals, magazines, and websites across Canada including Geist, The Walrus, The Malahat Review, The New Quarterly, Joyland, and Hazlitt.

Michael Ray is a poet and visual artist living in West Cork, Ireland. His poems have appeared in a number of Irish and international journals, including The Moth, The Shop, Cyphers, The Penny Dreadful, One, Southword, The Stinging Fly, Ambit, Magma and Numero Cinq.

Gareth E. Rees is the founder and editor of the website Unofficial Britain (www.unofficialbritain.com), author of *The*

Stone Tide (Influx Press, 2018) and *Marshland* (Influx Press, 2013). His stories and essays have featured in *Unthology 10* (Unthank Books, 2018) *An Unreliable Guide to London* (Influx Press, 2016), *Walking Inside Out: Contemporary British Psychogeography* (Rowman & Littlefield, 2015), *Mount London* (Penned in the Margins, 2014), *The Ashgate Companion to Paranormal Cultures* (Ashgate, 2013), *Acquired for Development By* (Influx Press, 2012) and the spoken word album with Jetsam, *A Dream Life of Hackney Marshes* (Clay Pipe Music, 2013). He lives in Hastings with his two daughters and a dog named Hendrix. Twitter: @hackneymarshman @britunofficial

Rhea Seren Phillips is a Ph.D student at Swansea University. She is studying how Welsh poetic forms and metre could be used to reconsider, engage and accurately represent the changing cultural identity of modern Wales. Rhea has been published in Cheval 10, Cultured Vultures and The Conversation. She runs Grandiloquent Wretches, a Patreon page that combines poetry, art and audio (https://www.patreon.com/grandiloquentwretch).

Louise Warren's first collection *A Child's Last Picture Book of the Zoo* won the Cinnamon First Collection Prize and was published in 2012. A pamphlet *In the scullery with John Keats* also published by Cinnamon came out in 2016. Her poems have appeared in many magazines including Ambit, New Welsh Review, The Rialto, Poetry Wales and Stand. She was a prize winner in the Troubadour International Poetry Prize (2013 and 2015) and this year her poem 'Geraniums' was highly commended in the Second Light Poetry Competition.

Anna-Marie Young is a doctorate student at Cardiff University in creative writing. She is working on an upcoming collection entitled *Flight* which was long-listed for the New Welsh Writing Awards: People, Place & Planet.

About the Editor

John Lavin has a doctorate from the University of Wales, Trinity Saint David, as well as an MA in Creative Writing from Cardiff University. The former Fiction Editor of Wales Arts Review, he edited their short story anthology, *A Fiction Map of Wales*, as well as their online series *Story: Retold*. His short fiction has appeared in The Incubator, Spork Press, Dead Ink and The Lampeter Review. His criticism has appeared in The Irish Times, Wales Arts Review and The Welsh Agenda. He is the founder and editor of The Lonely Crowd and The Lonely Press.

The Lonely Crowd is an entirely self-funded enterprise. Please consider supporting us by subscribing to the magazine here
www.thelonelycrowd.org/subscribe

Please direct all other enquiries to
johnlavin@thelonelycrowd.org
Visit our website for more new short fiction, poetry, critical writing & photography www.thelonelycrowd.org

'A joyous collection.' Amy McCauley, *New Welsh Review*

'Love words? Then follow, if you dare, Cornwell's intoxicated progress through the English language' **Robert Minhinnick**

ergasy
christopher cornwell

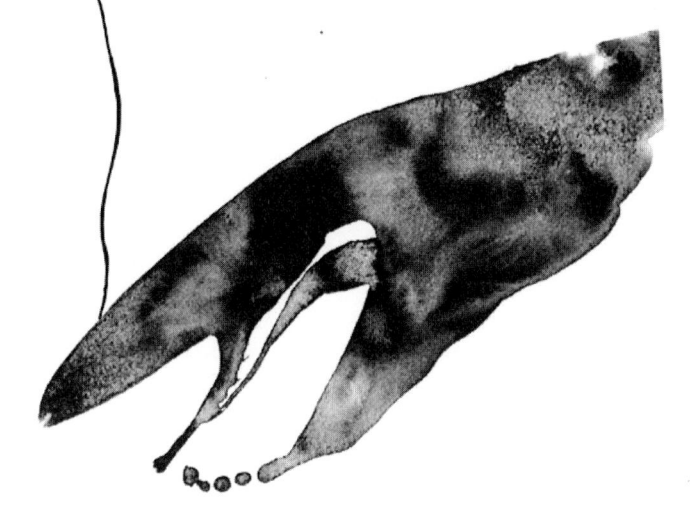

With an Introduction by **John Goodby**
And a series of Artworks by **Constantinos Andronis**

Available now from our online shop,
www.thelonelycrowd.org/online-shop